SUCH A LOVING COUPLE

BOOKS BY HAYLEY SMITH

The Perfect Girlfriend

SUCH A LOVING COUPLE

HAYLEY SMITH

bookouture

Published by Bookouture in 2023

An imprint of Storyfire Ltd.
Carmelite House
50 Victoria Embankment
London EC4Y 0DZ

www.bookouture.com

ISBN: 978-1-83790-284-2
eBook ISBN: 978-1-83790-274-3

For Michael, my soulmate in this crazy world.

PART ONE

ONE

'It's OK, love, don't panic. Just stay still. Let's have a little look at you.'

There's the strobe of a blue light coming from somewhere. Crackling voices. Some sort of interference. Bleeps. I can't remember what the thing is called that makes the noise. Above me there are lots of staring eyes. Acid burning my throat, choking me. I launch into another coughing fit and my chest feels like it has been ripped open.

'What's your name, love?'

More crackling. Police things. You hold them in your hand and speak into them but they're not phones. You say things like 'over and out' and press a button at the side.

'What's your name, love?' The kind-voiced man gives me a little rub on the cheek with a warm hand, dry like old bone.

My chest and shoulders scream with agony, and I gasp at the air like I'm being suffocated. I try to focus on what's happening around me as adrenaline storms my veins.

'Can you tell me your name, love?'

Walkie-talkies, that's it. That's what the crackly things are called. I feel a token of satisfaction, clinging to the sound of the words in my head – *walkie-talkies, walkie-talkies* – to distract myself from the unrelenting pain surging through my body.

'Can you hear me OK?'

I nod my head. My teeth chatter uncontrollably.

'What's your name, love?'

I can't feel my toes. My legs are numb.

'I'm freezing,' I say. I squeeze the words out between lips like stone. There seems to be no space left in my mouth.

Someone rustles something and I see a woman holding out a big foil blanket.

'What's your name, love?'

What is it? My mind is blank. One side of my head throbs with agony and my hair is wet. I don't know who I am and I'm hurting, I'm scared and confused. It feels like I'm lying on gravel and I flounder to try and sit up, but a firm hand holds my shoulder to the floor.

'Keep still, love, don't try to move. Can you tell us your name?'

It must be there somewhere. I try to relax, to remember what it is. Yes, I'm sure I know it. It's on the edge of my mind, the tip of my tongue. I close my eyes and try to picture the letters so that I can tell the man. I imagine a page with writing on, with my signature. I scan my eyes around the remnants of my memory. Where is the name? I can't see my name anywhere.

'I can't see it.'

'OK, don't worry, love, just stay with us, we're going to have you out of here in no time. Nice and warm and dry. Get you checked over.'

The man wraps the foil thing over me. He holds my head, and then the woman passes him a collar, which, between them, they manoeuvre and clip around my neck.

'Stay with me now, love,' the man says, but all I want to do is sleep. Just sleep.

. . .

I know that I am somewhere different even though my eyes are closed. The bed is harder than the one I am used to: the sheets are stiff and heavy. An unidentifiable commotion is happening somewhere in the distance. The temperature is wrong. I have the sensation of being elevated.

Who am I? I think and think, but nothing is there. I am nobody.

I have the feeling of being drunk. Something tips and lurches behind my eyes.

White wine. An argument in a pub. Torrential rain, lashing so hard that it's blinding, it's bending the windscreen wipers. Surging water with roads like rivers, rising so quickly that it's in the footwell of the car, up to my ankles.

I part my eyelids carefully, aware of a stickiness on them. The light is synthetic, bluey-white, dancing like a miniscule strobe.

My heart begins to race. This is some sort of hospital room: I can tell by the white walls that have just a subtle hint of green; by the waterproof wingback chair in the corner; by the clouded plastic of the water jug on the locker beside me.

Something is beeping. There are tubes and wires around me and in me, and then suddenly there's a nurse next to my bed pressing a gadget by the computer monitor thing and saying, 'Hi lovely. You've finally decided to join us then?'

She strokes my hair and hangs her face over mine, the saggy skin of her throat and jowls falling forward. She pulls my eyelids up a little and examines my pupils, and I don't know if I'm supposed to look up or down or directly at her. She checks something that is attached to the back of my hand, and then my fingernails.

'Can you remember anything? Do you know why you're here?'

I attempt to say the word 'water', but it comes out as a croak and so I clear my throat and try again.

'Water. I was in some water.'

'OK. Anything else?'

I can't find an answer. There is nothing else in my mind. It's like a television that has been switched off. How did I get here? What happened with the water, before the water?

'Well, you're safe now. You're in hospital and we're checking you over and making sure that everything works as it should. So, what shall I call you? Can you tell me what your name is?'

Surely I should know it. How can someone not know their own name? Perhaps I'm trying too hard, and maybe if I try to relax and not panic then it will just come. I take a deep breath and open my mouth, waiting for my voice to speak.

'It's... er...' I'm scared. What's happened to my brain? I fidget and feel my heart pounding.

'Don't worry.' The nurse must sense my distress. 'It'll come. It's still early days.'

I watch as she adjusts the line from a drip hung beside me. How can I know these words – drip, nurse, computer, tubes, green – yet not know my name?

* * *

I sleep again until the sound of screaming jolts me awake, but then I realise that the noise was in my head, locked somewhere in a dream or a nightmare. I am breathless, like I have been running. My body aches because I am lying on my back while attached to all the tubes, when all I want to do is curl into a foetal position on my side. The sheets rustle as I slowly worm my legs around, trying to move my feet and ankles under the weight of the blankets. I can't turn myself over. There is just not enough energy in my body.

It is dark apart from the glow of the machine that beeps beside me. I have the vague suspicion that someone is sitting in the chair next to the bed but my head hurts too much to turn and look. I am certain that I can hear breathing, though.

A man. It definitely feels like a man. I can't see him but I have the sensation that he is there, watching me.

Waiting for me.

TWO

The next time I wake, light is streaming through the big window in my room. A sense of traffic outside, aeroplanes in the sky, people going about their lives. The astringent smell of bleach in the corridor outside my room.

The jowly faced nurse comes in and checks me again with a weary smile. Is this the end or the beginning of her shift? I don't know. I feel like I don't know much about anything.

'So, what do we know this morning, then?' she says.

What *do* I know?

I was in some water. Now I am in hospital. My own name still eludes me.

'My head hurts,' I say.

She looks at the monitor and presses something on it. 'OK, we'll get you some more pain relief. Just give me a mo.'

'Am I all right?'

'Well, you're in the right place, and you're looking good so far.' She gives me an ardent wink.

'Was there a man here earlier?' I ask. 'Sitting by the bed?'

She pinches her lips and gives a sympathetic stare. 'You had a visitor for a little while.'

'Who was he?'

'Didn't you remember?'

'I didn't really see him. It was dark.'

'Well...' That pitying smile again. 'Maybe we should wait and see if his name comes to you.'

'Does *he* know my name?' I ask her. 'Surely, if he's a visitor he must know who *I* am?'

She shushes me with a gentle hand on my shoulder. 'Let's not get you into a tizz. Rest is what you need. The names and everything else will probably follow.'

I watch as she checks the tubes on my drip. 'What's *your* name?'

'I'm Adele. I'm your key nurse. You might get Sana or Grant during the night shift.'

'OK.' Adele. I must try to remember that for next time.

* * *

I don't know how much time passes before I see Adele again. Three hours. Three days. It seems like one minute I'm here, conversing, then the next I have slipped into oblivion. My head feels better though, if a little groggy.

'When can I go home?' I ask after I have impressed her by remembering her name.

Her face brightens. 'Do you remember your home? Where you live?'

Something slams shut in my head. 'I don't know.' Vague pictures of houses and bungalows float around but I'm not sure if one of them is mine. I see a fireplace, a hallway, patio doors to a garden. Then the images are gone again.

How can I go home when I don't know where it is? My throat starts to ache because I want to cry.

'Do you think you're able to have a little sip of water? Is your throat feeling OK to swallow?'

Adele pours water into a plastic beaker as I nod, and brings it to my lips. It's tepid and limey as I hold it in my mouth before swallowing, and it's just at that moment as I feel the bubble of liquid travel down my throat that I suddenly have the revelation.

Yes!

The utter joy, the relief!

'I've remembered,' I splutter, dribbling water onto the bedding.

'My name,' I tell her. 'It's Becka. My name is Becka.'

THREE

BECKA

A porter wheels me on a trolley along corridors, into lifts, past waiting rooms and a café, and I track the stained ceiling panels into each department as I am sent for scans and X-rays.

Later, the nurse called Sana spoons thin, watery soup into my mouth and asks me questions about where I am, where I was, what day it is and if I know the name of the prime minister. I am baffled by all the questions. My location is some vague hospital. I don't even remember my own surname.

Water. That's all I remember.

And Becka. My name is Becka. I cling onto this knowledge for dear life. Please, God, don't let me forget it.

* * *

I sleep again, hooked up to the machines and tubes. For how long, I don't know. Nurses come and go: they adjust things, check my blood pressure, ask me questions. The questions are a mixture of the same ones – name, date, location, birthday, where I live – and sometimes new ones are added, like earlier they asked if I could describe my partner.

'Partner?' It was only after the suggestion that I considered I might have one.

'You know, husband, significant other?' The nurse shone a torch into my eyes.

Again, my mind was blank. Although I knew in general terms *what* a husband was, I didn't specifically know if I had one or *who* he might be. I checked my left hand and yes, there, on my third finger was a band of gold. Did this mean that I definitely had a husband? I asked the nurse this question but she just rubbed my arm and didn't answer.

Sometimes it feels like they are playing games with me.

* * *

I sleep quite a lot in here. When I ask how long I have been here, the nurse says, 'How long do *you* think you have been here?' and again it is like a trick question that I can't get right. Some things I am OK with. Like, I can identify the staff members: Adele on the day shift, Sana or Grant on the night shift, and also Whitney who sometimes covers the changeovers and always writes with a green pen. I can generally remember what I have for breakfast – usually toast with marmalade, although I did try the poached egg once to find it dry and rubbery – and I know that if the hot tap in the bathroom is not switched off with an extra forceful twist then it will drip tortuously for hours.

It has been presumed that I will be able to retain information going forward, and the consultant – whose name is Mr Ali – is pleased with this. Whether or not my past memories will return is yet unclear.

Some of the tubes have been taken out now. There are plasters and bruises where my skin was pierced to insert them, and my body and limbs bloom with an array of colours. I try to avoid looking in the bathroom mirror: the first time I caught my reflection and saw the horrendous swells and scrapes made me want to be sick.

I don't know what medication I am on. There is a tube that goes into a cannula on the back of my hand; the nurses also bring me small paper pots of pills regularly, which I have to swallow while they watch me. Really, I should remember to ask them what it is all for and if it can be reduced. At times I feel so incredibly spaced-out, in a semi-conscious limbo where my eyes are closed but I hear people talking in my room.

They are there now, at least four of them in white coats, standing around my bed. I listen as they discuss dissociative seizures, retrograde amnesia, fugue state, head injury and severe concussion, extensive damage to the hippocampus...

Hippocampus makes me think of a big grey animal wallowing about in water.

Water. In the footwell, up to my ankles, filling quicker than a bath. My car door unable to open as I'm pushing, shoving, ramming my shoulder against it...

Then the memory disappears, extinguished as if a fire blanket has been thrown over it.

* * *

I open my eyes to the white walls. Have I been sleeping? It is quiet and all the doctors that were here earlier have gone.

It's different in my room this time though.

There's a man standing at the end of my bed. He's dressed in jeans and a grey jumper: he's obviously not one of the medical staff. But he's watching me.

Waiting.

'Honey, I've been so worried.'

The voice provokes a rush of tears from me but I don't know why.

And the man that has been standing at the end of my bed is

now beside me, pushing my hair gently back from my forehead, gazing at me with such an expression of disquiet that I am suddenly crushed with an awful fear.

What has happened?

And who is he?

FOUR

BECKA

I scrutinise the man from my hospital bed. He's probably around his mid-forties. The pull of his jumper across his chest and shoulders divulges that he undoubtedly works out and keeps himself in good shape. His hair is short, close-cropped to his head, a salt-and-pepper colour that suits him. His skin is taut, olive, with an attractive smattering of stubble. Sexy.

'Becka... oh God... they told me that you've lost your memory. That you can't remember anything about what happened.' His dark lashes are long. His flint-grey eyes hold mine for an intense length of time. 'Is it true? Can't you remember anything?'

I can't speak. I stare up at him. There's a prickly feeling spreading in my chest.

Who is he?

Dusk drifts through the expansive window and brings with it the rumble and splutter of unnecessary random fireworks outside. Then Nurse Adele strides into the room with her usual squeaky shoes, carrying a fresh jug of water for me.

'Look,' she says, 'you have a visitor. We thought it would do you good to see him, just briefly, if you're up to it?'

'She seems better today. More alert.' The man in the grey jumper directs the statement towards Adele.

His voice is deep and gravelly with the hint of a northern accent. He goes to lean against the windowsill and gazes out while Adele adjusts my position and plumps my pillows.

'Everything OK?' she asks. 'Freddie's basically moved into the waiting room downstairs. He's been frantic with worry about you.'

'Freddie.' I say the name as if this might coax the memories to return. I'm intrigued by him: he's a good-looking man, but why is he here?

He spins on his heels. 'Surely you remember *me*?'

His tone makes me teary again and I look towards Adele for help.

'You've had a serious head injury, love, and it's going to take some getting over. Remember when I was asking you the other day about your partner? If you could describe him? Well, this is him – he's been here for days and days – waiting for you to properly wake up because you've been in an induced coma. And although your body is on the mend, your memory seems to have taken the brunt of your little adventure.'

'Little adventure?'

It's a strange turn of phrase. But it seems that six nights ago, late on Saturday evening, I was dragged unconscious from the River Trent. The river had breached its banks in numerous places after flash flooding, causing vehicles to be abandoned and washed away. I had been pinned up by the force of water – along with a small shed and suite of rattan furniture – against the thick stone wall of a pub beer garden just long enough for the bar staff, who had been videoing the floods from an upstairs window, to pull me out and administer CPR until the paramedics arrived.

Physically, I had suffered mainly superficial injuries – three broken ribs, cuts and bruises to my head and hands – and hypothermia. But brain scans showed damage as a result of oxygen starvation and, although I have made good progress since being brought to hospital – I am able to retain most new memories – the doctors are unable to tell me if the amnesia is permanent. Maybe I will never regain my memories from the time before my *little adventure*.

'So, you're my partner?' I ask the man called Freddie.

His eyes look at the floor. Embarrassment, or distress, or pain. I'm still sussing out how to decipher emotions.

'I'm your *husband*.' He pulls a chair to the side of me and holds my hand. I feel his fingers trembling.

'Ohhh. OK.' There's the tingly sensation in my chest again and the room seems to spin. I look at the ceiling and breathe deeply.

'I'll give you five minutes alone,' says Adele as she leaves the room.

There's a silence then, when it feels like everything outside the window and in the corridor stops to wait for something to happen. The monitor beeps and I turn to look at the numbers. My heart rate has gone up to ninety-two.

'How are you?' Freddie says, eventually.

'Well... I don't know. I'm alive, at least.'

'Don't you remember anything at all? I don't just mean about the accident, but about your life before it? About *us*?'

I bite my lip. 'It took me days to remember that my name is Becka. I don't even remember my surname. That's everything I know about my life. And the accident was something to do with water.'

'Really? That's the extent of your memories?'

'More or less.' I look at him again, focusing on a tiny scar on the left side of his chin where the stubble doesn't grow. His eyes connect with mine for a few seconds and there's a definite magnetic pull between them.

'Do you want to sit up a bit more?' he says. 'I could move

your pillows and help you up? You could look out of the window.'

Suddenly I am drained. I struggle to keep my eyes open, and try to breathe out the weird feeling in my chest.

'No thank you. I'm... I think I'm tired again.'

'Sorry.' He stoops to kiss the back of my hand before returning it to the bed. 'I'll leave you alone now.'

He goes to the door where he stands and lingers. 'Can I come back later? Or tomorrow?'

'Yes,' I whisper as I close my eyes. 'Tomorrow.'

FIVE

BECKA

Later – I don't know if it's the same day or a week afterwards – Freddie returns to my room. I have more energy this time. I feel as if I am ready for him, because he could be useful in helping me to sort my head out.

We talk.

It is like a cautious blind date, although I see something familiar in his mannerisms, hear something in his accent that I vaguely recognise.

'So, what happened with the flood, the river? Why was I there? Were you with me, too?' There are so many questions I need answering.

Freddie tells me that I had been to meet up with a friend in a pub. An old university acquaintance that lived out near Newark. Freddie hadn't been with me, but when I didn't arrive home on time he rang the pub and was told about the flooding. Vehicles had been abandoned; a couple had been swept away in the water and taken to a hospital in Lincoln; a dog had died; and another woman pulled from further down the river had been taken to a different hospital. It had been a chaotic night: homes had been evacuated, the power had been cut off in places and the emergency services had been inundated. Freddie rang around all the hospitals but there was no one with my name at any of them. Finally, he found an unidentified female patient that had been taken to Mansfield, so he drove like a maniac to the inadequate hospital car park, where he ended up blocking someone in and getting a parking ticket. He was allowed into the critical care unit in order to identify me, and over the next few days spent an inordinate amount of time in the downstairs café and waiting room, napping in a chair that cricked his neck.

'You've been unconscious for most of the time,' he says. 'But I've been by your side, talking to you, waiting for you to wake up.'

I want to know everything. When my birthday is, where we live, how we met, how long we've been married, if we have children, information about my family and my past.

Freddie smiles affectionately and rolls his eyes. 'Oh my God. The whole back catalogue. Where to start with it all!'

So, I listen as he recounts the story of my life.

It turns out that I'm forty years old.

'Forty? I don't feel forty.'

Unfortunately, yes, but apparently still good for my age. We rented a Cornish beachside cottage with a hot tub last June to celebrate. Near St Ives. It was a favourite place of mine, with all the galleries, all the arty connections.

And us. Me and Freddie. We were childhood sweethearts: I had still been doing A levels when we met. All those years ago.

He takes my left hand in both of his, looking at my wedding ring. 'You were my proper first love and I'm not ashamed to say it. When I first saw you I knew that I'd never want anyone else.'

His eyes are not only gorgeous, but they hold such depth and honesty.

'Kids?' I ask, but he tells me that we don't have children. He says they didn't fit in with our lifestyle. I don't know whether to feel disappointed.

'You claimed not to be a very maternal person. You'd been an only child and never really had babies around you. Your parents were great: very active and into gardening. Your dad had an allotment and grew fantastic vegetables: he used to win trophies at shows for giant marrows and stuff like that. They both died – must be five years ago – within months of each other. It was such a stressful time,' he tells me. 'Your mum first with cancer, then your dad with a stroke in the same year. We sprinkled their ashes on the top of Mam Tor.'

A lump lodges in my throat. I feel suddenly sad. Not just to know that my parents are dead, but that I cannot remember anything about them at all.

'Tell me more about us,' I say.

'Well, we've been married for nearly seventeen years and live just south of Chesterfield in a nice area. It's almost in the Peak District.' He laughs. 'We'll cross that border one day and live the dream. You always wanted to be in Bakewell.'

When Nurse Adele pops in to do my hourly checks she suggests that maybe Freddie should show me photographs to jog my memory, and so he says he will bring some in tomorrow.

'And what about getting in touch with old friends? They might like to come and visit.' Adele's words provoke a little frown between Freddie's eyes, but then it's gone in a flash.

'Oh,' I say. 'Can I have extra visitors now?'

'Yes, of course you can. It would be good for you to speak to friends, and they could help you fill in a few extra gaps, trigger some more memories.'

'I don't know who my friends are.' I laugh and look towards Freddie.

He leans his elbows onto his knees and rubs a hand through his hair. 'Well. To be honest, I didn't have a great deal to do with your friends. You didn't really have that many close ones. Obviously, there was Rhianna who came round quite a lot...'

'Maybe you could contact her,' I suggest.

'She's not here any more though,' says Freddie. 'She emigrated to Australia just before Christmas. And Vina was probably your closest friend but' – his face grimaces – 'she died in September. We were gutted – completely in shock – that it could happen so quickly. Breast cancer' – he looks up at Adele for a moment – 'a particularly aggressive one. Five weeks from diagnosis to death. Horrendous. It really makes you think.'

'Oh poor thing,' I say, even though I don't know who we are talking about.

'Hmm,' says Freddie, reaching across the bedcover to sympathetically rub my knee.

'But what about the person I was with on the night of my accident? You said I was in a pub with an old friend.'

Freddie pulls his hand away to scratch his eyebrow. He looks at the floor and shrugs. 'I don't know what their name was. It was just someone you said you knew from university. And obviously, your phone got washed away with all your contacts on it.'

So all my friends and colleagues have disappeared with the outgoing tide. There must be someone. Maybe there are things at home – address books, letters, that sort of thing – that will lead me back to them.

'I might be able to sync your files to the computer,' says Freddie, looking pensive, 'if you bear with with me I can certainly give it a go and see what we can retrieve for you.'

I don't know what he means about syncing files. But he's obviously doing all he can to help my memory.

How long have we been talking for? I suddenly feel exhausted. I need to sleep again and give my brain a rest. I smile at Freddie and he lifts my hand to kiss it.

He seems so caring, so doting; the perfect, handsome, lovely guy that any sensible woman would want to be married to. Faultless almost.

I'm so lucky that he's my husband.

Because the thought strikes me that I have absolutely no one else I can rely on.

SIX

BECKA

Freddie is here again when I wake. He asks me if I remember him this time and when I tell him that I do, he tests me on all the other information like my birthday and where we live and our wedding anniversary, and we're both delighted when all my answers are correct.

He gets his phone out and tells me that he took photographs of our house and garden to help trigger my memory.

'You're not supposed to be using screens yet because of your head injury and concussion, but they might let me show you a few pictures,' he says.

'Go on then,' says Nurse Whitney who has arrived with a fresh water jug, 'just a couple of minutes and I won't say anything.'

Freddie shows me how to swipe through the images, and I examine the spacious rooms and high ceilings, the soft grey walls, quality furnishings, sleek kitchen with black marble-topped island and Belfast sink. The garden is newly turfed – Freddie says that it was only finished last week – edged with tasteful shrubs, with a large square of decking and pagoda strung with fairy lights. Built-in pizza oven and seating area.

Attractive architectural planting with a variety of colours, heights and textures. I feel the serenity of it all from my bed.

'Gorgeous,' says Nurse Whitney who is beside me, peeking at the pictures of the lounge. 'Now, just imagine a room half that size with kids' toys everywhere, and ketchup on the carpet and handprints on the walls, because that's what photos of *my* house would look like.'

'She's got a good eye for design,' says Freddie, nodding towards me and winking.

'Me? Really?'

'You got a degree from Glasgow School of Art. Your paintings and sketches are amazing.'

'Oh, wow.' I look down at my hands that must have used paintbrushes and pencils. I imagine a paint palette and jars of solvent on a desk, trying to picture myself using them. There is a big space in my head that should hold memories of being at university, student life, learning and partying. Maybe I will remember in time...

I look again at Freddie's phone. I love the idea that I have created these spaces. I go through the pictures once more and visualise myself in these rooms and, yes, maybe there is a tiny flicker of recognition of the way that I have set out the furniture and combined the soft furnishings in a stylish but slightly quirky colour scheme.

'I bet you can't wait to get home now you've seen what it looks like,' says Nurse Whitney.

Freddie squeezes my hand. 'I can't wait to get you there.'

My heart skips and flutters. I pass the phone back, taking in Freddie's striking presence, his alluring demeanour, and although it ought to feel like being in a dream I'm suddenly shivering as a pain stabs through the top of my head.

I slump back onto my pillow and close my eyes.

'Sorry,' I whisper. 'I need to sleep.'

* * *

I am free from the tubes and the monitor. Nurse Adele helps my stiff, bruised body out of bed and I hold on to her as I hobble out of my bedroom door for the first time. My ribs hurt with every step and my legs struggle with the short journey. We venture through the main ward and past the nurses' station to the end of the corridor and back. The distance and the staring faces are exhausting and overwhelming.

'You're doing great,' she tells me as I sink back into bed and fold my weak legs under the sheets. 'We need to get you in practice for when you go home.'

'Home.' I don't know why the word conveys such trepidation. I've seen the photographs and it looks beautiful.

'Yes.' Adele smiles. 'You've got a gorgeous place to go back to, and Freddie will look after you, won't he?'

'Will he?'

My belly is churning and I feel sick. There is a dark shadow behind my eyes but it could be due to my head injury.

Adele rubs my shoulder. 'Of course he will. It's clear to everyone how much he loves you. All the nurses think he's brilliant.'

There's obviously apprehension all over my face because Adele sits down on the bed and looks me in the eyes.

'I know you're worried. Memory loss is a scary thing. For you it will feel like a stranger has just walked in off the street and offered to take you home. That's it, isn't it?'

I nod.

'Shall I get him to bring your documents in just to prove he's not some random weirdo?' She winks and ruffles my sleeve.

I laugh. 'Am I being stupid?'

'Of course you're not.' She puts on a matronly voice. 'I will make sure that you're not let out of here until we've seen them. OK?'

'Thank you.'

She stands and gives me a thumbs-up before she leaves me alone.

Am I being stupid?

What woman wouldn't want a gorgeous, kind and caring man like Freddie?

I realise that I am just being irrational. It must be the medication, the head injury, the time I have spent being cooped up in here.

It will be fine, the calm and logical part of my brain tells me. There's absolutely nothing to worry about.

SEVEN

BECKA

The next time that Freddie is here he has brought more pictures. Proper old-fashioned glossy photographs that have been thumbed and looked through, laughed over.

This is a good sign, I tell myself. We have history, even though I cannot remember it. I resolve to make an effort with him, because he is obviously doing all he can to help me.

'Oh my God,' I say. 'Surely this is not me!' But it definitely is: a young, fresh-faced seventeen-year-old me with long hair and a curtain fringe, in school uniform, posing next to a sporty red car. Me, with pouting lips, willowy legs and a confident hand on the hip. 'That surely can't be a regulation school skirt. Not that sort of length. It's far too short.' I lift the photograph higher and examine my attire: the tie has been loosened enough to undo the top shirt button, and the sleeves of the navy blazer have been pushed up to my elbows.

'You were always so gorgeous,' says Freddie.

But he's some need to talk. Here are photographs of him with black hair flopping over his face, muscles bursting out of his vest top, lips framing a grin that could tempt anyone into bed.

'Young lovers,' Nurse Adele comments. She's become a bit attached to us, says she will miss us when I go home. 'Look for me on Facebook,' she comments while Freddie pulls a grimace behind her back.

I have heard of Facebook and have a vague recollection of what it looks like. Social media, laptops, phones, all this technology that needs to be used and could prove to be a mystery may be a challenge, but I am willing to take it on. Whatever I need to do to get back to my life, I will embrace fully as soon as I can. The doctors have told me to avoid computer screens and phones as much as possible until my next scheduled scans in three months' time, and I am happy to take their advice if it will help my memory in the long term.

'Oh, I should have thought,' says Freddie, clapping a hand to his forehead, 'I could have downloaded some music for you.'

He's certain there are some songs that would trigger memories of our early years together when we were youthful and fervent and couldn't get enough of each other. *Our* tunes.

'What sort of music is it?' I ask, and he laughs as he tells me that we were into dance music, clubby stuff that had a beat, that caught the attention of everyone when we rode around in his car with the windows down.

There is a rich warmth in his voice. And he has such love in his eyes. I see it every time I look at him. He has it for both of us – it can carry us through this fallow period where I am unsure and unremembering. In some ways it is like we are young again, in one of those new relationships that makes you catch your breath, wanting to spend every spare moment in each other's presence.

I find myself tentatively smiling, being somewhat nervous in his company, thinking about the photograph of our bedroom and what it will be like to be back there. What will he expect from me? How did we used to be with each other? Can I trust him to be patient and gentle while my memory is healing?

Anxiety starts to creep back in and I find myself digging my fingernails into the top of my thigh.

Stop it, I tell myself. A new start lies in front of us.

I may not remember anything of the last seventeen years of our marriage, but I will give everything I can to make our future wonderful.

* * *

The bruising on my ribs is a rainbow of green, blue and purple. Scabs have formed over the cuts on my scalp and are becoming increasingly itchy. But things are looking good. I am eating properly. I can walk to the toilet without assistance. Pain relief is only necessary for the intermittent headaches that take hold much less often now. The consultant has asked me an intensive range of questions as part of a pre-discharge assessment and decided that I should be fit to go home in the next couple of days. There will be follow-up appointments plus the opportunity for counselling sessions if I wish, but it looks like I have had a lucky escape. It is still not known if or when my memories will return, but as my brain is able to recall practical and motor skills, and can retain new information going forward, then life with a supportive partner should not be a problem.

* * *

The psychologist has told me to exercise my memory when I get home. I should avoid stress. I should relax in a warm room with soft music and imagine being in a group of people. I should look at the faces and try to put names to the faces. I should visualise myself walking around places and try to identify roads and buildings that might be familiar. There is a chance that my memories might return at some point.

'Think about what you remember and write it all down,' he

told me. 'It will help to coax out the missing bits.'

I smiled and said that I would, and didn't even become disconcerted when he added with a flippant laugh, '...that is, if you *want* to remember the missing bits.'

* * *

In my hospital bed, during the night when the wards are relatively quiet, I try out the mind activity. I imagine myself in stiletto shoes and a classy black coat walking down a street. Weaving in and out of people with shopping bags, kids on scooters, and pensioners holding scurrying dogs on leads. I search their faces for any feature that might be familiar. But there's nothing. Men, women, children: all of them are unrecognisable.

I try to relax. To not look too intently. To take more notice of the buildings and the signs instead.

There's a row of cottages. A red postbox in a wall. The shops have disappeared and the clusters of people have thinned out. It's dark, raining, and I sense myself feeling angry. I look back and there is a pub behind me with a straggle of customers spilling out onto the pavement. Then, suddenly, my feet are cold. Wet. Legs sloshing through water. I'm shouting. Not just shouting, but shouting at *someone*. He's in front of me but I can't reach him to see his face and I don't know what his name is. I stumble over a kerb submerged in the water and throw out a hand to stop myself falling...

I jump.

The image is gone in a beat.

My eyes open in the darkness, I stare towards the sliver of moonlight that spies through the chink in the curtains and try to slow my increased breaths.

I lie still, fearful of what sleep might bring, and where it might take me to. My eyes remain open until Nurse Adele arrives at six o'clock to do my morning checks.

EIGHT

BECKA

Freddie brings a holdall of clothes into the hospital for me. Underwear, baggy yoga pants, gym vest and fleecy hoodie. They are not what I expect, and look as if they have rarely been worn, if at all. I push my face into them and take a deep breath to try and get a sense of my old self, but they smell of nothing.

'I can't remember being sporty,' I tell him. 'Somehow, my body doesn't feel like I used to work out.'

'Your downward dogs were great,' he laughs. 'But you didn't have a gym membership. Sometimes you went to an aerobics class if you were in the right mood. Swimming was more your thing, really. Perhaps that's what helped you survive in the river. But I thought that bringing loose clothing would be best for your bruising.'

So, he was just being considerate.

But when I get dressed, I find that the bra doesn't fit properly – it's considerably tight around the back – and the trainers look brand spanking new with not a mark on them. I re-thread the laces to take out any slack because they are far too sloppy on my feet.

I take Freddie's arm and we walk slowly, steadily, around

the hospital. We get a coffee in the café downstairs. I find that I remember how to use a lift and I'm able to read a menu. Freddie shows me the waiting room where he spent many anxious nights while I was in a coma.

'That chair has wrecked my neck,' he jokes, pointing to a grubby seat in the corner.

Outside, we shamble together along the front of the building, passing people who are smoking, texting, eating and crying. The car park seems like a terrifying maelstrom of dangerous moving objects.

'Do *I* drive?' I turn and ask Freddie suddenly. 'I mean, am I able to drive?'

He blinks and there's a couple of seconds spare before he says that, yes, of course I can drive. I used to have a car for a while but gave it up a year ago in favour of using public transport and doing more walking. Then he laughs and pulls me into him and calls me an eco-warrior.

A brief moment of confusion spills over me. Something half-remembered, like being in a car – even *driving* a car – as it is filling up with water. But I am unable to hold on to the scene, and just as we return to the entrance it flits quickly from my mind as an ambulance wails into the emergency bay.

* * *

Nurse Adele pops her head around my door at teatime. I am in the process of eating some cold and unidentifiable sponge pudding when she grins and gives me her trademark thumbs-up.

'It's all legit,' she tells me. 'Freddie brought in your passport and marriage certificate. I think hospital records still had you at a previous address – or was it we still had you down with your maiden name? I can't remember – but anyway, it's all been sorted, so you're safe to go home with him.'

'OK.' I give a weak smile and stick my spoon in the congealed custard. I'm not hungry any more.

'It's normal to feel some anxiety after being in here for so long, but really, it's all going to be great,' she assures me. 'You really don't need to worry. And if there's anything specific, medically, that you are concerned about after you get home, then you can always ring and speak to the consultant if you don't want to wait until your next appointment.'

I smile again; she seems to expect it.

'I know.'

She's right. I have become like a prisoner, feeling safe within the confines of my four walls here, afraid to break away from the routines and go out into the world.

It's normal. I will be fine.

I have Freddie to look after me.

* * *

Tomorrow. That's when I can go. I will get a final appointment with the consultant, then Freddie will be free to take me back home.

Grant and Sana bring me a giant chocolate muffin with a candle in the top to celebrate my departure and wish me luck.

'Don't forget about *us*,' says Grant cheekily.

I bite my lip, having no idea what to expect from tomorrow.

It's as if Sana recognises my uncertainty, just like Nurse Adele did.

'Don't be anxious,' she says. 'Everything will fall into place once you get home. I bet all your friends will be round to visit and all your memories will come flooding back. And if they don't, well, you can just make some lovely new ones.'

'Yes, you're right.'

I smile and look down at my wedding ring. Love will surely get us through all this.

NINE

BECKA

Leaving the hospital is a challenge. Twice I have to find a toilet on my journey down to reception because the nausea is so bad that I really think I am going to throw up. I become tearful as I step out of the doors, and Freddie has to set down the holdall so that he can envelop me supportively, until it becomes evident that we are blocking the entrance to wheelchair users.

'Should we go back in and sit in the café for a while until you feel OK?' he suggests. 'We could get coffee and cake? We don't want to rush you.'

It's lovely that he is so caring. But I shake my head. Despite my fraught emotions I know that once I have taken this step I will be properly on the road to my future. I need to get home. I need to get back to a level of normality. Taking deep breaths, I walk as calmly as I can with him towards his waiting car.

* * *

It's a gloriously bright and sunny day as we travel home. Freddie brought more clothes for me to wear: this time a woollen dress in grey (it feels much more *me*), tights, black court shoes and a stylish double-breasted black coat. He admitted that he had been out to Next and bought everything brand new. It seemed significant, he said, that a new start and new memories should be accompanied by a new outfit for me.

Thankfully, all the clothing and shoes fit perfectly this time.

I can't help but look at him during the journey. There's a sense of déjà vu being beside him, watching the way his thumbs stroke the steering wheel, and although it's not a memory as such, it gives me hope.

Dusk is settling in as we arrive home. There's a distinctive frosty chill in the air as we step out of the car onto the drive.

Freddie holds out his arm. 'Shall I carry you over the threshold?'

I squeeze his hand affectionately; he puts the key in the front door and we step inside. He picks up post from the floor and glances at it.

'Just junk mail for you,' he says, tossing it onto a table in the hall.

I glance at the envelope. It's a home furnishings catalogue addressed to Mrs Rebecca Anthony. Me. The name I almost couldn't remember.

'Well, here you are,' Freddie declares, sweeping his arms out in a flourish. 'Again. Obviously.'

I look around the hallway: nice parquet floor that looks like it has been restored; staircase with a blue and grey stripy carpet; clean white walls.

'Do you want to go and have a look round on your own?' he says. 'Or shall I come with you? You might want me to show you where things are.'

My chin wobbles a little and I feel somewhat overwhelmed. I don't know where to start.

'Could I just have a cup of tea, please? For now.'

He goes through a door at the end of the hall, and I follow him. There's the stunning kitchen with a view to the garden through the bi-fold doors. Subtle lighting around the patio and shrubbery is already switched on. I love everything about it all and can't get my head around the fact that it is mine.

There's a special tap that dispenses boiling water, and I say 'wow', as if I have never heard of such a thing before. Freddie takes mugs from a cupboard – one of them is pink with *Becka* written on in swirly script – and puts teabags in. I watch in silence as he makes the drinks and goes to the huge, silver fridge for milk.

A thought strikes me. 'Have I always had milk in tea?'

Freddie is puzzled. Hesitant. He hovers the carton over the waiting cups.

'I just wondered. I only drank coffee in hospital, but for some reason I just fancied tea – sort of unconsciously, you know? – and now I can't remember if I have it black or not.'

'Yes,' he says without looking up. He quickly tips a drop in each cup. 'Yes, you've always had milk. But maybe your taste buds have changed since the accident?'

We sit on the high stools at the kitchen island. Freddie gets a packet of chocolate chip cookies out and puts some on a plate between us. I feel like a guest. The tea tastes wrong. Maybe I will just drink coffee in future.

* * *

I tour the house with him and he takes me upstairs to the fantastic bedroom that I recognise from the pictures on his phone. The bed is immaculately made, with a huge canvas photograph of our wedding day looking down on it, and I gaze at it, at the young version of myself in the picture, thinking how happy I looked.

He shows me the en suite and demonstrates how to work the shower. Everything is gleaming, and when I mention this he tells me that he likes things to be clean and orderly, always has.

Across the hall there are two smaller bedrooms, simply and elegantly decorated with plush carpets. One of the rooms is empty; the other contains a chest of drawers and a bed that has been stripped to the mattress. There is a fixing on the wall that no longer holds a television. A guest room where people don't stay often, by the looks of it.

'We'd been having a clear-out before your accident,' says Freddie. 'With a view to moving on.'

'Really?' I'm surprised that we would want to leave such a lovely place.

We return to the landing and look over the banister to the hallway below.

'What do you think?' Freddie asks, as if it is the first time I have seen the place. Although, I suppose, my damaged brain thinks it is.

'It's amazing.'

'You did all this,' he tells me. 'Your ideas, your designs, everything.'

I smile. My insides feel warm. I go back into the master bedroom to take it all in once again, and maybe there is a glimmer of recognition at what I have created and it's not just that I have seen the photographs beforehand.

* * *

We spend the evening in the sitting room. I browse through the furnishings brochure that came through the post, and Freddie scrolls through news items on his iPad. It feels comfortable, companionable, and my earlier bouts of nausea and panic have subsided. We chat at times, about what we might do tomorrow, what kind of food we might want to eat, where we might go.

The conversation is relaxed, and Freddie doesn't pressure or pester. He lets me go up to the bedroom before him, to change into the silk night shirt that he earlier folded and put on the left-hand pillow of the bed. I assume that is the side that I sleep on, although when I slide between the sheets it somehow feels wrong.

'Everything OK?' Freddie joins me after he has locked up the house.

'Yes, good.' I yawn and try to organise my pillows so that they are comfortable: the top one is far too rigid for my liking.

Freddie goes into the en suite before returning in a modest pair of boxer shorts. I throw the unyielding pillow onto the floor and settle down with the softest one.

'How are you feeling, babe?' Freddie climbs into bed and strokes my hair.

Suddenly, the nausea is back. Is he expecting sex? Was it a regular thing in our marriage? It's something that we haven't talked about. Yet.

I close my eyes and swallow down the biley saliva that has filled my mouth.

He kisses my forehead gently. 'Goodnight, darling. Sleep well. It's wonderful to have you back.'

I relax. It's OK.

I'm home.

TEN

BECKA

In the morning, after a solid, dreamless night, I wake refreshed to find Freddie standing over me with a tray of croissants and coffee. He shuffles the discarded pillow behind my back as I sit up.

'Good morning, sleeping beauty.' He places the tray onto my lap and kisses the top of my head.

'Well, this is preferable to the service I got in hospital,' I say. 'I've had a much better night here.'

'You always sleep well in your own bed.'

Freddie breaks the croissants into chunks and smothers strawberry jam onto them. I sip the coffee and eat the breakfast that he proffers, piece by piece, dropping crumbs all over the duvet.

'Bloody messy woman,' he laughs, brushing off the bits. 'You never change.'

It's another morsel of information about myself that I have just learned. Slowly, I am doing a jigsaw without a picture, fitting together all the pieces of myself so that I can find out who the real me is.

We discuss potential plans for the day: a visit to Chatsworth

House which Freddie tells me is a stately home not too far away. There are lovely grounds to stroll in, a farm shop nearby, and the drive out won't require using busy roads through the town. It sounds like a pleasant way to spend an afternoon, and Freddie suggests that I have some pampering time in the bathroom while he checks his work emails downstairs in the study.

So I familiarise myself with the contents of the bathroom cabinets and drawers, relearning how to get the right temperature on the shower, and giving my hair a good wash and conditioning treatment. Eventually, wrapping myself in a huge bath towel, I return to the bedroom to examine the contents of the wardrobe and drawers. Underwear (mainly black and red, including some kinky thongs), socks, tights, suspenders and stockings – six pairs of black ones: really? – some assorted tops in different styles, more sportswear, two pairs of jeans, a sweatshirt and a cardigan, and three dresses that would be suitable for a restaurant or party. I slide the things along the rail and move them around in the drawers. Nothing jogs any memories. The quantity of clothing seems quite meagre and I wonder if there is an overspill wardrobe elsewhere. I check out the guest room where a cupboard is built into the recess of the chimney breast, but it is full of bedding and towels.

I go back to the master bedroom wardrobe to select items from the bizarre collection and hold them up against myself, standing in front of the full-length mirror. Is this really *me*? Did I used to wear party dresses with slinky knickers and black stockings? I am forty years old. Should that be normal? I genuinely don't know.

Why am I having doubts? I ask myself. Is my subconscious wanting to leave an old life behind? Am I a different person now, someone who doesn't want to wear these colours, these things? And if so, why?

I choose a pair of jeans and a top with the cardigan. First, though, I need to dry my hair. I pull open more drawers to look for a hairdryer and find Freddie's clothes neatly folded, socks paired, boxers rolled into tight cylinders. Where would I keep a hairdryer? Frustrated, I look around the room, under the bed, in all the cupboards and containers.

I go to the top of the stairs.

'Freddie,' I call down over the banister, to where I can see him through an open door, sitting at a mahogany desk. 'Freddie, I can't find a hairdryer.'

He leaves his study and comes into the hallway scratching his head. Somewhat puzzled, he joins me in the bedroom and I show him the drawers I have looked through, and he rubs his face and keeps saying, 'Well, it must be somewhere, there must be one, I'm sure I've seen it,' and when I suggest we look in the other rooms he has a reluctance about him, but we go through to the guest bedroom where the drawers in there contain nothing but fluff and a Monsoon tag for something that cost £29.99.

'Do you really need a hairdryer right now?' he asks. 'Could you just manage with a towel and we'll call and get one from the retail park later?'

'OK,' I say. 'I just thought I would have had one.'

'Yeah,' says Freddie, still scratching his head. Distracted, he leaves me to get dressed, and I hear him rummaging around in the smaller room before he goes back to his study.

I choose the black jeans and a purple top with the cardigan. They are all a size twelve and the jeans are stiff and uncomfortable. I struggle to zip them up. Maybe I put on weight while I was in hospital. I look again at the sportswear and resolve to get more active, to rebook the aerobics sessions that Freddie told me I used to attend.

In the bay window of the bedroom I stand and survey the front garden and the desirable, tree-lined road. Most of the properties are elegant and impressive, well maintained with swanky cars in the drives. But the house across from ours is tired, with yellowing nets, peeling paint and sagging gates.

Their wheelie bin is still out on the pavement. As I gaze out, I notice the curtains across the road tweak sharply and the face of a white-haired lady peers through. She stares straight at me and I take a step back. But... maybe we know each other.

Does she know what's happened to me? Will Freddie have told her about my accident, about how I have lost my memory?

I step into the window recess again and give her a little wave. She seems reluctant, but tips her hand quickly before retreating and pulling the curtain back. Maybe I should go over later and take her dustbin back up the drive.

The sound of conversation drifts upstairs. I quietly go to the banister again and listen as Freddie speaks to someone on his phone. Work talk. The discussion of contracts, start dates, time schedules.

I go into the main bathroom to look for make-up, as there seems to be nothing in our en suite. There are odd bits here in the cabinet and drawers – foundation in quite an orangey shade, pink lipsticks, a huge blusher brush but no blusher, and two mascaras that have dried up – but no proper toiletry bag or box that contains everything together. Was I more of a 'natural' person? It seems an insignificant question to bother Freddie with while he is working, so I make do with moisturiser that I find in my underwear drawer. While I am applying it to my crows' feet and the subtle frown lines on my forehead, I am struck by the thought that I don't know what Freddie does for work. I don't even know what I do! My past has been completely stolen and dumped somewhere so that I can't find it, leaving me to question every aspect of *who* I used to be and *how* I used to be.

It's a lovely afternoon at Chatsworth House and gardens. I feel so much better already, both physically and mentally. We hold hands and stroll through the grounds, and I feel that I can ask

Freddie about anything. He doesn't laugh or mock me when I present him with questions like 'do I still have periods?' (yes, but sometimes they are irregular) or 'what sort of films do I like to watch?' (most things apart from horror and war) or 'tell me about my food likes and dislikes' (I'm not a fan of shellfish and pork, but I love Italian food and have dabbled in the past with Veganuary).

Freddie tells me that he is a freelance photographer now – *'remember when we first met and I was so proud to show you my pictures when I worked for the local rag'* – and his work regularly appears in *National Geographic, Vogue* and *Good Housekeeping*. He's done commissions for Jamie Oliver on a number of cookery books (I have never heard of Jamie Oliver but Freddie explains that he's a celebrity chef) and spent a number of years doing wildlife photography all over the world. 'Did I go with you?' I ask him, and he tells me that, unfortunately, he wasn't able to take me along and has always regretted having to spend weeks away while I was at home alone. He's done some high-profile weddings – famous singers that I probably won't remember – and portraits of politicians and lesser royals.

'What about me?' I ask, and he looks puzzled.

'What... have I photographed you?'

I laugh and explain. 'No, I mean, what do I do for a job? Rocket scientist? Brain surgeon? Like, am I supposed to be at work or something?'

Freddie looks at me and makes a lengthy hmmm. 'Well...'

'Don't tell me I'm a bloody cleaner or a waitress...'

'No. Nothing like that. You used to do a lot of sketching and painting. Watercolours in particular. Then you'd sell your art at craft fairs. Although for the last few years you moved away from all that and became part of my photography business, doing admin work, invoices, emails, that sort of thing.'

'Oh, OK. Is that still doable with my memory problems?'

Freddie thinks that in due course it will be fine, although

he points out that I'm not really supposed to be using screens until I have been assessed at my next appointment. But when I get the go-ahead he will give me a refresher course on the computer and printer and remind me how to file everything. He swings my arm and then pulls me into a hug and calls me his right-hand woman, and I joke with him and ask if I am actually left or right-handed even though I already know – I applied the moisturiser and picked up my cup and fastened my buttons with my right hand – and he laughs loudly for a long time and then says that he loves what I do to him with both of my hands. It's the closest thing he's mentioned to sex, but it suddenly feels inappropriate and then Freddie backtracks by babbling about the overpriced stuff that we might find in the gift shop.

* * *

Later, we go to the café to eat scones with jam and cream, watching with amusement as a young couple tries to deal with a baby and twin toddlers who won't sit down.

'Kids,' says Freddie, rolling his eyes.

Something knots in my stomach.

'Why didn't we have any?' I ask him.

His mouth twists and he glances away for a second. His shoulders shrug loosely. 'Neither of us were that interested. I spent time away with work – sometimes two or three weeks at a time – and that wouldn't have been ideal with a family. We just made the decision to enjoy our lives in a different way. Go places and have fun.'

'So, where did we go? Tell me about the fun we had.'

He looks again at the bickering tots who are involved in a dispute over a plastic cup of juice. Someone bumps his chair as they squeeze through the tables with a tray loaded with cake and Cokes.

'Everywhere,' he says, shrugging again. 'Holidays, weekends away. You name it, we went.'

'Well, you name it,' I tell him. 'Then maybe it might jog my memory.'

He sits stiffly, and suddenly it feels like there's something between us, not something significant but just awkward, like when you get a piece of grit in your shoe. He looks again at the family, obviously irritated by them.

'Well, all the usual places. Majorca, Tenerife, Rome, Benidorm. We had weekends in Paris, in Amsterdam, a nice apartment in the Grand-Place in Brussels. We went to Goa for a fortnight, but you didn't like it. The sickness and whatnot.'

The list doesn't connect, doesn't make any stirrings within me. I want to know what we did, what we ate, quirky things that happened on beaches and in city streets around us, how heat and sangria and romance swallowed us up and made us happy. But Freddie has had enough of the café, of the noise and clatter.

'Come on,' he says, pushing back his chair. 'Let's go and see the house now.'

We escape the bustle and find ourselves awed by utter grandeur: magnificent rooms with ornate ceilings, works of art and pieces of furniture hundreds of years old.

'How the other half live,' says Freddie. 'It's like a different world.'

But we can't complain, really. Our house is perfect for what we need – impressive to some – and is in an area that appears to be affluent and accessible to nice countryside.

'You said we'd been thinking about moving away,' I say to Freddie. 'I can't believe we would want to leave such a lovely place.'

'Well, yes,' he replies. 'It was seriously on the cards. Although with your accident things were put on hold.'

'So have we been there long?'

'The house belonged to my father,' he tells me. 'I was actually born in that big bedroom. So it got passed down to me. Just like Chatsworth.'

He talks about his dad, who died before we got married. A brain tumour lingered for nearly a year before snatching him harshly at the age of fifty. He'd been a strict but gentle soul who worked in a bank approving mortgages, a teetotaller who took pleasure in hillwalking and restoring old gramophones. His wife, Freddie's mother, found him boring and ran off to London with an actor when Freddie was six years old and they never saw her again. Freddie regretted never making an attempt to find her – probably because his father had poisoned his mind so completely against her – and after doing some research a few years ago discovered that she died only a year after abandoning him.

'Do we have photographs of our parents?' I ask, and Freddie says that he's certain there should be some somewhere, most likely packed up with other possessions that we put in storage a few weeks ago.

We wander around the formal gardens, and I steep myself in all this information. Forgetting to stop and admire the sculptures, the waterfalls, the clipped box hedges, we immerse ourselves into Freddie's history and the past I don't remember. The talking takes over and without realising, we have walked miles around the paths and gardens and woodlands, sweeping round to the back of the house and into the car park.

Freddie's nose is red. He blows into his hands then looks at his watch. 'We've been out for hours,' he says. 'It's half past three. Do you fancy a visit to the farm shop before we go home?'

I shake my head. 'No, let's just get home and get warm.'

Freddie hugs me and rubs his hands on my back. 'I'll rustle up a spag bol for tea. Your favourite.'

'OK, I say,' trying to remember what spag bol is and trusting that he knows I like it.

ELEVEN

BECKA

For the next few days, we settle into a routine of meals and menial household chores and dreamless nights, and popping out to places of interest like tourists. Freddie presents me with a beautiful box of pencils and pastels, and I sit in a comfy chair by the bi-fold doors to make sketches of the garden. He flits around with his camera, snapping me from different angles, until I become unnerved and distracted and have to tell him to stop.

Then, early on Wednesday morning Freddie tells me that he has to go into Derby: he's been commissioned to do a job at Rolls Royce that will last for the next few weeks and pay a handsome fee. Unfortunately, it was arranged months ago so he can't really get out of it.

'Why would you want to get out of it?' I ask.

'Well, because I'm caring for you at the moment.'

I burst out laughing, feeling slightly offended. 'I don't need caring for! It's not like I'm ill or anything. I'm perfectly capable of staying here and doing some cooking and reading and sketching. You don't need to be with me all the time.'

Freddie purses his lips and looks somewhat hurt. I reach out for his hand.

'Sorry. Look I was just trying to point out that we can get back to normal, where you go to work and I do whatever I'm supposed to do here. Decorating, home things, and eventually your office stuff and emails. Just like before. You still need to go through all that with me, but I'm willing to get back to doing everything I used to do.'

'But I want you to take it easy for a while,' he says. 'You've had a serious head injury and I worry about you.'

I kiss him warmly. 'Go. Do your work and don't worry about me. I won't overdo things, I promise.'

'Just put your feet up and chill out,' he says. 'I'll be back as soon as I can and I will bring a takeaway so you don't have to lift a finger.'

As I stand on the doorstep and watch him pull his car out of the drive, I see the lady across the road peering through her window again. Maybe I should have asked Freddie about her. I lift my hand and give my fingers a wiggle in her direction. She stares for a while before waving back, and I consider going across to say hello, but I don't know her circumstances and I can't think of an excuse, so I assure myself that I will do it some other time.

I go back indoors and wander around the house, enjoying the space. It's nice not to be followed around. Upstairs, I check the cupboards again because – maybe it's my mind playing tricks on me – things feel somehow incomplete. Like, I don't seem to possess gloves or a scarf. Or a swimming costume despite Freddie saying that I used to swim regularly. Or tweez-ers. Perhaps I always went to a salon to get my eyebrows done, I don't know. There are no mismatched socks, tights with ladders in, tatty leggings or paint-spattered clothing that I would have worn for decorating.

Everything is so *meticulous*.

Apart from the guest bedroom, which seems kind of abandoned.

I decide to make up the bed just to improve the look of the room, because surely it will help if we are going to put the house on the market. And maybe I could select one of my sketches for framing, because this appears to be the only room that has empty walls.

This bed is smaller than ours in the master bedroom – just a double – so I rummage through the linen cupboard for the appropriately sized sheet and duvet cover. White sheet and a cool sage green cover with matching pillowcases. There are no spare scatter cushions and I make a mental note to buy some in a striking colour, burnt orange maybe.

I take the bedding downstairs so that I can iron it in the kitchen. It feels satisfying to be doing something productive.

When it's done, I carry everything back upstairs and fit the sheet onto the mattress. It's only then that I realise there are no pillows or duvet on the bed. I check the drawers of the divan but they are empty. Puzzled, I open up the linen cupboard again. Surely there must be a double duvet to go inside the cover? Surely there will be spare pillows?

I remove the folded piles of bedding to see if there's anything behind. But no, just more pillowcases and a fleecy blanket. I scratch my head. Then I notice the edge of a black bin bag poking from behind a stack of towels. That's where the quilt must be. I pull the towels out so that I can get to the heavy-duty bin bag. Immediately, I know from its weight that it is not a double duvet.

Dropping it onto the floor, I untie it and open the top. Ladies' clothes: jeans, leggings, trousers. I pull out a pair and look them over. Size fourteen, clean and good condition although not new. I hold them up against me and they look like the right size, and I am suddenly struck with the thought: did these belong to me? And if so, why are they here? And if they are not my belongings, then whose are they?

I rummage further into the bag to find more stuff: blouses, mint green cotton pyjamas, tubes of old make-up, eyeshadow sets, a half-used bottle of perfume. Then, at the bottom, underwear: cotton knickers that look practical, in various colours, some pairs slightly frayed or saggy; tights and socks that are all balled into pairs; bras, some of which are bobbly in places and smell strongly of fabric conditioner. I pull one out to inspect the label and find it's bigger than the one I am wearing, the one that pinches my back. I frown and stand back to stare at the stuff, not knowing what to make of it all.

Logical thinking tells me that it must be mine. But why is it in a bin bag? Did I intend to throw it away?

I sniff the perfume and squirt some onto my wrist. Chanel Coco Mademoiselle. It looks and smells expensive. Why would anyone get rid of half a bottle of luxury perfume?

The gaps in my brain start to fill with scenarios as I try to imagine why these things are in a rubbish bag.

Me, dragging my belongings out of the wardrobe and drawers, stuffing them into the black sack while Freddie watches, begging me to put them back.

Then another one...

Freddie, angrily throwing my things into the bag after finding out that I have been unfaithful to him, vowing to never let me back in the house again.

Was this stuff put here before I had my accident? Does this mean that our relationship wasn't good, that something happened before which meant that I had to leave? Has other stuff of mine been thrown away and that explains why I don't have a hairdryer or a swimming costume or gloves?

I go through to the master bedroom where I check through my wardrobe and drawers. All the clothes within look much newer – maybe even *unworn* – than the ones that have been packed away. Why would this be? Something doesn't add up.

I check out the other empty bedroom, but the cupboard in there contains nothing but an old vacuum cleaner.

Nausea begins to rumble through me again. This puzzling discovery is unsettling, unhelpful with my anxiety and memory loss.

Stop overthinking, I tell myself. There will probably be a simple explanation.

But I struggle to think what it might be. Abandoning the ironed duvet set on the mattress and the old clothes and make-up scattered on the floor, I leave the room and close the door behind me.

Freddie arrives home just before six, bringing the chill of the evening inside with him. He has a Chinese takeaway and a huge bouquet of lilies in his arms; a hopeful smile on his face. I take the bag of food and the flowers, and he goes back to the car to bring in his photography gear.

My hands are trembling. I don't know how to approach him with my questions. He moves in and out of the house, putting equipment in the cupboards in his study, wheeling in cases, wiping his feet each time at the front door. I listen as the car boot slams shut. My heart is thumping, kicking like a captured animal in my chest. Will he tell me what happened? Will he get angry with me? Do I even want to know?

Maybe I should just leave it. Perhaps I did something bad. But things are good now, however they were before. That's all that matters, isn't it? We've started a blank page.

I find a vase for the flowers and display them on the sill of the bay window. We share out the food – special chow mein, fried rice, sweet and sour chicken – and eat it on our laps in front of the BBC News. Freddie tells me that it's been a good

day, easier than he expected, and he's likely to get further
contracts if he delivers all the proofs on time.

'Great,' I say. I pick the prawns out of the chow mein and
slide them to the edge of my plate because he'd told me before
that I don't like seafood. Should I say something about the bin
bag or not? Should I just go for it?

'What have *you* been up to while I've been out?'

'Oh, nothing much. Did some sketching. Cleaned the bathroom. Wasted my time ironing bedding. Found a bin bag of
women's clothes in the linen cupboard.'

He looks up at my tone, a chicken ball on his fork like a
lollipop, a quizzical cleft in his forehead. 'What do you mean?'

I shake my head and stab at noodles. 'Just being silly.'

'No. What bin bag are you talking about?'

My face is red. I can feel the burning in my cheeks, my
nose. I'm going to go for it though, because keeping it in feels
wrong, it feels like it's tainting me.

'In the linen cupboard, behind all the towels. There was a
bin bag full of what I assume is my stuff. Underwear, make-up,
that sort of thing. It looks like it's waiting to be thrown away or
something. And since I can't remember anything about what
happened with us before my accident, I just wondered why.'

Freddie twitches his nose for a moment before rubbing it
aggressively. He puts his plate to one side and stares at the floor.
He rubs at the collar of his jumper and breathes deeply, in and
out, in and out. I wait for his answer.

'Oh God.' He rubs the palm of his hand across his mouth.
'You're going to take this the wrong way.'

'What?'

'Well... before.' He looks up at the ceiling. 'You got this
thing about losing weight and getting fit. Look, don't get
offended or anything because it used to be a tricky subject, but
you thought that if you got rid of all your stuff it would be like
an incentive and so you cleared everything out and bagged it up.

It was around the same time that we were sorting some of the contents to put into storage, so some of the bags probably got mixed up. I took some stuff to the tip. I didn't want to say because you got it into your head that I thought you were fat, but I've never thought that at all – you're gorgeous as you are – but it sort of went a bit wrong and we had a fallout and you threw most of your clothes away. And then you bought new stuff in a smaller size. And sporty stuff for you to exercise in. That's why I brought it to the hospital. But you clearly didn't remember and I didn't like to mention it.'

I watch him and it's obvious that he feels awkward telling me this. Perhaps it was something that came between us. But it is an explanation that I hadn't thought of, and there's a calming relief that settles through my body like anaesthetic. It seems ridiculous how I worried that we were on the verge of splitting up.

He smiles enquiringly and I mirror his expression.

'I thought you were throwing *me* out,' I laugh. 'I couldn't work out why my stuff would be packed up.'

He shakes his head and rolls his eyes dramatically. 'Oh God. What were you thinking? As if I'd ever do that!'

We joke about my lost memory and the potential trouble it might cause. We finish our food and I feel guilty afterwards for eating too much when I am supposed to be losing weight so that the outfits in my wardrobe will fit properly. Maybe I should take some of the stuff back out of the bag – just some of my favourite things – so that I can feel more comfortable for now.

There's a film on television and we settle down on the sofa to watch it. I relax onto Freddie and he wraps his arms around me and I wonder if this is new or if it is how we used to be two months ago. If anything, our current behaviour feels a bit *teenage* rather than middle-aged. But it's nice. It's fresh. Maybe my accident restored something lost in our relationship. I'm speculating really, and there's no need to make comparisons with a past that I can't even remember, so I tell myself that all I should do is enjoy it as we go forward. I snuggle further into his warm body and he kisses the top of my head.

And it's only after we have gone to bed, and it's in the middle of the night, when something jolts me awake...

Why would I throw away the perfume?

TWELVE

BECKA

Freddie goes off to Derby early the next morning. I return to the guest room to examine the contents of the bin bag again. Really, it's stupid to throw things away that still have plenty of wear in them, and I obviously need to make more effort with my fitness regime before the new garments in the wardrobe will be my perfect size.

I pick out some items of make-up, even though they don't seem to quite match my skin tone, along with the bottle of perfume, and put them with my meagre collection in the bathroom. I sort through the clothing. Jeans, jumpers, big comfortable knickers, a zip-up fleecy top. These are the things that look the most useful, and I put a load into the washing machine to freshen up and get rid of the strangely sweet smell – some kind of scent or deodorant? – that lingers on everything.

I put all the unwanted stuff back into the bag and take it outside to dump in the bin. And again, as I glance over the road the old lady has her net curtains pulled back, watching me.

This time though, she's the first to wave.

* * *

I fold the clothes out of the tumble dryer, pressing my face into each sweater. They do smell better but, I don't know, there's an enduring aroma that is messing with my senses. Nothing identifiable, and not necessarily bad, just different. It's not the Chanel perfume, it's something else. It must be from being sealed up in a bag: some kind of sweaty fustiness mixed with a floral scent.

I take the pile upstairs to transfer into the wardrobe and drawers.

At least I remembered to ask Freddie about the perfume this morning. It had kept me awake for a substantial part of the night.

'Oh God, that stuff,' he said. 'You were allergic to it.'

I pulled a quizzical face. 'Really? Allergic to perfume?' I checked my wrists, which I had generously squirted the day before. 'Look, I sprayed some on and they're fine. No rash.'

'Well,' he replied quickly. 'No, what I meant was that it seemed to make you, like, asthmatic. It affected your breathing, the smell of it.'

'It seemed to be all right yesterday.'

'Well, if you only sprayed it on your wrists and not your neck then it might be fine...'

'I sniffed it. It smelled lovely.' The conversation had seemed to be edging towards a bizarre disagreement. It was unnecessary, really. Because when all was said and done, I had only thrown away some perfume and forgotten why.

'Perhaps your senses have changed since your accident. Who knows? Anyway, it's not a problem: we could go to a nice shop so that you can try some fragrances and buy some more. Tuh! What are you like! All the stuff you have for your pampering.' He laughed and ruffled my hair.

I gave him a weak smile. The issue had been sorted.

It's ten days since I came home.

There have been ups and downs, as moments of anxiety and confusion are balanced with moments of bliss and contentment. Freddie says I'm doing brilliantly, the way that I'm coping with getting back to normal. But he has been the perfect husband, loving and patient, as my memory is restocked with happy occasions. I feel like I am falling in love all over again.

Sex hasn't happened yet. That first week back, I was awkward and demure, dressing and undressing behind the closed door of the en suite, shying away from encouraging any act of sensuality beyond a hug or a brief kiss.

But now...

I caught myself watching Freddie dress this morning, a flush rising in my cheeks. I felt a stirring in the depth of my flesh that made my muscles clench and my breath catch. I kept my lips pressed to his for a second longer before he went to work.

And then tonight...

We eat at the kitchen island, perching on the stools. Mushroom carbonara and a glass of crisp Pinot Grigio. Between us, the flame of a chubby candle bounces and wavers.

'Remember this?' says Freddie, suddenly, pressing something on his phone so that music comes out from speakers which are hidden all over the room.

A trance beat, a female voice, something that sounds clubby. And then... my heart skips; the song connects with me, with the nerves in my body so that I feel some kind of exhilaration, some kind of anticipation, arousal even.

'Hey, I think I know this!' I tap my hand on the worktop in time with the beat. Words come back to me and I sing along with them. 'I... *want you back in my life*...'

Freddie turns up the music and gets off his stool to come and pull me off mine so that we are dancing, laughing, twirling around on the kitchen floor, and he does something else with his phone that dims the lighting and changes the colours under the cupboards, and I feel like I am seventeen again. Is this the start of my memory returning?

'It's our song,' he says. 'It always has been.'

'I remembered it!'

Then we kiss, and it must be like the very first time that we kissed when we were young: edgy and electrifying, with our bodies pressed so close that we can feel the bones of each other under the skin. I wind my arms around his neck and into his hair, and he touches my face, my shoulders, the outline of my waist and thighs, then up again to my breasts and we are hungry and breathless like tormented animals. He pulls his lips away to bite my neck, my ears, and I whimper with pleasure, wondering if it has always been like this or if something has been reset so that it now feels fresh and rediscovered.

'Do you want to go upstairs?' he murmurs. 'We don't have to, though, if you're not ready yet.'

But I am ready. I want everything he is offering. I kick off my shoes and follow him to the bedroom.

* * *

We watch our older selves from the younger eyes of our wedding canvas as we undress each other, clawing and sucking and licking and grasping at skin and hair. I ignore the gnawing ache in my injured ribs, and we wrap quickly and easily around each other. We rip back the sheets and throw ourselves onto the bed, desperate. It's a sex scene from a film, packed with passion and action and craving and lust. Everything feels so new and thrilling; nothing like you would expect middle-aged sex to be in a seventeen-year-old marriage. We cling to each other and rock, moaning, to a shuddering level of ecstasy, to Freddie saying, 'I love you, I love you, oh, Becka, I love you so much.'

I look at him, to see his face wet with tears, then suddenly it's as if he's embarrassed; he's burying his face in my shoulder and sobbing as I grip my arms around his broad back and press my cheek against his head.

'I thought I'd lost you,' he says. 'I thought you were gone forever.'

'I'm here. I'm right here,' I whisper, raking my fingers through his hair. 'I'm back and I'm not going anywhere.'

We are linked in love and satisfaction and silence, and time freezes even though the dusk turns to black and pours in through the windows whose curtains we forgot to close in our moment of desire.

THIRTEEN

BECKA

Maybe I have overeaten at lunch, but my outfit is causing me some discomfort. I really do need to find out about the gym sessions and start doing some exercise. Or even just do half an hour walking briskly every day. I undo the button on my jeans to lessen the pinch.

Actually, I think, I will change my clothes. The size twelve stuff I have been wearing is too tight and makes me feel fat. Perhaps if I go back to my old outfits for now but attempt to lose a few pounds then the new clothes will fit me better in a couple of weeks.

I go upstairs to rummage through the garments that I washed the other day.

There's a nice green jumper that feels snuggly and I like that the sleeves are a little longer. I pair it with jeans, and although they are a welcome change from the ones that I step out of, they are not a perfect fit, sagging on the buttocks as if my bum used to be bigger than it is now. Also, I could do with a belt but don't have one in my drawers. Maybe they were thrown away, too. I really should sort out this wardrobe chaos and go shopping for all the things that are missing.

. . .

Freddie does a double take when he gets home and sees me wearing the clothes that I had previously discarded. He seems sheepish somehow and doesn't comment on them. But he comes up and kisses me, telling me that I smell nice. I have overdone the Chanel a bit, in an effort to mask the old jumper scent. It doesn't seem to have caused any of my previous asthmatic symptoms.

'You probably think I'm mad, going back to this shabby stuff,' I say. 'But I just wanted to be comfy. My body isn't ready for the new clobber yet.'

'Your body is gorgeous,' he says, twining his arms around me.

'I will get fit though. I've decided that I'm going to go out and do more walking. You know, intense bouts of walking are more beneficial than, say, jogging. There was a radio programme on about it.'

But Freddie isn't really listening to my fitness plans. He's nuzzling my neck, squeezing my arse, pressing himself up against me so there's no point in carrying on with the conversation as we're both getting so turned on that we'll end up in the bedroom again before our evening meal. It seems to be our new routine. Maybe my fugue state has returned me, like a time machine, to our newlywed period so that we can start our marriage again from the beginning.

Friday is bin day. I'm remembering all these little things that make up my life. So, when Freddie goes out to work the next morning, he drags the wheelie bin out to the side of the road. The house across the road already has its bin in position on the pavement. The lady must have put it out the night before. I resolve to watch out for the recycling lorry so that I can go

across and take her bin back in order to knock on the door and
say hello.

During the morning I vacuum all the rooms and the stairs,
clean the living room windows and dust all the surfaces. In
Freddie's office I polish his desk and wipe over the computer
monitor and keyboard. Something gets knocked: I think it is
called a mouse. It brings the computer suddenly to life and a
picture appears on the screen, the photograph from years ago of
teenage me in my school uniform standing by his car. It makes
me smile to think that he treasures this image, to think that we
have been together all this time with a marriage going stronger
than ever.

I pick up the mouse and shuffle it around the desk and there
is an arrow that moves simultaneously on the screen. Sometimes
things flash up when the arrow touches some of the pictures but
then they disappear when the arrow moves away. I really need
Freddie to give me a refresher course so that I can remember
how to use this.

I tidy up some paperwork – it looks like junk mail and
adverts for computer and photography equipment – into a
stack. I leaf through some receipts to see that he has recently
bought photographic paper, a large image on canvas, batteries
and flash drives. On the shelves are ring binders and old diaries
going back four years. Maybe there could be something in them
to jog my memories? I remove the one for 2020 and see appointments crossed out and cancelled everywhere. Flights from East
Midlands and Gatwick with squiggles through. Whole weeks
with lines through in black marker, meetings, courses, photo-
shoots and events all deleted. Obviously, something weird
happened for a big chunk of time that caused him to stop working. I will ask him later. This year's diary is busier: there are lots
of entries for work throughout the year. There's no mention of
my name anywhere, though, in any of them.

Suddenly, I hear the rumble of a lorry, the smashing of

bottles. It is the recycling truck, working its way down the road. I go outside to bring in the bin, then put the door on the latch while I venture across the road.

* * *

The net curtains move, and I feel eyes upon me as I wheel the bin up the cracked concrete drive. I leave it beside the garage and then knock on the front door. At first, it seems like I am being ignored, until a light finally comes on in the hallway and a bunch of keys is shuffled before the correct one is turned in the lock.

'Hi,' I say cheerfully to the frail old lady who is swathed in beige trousers and a number of oversized cardigans. 'I'm Becka, from across the road. I just brought your bin back for you. I thought I would come and say hello.'

'I know where you're from.' She points a bony, trembling finger towards my house on the other side of the road.

I smile. 'Just wanted to check on you, really. Do you need anything at all?'

'Well, not that I can think of. But I did enjoy the cake you brought last time. I think it had walnuts in it. I do like walnuts, you know. And home-baked cakes are so much nicer than the shop ones.'

'OK.' More new information then. I bake cakes with walnuts in.

'Do you want to come in? I could make a pot of tea for us.'

It is exactly what I am hoping for. 'Thank you. That would be lovely.'

I follow her through a cold, tiled hallway that smells of vinegar and cooked cabbage, noticing how the wallpaper seams are curling away with the damp. We go into the front room, with the window that looks across to mine, and I see how her chair is decayed with the imprint of her body; the right-side of the net curtain discoloured by her frequent adjustments. I sit on the fawn sofa that looks like a recent purchase: plastic covers adorn the arms and the seat is firm.

She makes tea and puts two sugars in my cup before handing it to me, as if she already knows how I take it. I sip politely, trying not to grimace at the sweetness.

'How's the business?' she asks when she's got settled back into her chair by the window.

'Oh, pretty good. Freddie's been working for Rolls Royce this week on a big contract.'

She frowns. 'No. I mean the cakes.'

'Cakes?'

'I thought I hadn't seen anyone calling for a few weeks. You know, coming away with the big boxes. They always leave with a smile on their face. I love seeing the photographs but you haven't brought any over for a while.'

I smile courteously, wondering what she is talking about. Maybe she has dementia.

'I've been in hospital for a while. Nearly three weeks, actually. I had an accident while I was out with a friend.'

She clicks her fingers at me. 'Ahh. That will be why I haven't seen much of you. Three weeks? That's a long time to be in hospital. Did you have a fall?'

'No, I got caught up in a flood when a river burst its banks. Hypothermia, cracked ribs, lots of cuts and bruises. And quite a serious head injury that affected my memory.'

She holds her own head in sympathy. 'Ohh, not your memory. I have problems with mine, too.'

I force myself to swallow some more of the dark, sugary tea, before she suddenly grabs the net curtain and yanks it a face-width open. She watches for a few seconds before letting it fall back into place and turning to me again.

'Just a parcel for number sixteen. They're forever having stuff delivered. I think they get it from the computer. People can't be bothered to go to the shops any more, but I like to look at things before I buy them. Surely, you need to try them on because there can be such a difference between sizes.'

'I was saying about my memory,' I explain. 'So there are lots of things I can't remember that I need to learn again. Like *your* name.'

She puts a claw-like hand to her chest. 'Me? I'm Grace Wardle. I don't mind you calling me Grace, although if you were younger I think I would prefer Mrs Wardle. It's just the generation I'm from.'

'Well, it's nice to be reminded of your name, Grace.'

'What did you say yours was again?'

'Becka. I prefer it to Rebecca. Well, I think I do. I must have done.'

She scratches her head. 'Becka? I thought it was... well I can't remember what I thought it was but not that. Although it must have been. But that's how *my* memory goes.' She laughs and her false teeth clack at the back of her mouth. 'We're a pair, aren't we? But Becka's a nice name. I will remember that. Well, obviously until I forget it again.'

I am unable to suppress a hearty chuckle at Grace's wisdom.

'So you still make cakes then?' she asks. 'Your memory hasn't stopped you?'

It is clearly a concern for her. 'Well, I haven't for a few weeks with me not being well, but if you would like cake, Grace, then I will make one for you. This afternoon.'

She smiles and folds her arms, satisfied. I finish as much tea as I can muster and put the half-drunk mug on the coffee table.

FOURTEEN

BECKA

How do I bake a cake? Flour, eggs and sugar sound like a good start. Butter? I can't remember. I open up the kitchen cupboards to see what ingredients are available. Tins to bake them in. Oh, and walnuts too. Grace likes walnuts. Rummaging around the shelves I find flour and sugar but no walnuts. There is a plastic tub with a selection of food colourings and flavourings, and I recall something about vanilla essence being in a recipe. Butter and eggs are in the fridge.

Get yourself organised, I tell myself, as I put everything on the worktop with a glass bowl ready to begin.

But I realise that I need instructions and weighing scales. And I still haven't found tins. I search through the cupboards again: there are flat baking trays and roasting tins but nothing round that I could use for a cake.

Maybe everything is in the utility room. I go and check the tall cupboard next to the washing machine and, hey presto, it's all there. Cake tins of all shapes and sizes, sieves, a box of silicone spatulas and measuring spoons, icing bags and nozzles, tubs of different sugared decorations, scales and bowls. It looks like I made a serious hobby of this.

I remove everything I need, and at the back of the cupboard find a selection of recipe books and laminated sheets. There is a photograph album – I assume that Freddie has taken the pictures of creations that I have baked – of impressive party cakes, some of which are five layers tall, and wedding cakes decorated with flowers and swirls, buttercream and petals. Wow! I swell with pride at the discovery. Have I never thought of doing this professionally? Perhaps coming back to it again with fresh eyes and a new motivation for life could be the start of a successful venture.

One of the laminated sheets gives me the ingredients and method required for a basic vanilla sponge, and I follow the instructions religiously before spooning the batter into tins and putting it into the oven. The timing is more tricky. Twenty-five to thirty minutes in the oven, or maybe a little longer, the recipe says. Check the springiness.

I open the oven door at least four times to press my fingers into the sponge. Worried that the cakes are getting too dark I remove them at twenty minutes. They seem quite flat and sunken in the centre as I turn them out to cool. Disappointed somewhat, I make the buttercream and later sandwich them together, topping with coloured sprinkles, and leave my creation sitting on the kitchen table. I return the photograph album to the utility cupboard.

'Something smells nice,' says Freddie when he gets home. 'Have you been baking?'

I show him my efforts and we both laugh hysterically after he tells me that it looks delicious. We cut into it to find the middle soggy, but Freddie takes a slice anyway and eats it, declaring that it is the best cake he's ever had.

'What brought on the baking session?' he asks, licking buttercream from his fingers.

'Well, I ended up having a cup of tea with Grace across the road, after I took her dustbin in for her. She said that I used to bake cakes for her.'

The smile has disappeared from Freddie's face. 'Don't listen to anything *she* tells you. She's completely batty, has been for a while. It's about time she went into a care home.'

'Well, she got a little confused about some things, but she didn't seem that bad. She was chatty, funny. I quite liked her. But I ended up telling her that I would take her some cake over, so I thought I had better stick to my promise.'

Freddie rubs the back of his neck and purses his lips. Flits his gaze around the kitchen. 'So, are you going to take *that*?'

We look again at the miserable sponge. 'Maybe not. I just assumed that I would be able to get straight back into the baking again. You know, like always knowing how to ride a bike once you've learnt.'

'But perhaps baking's not really your thing.'

'What?' I don't know if it's part of my memory damage but I'm starting to become confused. Why is he saying this? He *knows* that baking is my thing: there's the evidence of it in the utility cupboard! Or maybe he would rather I didn't make cakes. Perhaps there's more to all the argument about me getting fat and throwing my clothes away – it could be linked to that.

'If you really want to take a cake to Grace I could just pick something up from the bakery. Pretend that you've made it.' He puts the knife in the dishwasher.

What is this? Some kind of mind game? There's a bubble of resentment under my ribs at the thought that Freddie is using my accident to try and control some element of my behaviour, my eating. I stride into the utility room to get the photograph album.

'There,' I say, tossing it onto the table. 'Perhaps baking *is* my thing.' I flick it open to a sumptuous chocolate cake oozing cherries and cream.

He looks sheepishly at me. Why would he lie? I give him a killer glare and storm away to the bathroom. I may have temporarily lost my touch with the baking but I *will* get it back. I will practise and practise until I get it perfect.

I have been back at home for over three weeks and every night sleep has captured me, drawing me into a solid, dreamless blackout that I wake completely refreshed from. But not tonight. In the depth of the darkness, pictures of rushing water fill my mind and I find myself in a car, clinging to the steering wheel, my legs cold and wet as the river fills the footwell. There's the sound of screaming – is it me? – and a name, something like *Tony*, being shouted, pleaded, over and over – *Tony! Tony!* – and I'm jolted around, bumping into the car door, thrashing out at my feet being dragged under something until, suddenly, I'm awake.

My heart is racing; my body drenched in sweat. I am in bed whimpering from the back of my throat while Freddie is shaking me by the shoulder.

'Becka, Becka, wake up. It's OK.' He strokes my wet hair away from my face, then clicks on the bedside lamp. 'You were having a bad dream.'

I kick away the duvet that has wrapped around my feet and lie quietly on my back as my battering heart subsides.

'It felt so real. I was in the water and thought I was going to die.'

'Some dreams do feel real. But it's all right now. I'm here. You're safe, at home.'

'Was I screaming out loud?'

'Like something out of a horror movie.' Freddie shuddered. 'That's why I had to wake you up.'

I consider asking him if he knows anyone called Tony – or maybe it's a female Toni – but something stops me. What if I was having an affair? What if Tony was my lover? It feels like there are snippets of information that I should hold back for now, that I should wait until other pieces of the jigsaw turn up and help me to see a bigger picture.

Freddie goes downstairs and makes hot chocolate for me, and I change out of my sweat-soaked nightdress. I try to think myself back into my dream, to examine the experience for more clues, but most of it has gone. My mind goes round in circles, and all it's filled with is water and fear.

'OK now?' Freddie sets the hot drink down beside me.

'Yeah, fine. I don't think I've had a proper dream like that since I got home. Perhaps I ate too close to bedtime. It could have been the cheese.'

He rubs my arm and adjusts the pillow behind me.

'It did make me think though... What happened to my car?'

'Well, you asked me about that before, didn't you? You haven't had a car for a while – we got rid of it over a year ago – so you could do more walking. It worked perfectly well just having the one outside. There were the odd occasions you'd use buses or trains, but...'

'So did I ever drive the one outside?'

'Well, no. You were a bit reluctant to drive after the incident... Well, you won't remember but you had a collision in the Tesco car park – it's not like anyone was injured or anything – but there was a bit of a hoo-ha with insurance and all that, so it put you off and probably contributed to the idea of getting rid and doing more walking.'

'Oh.' I sip the hot chocolate. It doesn't really feel like things add up. 'That dream just now, and a previous flashback in hospital... I keep thinking that I was driving a car. But if I didn't have a car then whose car would I have been driving?'

Freddie smooths my hair back again and strokes my neck. 'There *was* no car. You're assuming because you had a dream that it was a memory, that it was something that actually happened. And dreams aren't like that, are they? They might contain elements of your experience, but there's nothing to say that it's an actual memory of the event.'

He's right. I'm trying too hard to put the picture together and some of the pieces I have aren't even the correct ones.

FIFTEEN

BECKA

The next morning it feels like my head is different. I don't know how, but it reminds me of when you put an avocado stone in water and eventually it starts to crack and a root begins to grow out.

There are memories trying to resurface. I go downstairs and walk around the living room, looking at it from different angles. The bay window, the recesses by the fire, the door into the hall. Every shape and angle, every subtle join in the cornicing, the antique ceiling rose. Something about it all is talking to me. I close my eyes to feel the vibe of the room, to try and transport myself back to another time – five years ago, ten years ago, more – and imagine what it looked like then. Yellow. Heavy wall-paper with triangles on it.

An idea strikes me. Grace's house. I peer through the front window to her house across the road. It's like a mirror image of this one. Shabbier obviously, and without the new door and windows and kitchen extension, but the same structural design.

I pop outside to the end of the drive and see the familiar twitch of the net curtain. Waving to Grace, I make my way to her front door. With an undisguised look of disappointment that my hands are empty, she lets me into the hallway.

'Morning, Grace,' I say. 'I hope you don't mind me just dropping in. But you know how I told you about me losing my memory? Well, sometimes things come to light in my mind and I thought that as your house is probably the same footprint as ours, it might help trigger some recollections if I could have a look around. Obviously not upstairs or anywhere private.'

'Oh. Well yes, you could. What do you want to see?'

I scan around the rooms like an estate agent, taking in the position of the walls and connecting doors, the fireplace, the cupboard under the stairs. I realise that our house has had walls knocked out, the back wall moved and the original kitchen window at the side blocked up.

'Our layout must have originally been like this,' I tell her.

'I wouldn't know,' Grace says with a little prickliness. 'I've never been invited over there.'

Guilt flushes on my face. 'Well, you must come over sometime. For tea and cake.'

She looks me in the eye on the word 'cake' but says nothing else about it. We move into the kitchen and look through the window to the back garden that is overgrown with elder and brambles. I tell her that the back of our house has been extended to make a huge open-plan kitchen diner with bi-fold doors onto a patio.

'There was a lot of work done, I remember that. But it had gone to rack and ruin after the fire.' She fills a cup with water to tip onto a huge aloe vera plant on the windowsill.

'Oh, really? A fire? What year was that?'

Grace attempts to excavate her recollections, first mentioning the Queen's Jubilee in 1977 and then the attack on the twin towers. 'Twin towers?' I ask, and she tells me that it was a major terrorist incident in the USA. I doubt her reliability on the dates but file the information so that I can look into it.

Freddie has never mentioned a fire. Perhaps she is thinking of somewhere else on the street.

'Did you know Freddie's father?' I ask. 'He had the house before us, and Freddie was born there.'

'Hmm. Maybe vaguely. Did he have a beard?'

I shrug. There is no point in asking me.

'I remember the woman who lived there, though. Highly strung, religious type, Catholic I think. Someone told me that she had a stigmata on her hand.' Grace holds out her own wrinkled, speckled hand and rubs the area on the back where it was rumoured to be.

Something squirms in me. *Stigmata*. A fleck on the surface of my memory is scratched.

'Really?'

'Well, not that I ever saw it, but you know how people talk.'

Was this Freddie's mother who ran away to London with an actor? Surely not: even he doesn't remember *her*, so why would I know anything?

I walk around the rooms again, imagining being newly married. The sofa would be in this position with the television in that alcove. A gas fire that looked like real flames and coals. A stripped pine panelled door through to the hallway. I stand against the chimney breast and take in a different angle, seeing through to the bottom of the stairs where numerous coats hang redundantly. Everything feels fuzzy, ambiguous: I think it seems familiar but maybe not.

Grace waits near her place by the net curtain, somewhat confused by my analysis of her house, yet fearful of missing any action out on the street.

'She died after the fire you know,' she announces suddenly.

'Who died?'

'Her with the stigmata. I can't remember if it was deliberate or not or if someone was charged with anything. I'm pretty sure that it was in November because it all got blamed on one of those Guy Fawkes things, you know...'

'Bonfire? Fireworks?' I suggest.

'Yes, it must have been put through the letter box. A rocket, that's what it was. And I'd like to say that the Catholic woman was called Marilyn but I think I'd probably be wrong.'

'OK.' This is a lot of information to take in. I realise that much of it may not be reliable, but I will ask Freddie about it all later.

Grace doesn't offer me tea this time, probably because I have defaulted on my promise of cake, and so I leave her to settle back into her little watch tower area.

Something has worked though with this exercise. I cross the road and step back into my house, the hallway, the living room. Suddenly a memory is there, full and vivid.

It's the same room and I am standing in the same place: there's the view of the monkey puzzle tree through the front window. But it's from a different age. Yellow wallpaper with a geometric seventies design. Plants hanging in macrame pots from hooks in the bay window. The room crammed with furniture: a huge brown four-seater settee against the back wall, three dining chairs in the window, and an armchair, a pouffe and a kitchen stool on the opposite wall. The television pushed into an alcove with a towel draped over the screen. A tiled open fire the focal point of the room above which is displayed a picture of Jesus holding out his hands.

Then more comes to me: a stiff, wiry lady, early-fifties, in a floral apron wearing pink rubber gloves on her hands. Her face is curdled with condescension as she looks at me and I get the sense of being unwelcome.

I shiver and hug my arms around myself. Then the memory is gone, evicted, and I find myself standing in my own room, with soft grey walls, clean modern furniture, no sour-faced lady and no staring picture of Jesus.

. . .

Walking is good for me, I tell myself as I stride briskly along the main road towards town. Freddie has bought me a watch that monitors my heart rate and counts my steps. I need to aim for ten thousand a day and maybe it will help my mind as well as get rid of a few pounds.

Freddie has suggested that I treat myself, and given me cash and his bank card – he's still in the process of cancelling and reissuing mine that were lost in the water – so that I can buy some new earrings or a book or clothing accessories, or maybe get my nails done.

It's a twenty-minute walk into the main part of town. Some of the shops feel more familiar than others: Marks & Spencer, WH Smith, Boots, and I browse leisurely in and out of places, touching the fabrics of stylish frocks, sniffing bath oils, spraying perfume samples onto my wrists, flicking through cookery books and trying to remember if I like goat's cheese.

Inside another clothes shop, I am attracted to the family of mannequins that are sporting a coordinated assortment of spring fashions. I make my way through the displays towards the huge front window to feel the thickness of a luxuriant black coat. It's lovely. Although I'm not sure about the brash silver-coloured buttons.

Suddenly, my attention is caught by someone outside: a man across the street is trying to remove the plastic lid of a take-away coffee, the steam rising to blur his face. He's wearing faded jeans and a black leather jacket, and one of those hats where flaps fold down over the ears. Clean-shaven, deep-set dark eyes, taut skin and thin lips.

I know him.

I mean *really* know him. From before I lost my memory.

My heart starts racing and I watch him sip his hot drink and check his watch. The way he rubs a finger across his lips and pinches the bridge of his nose: I recognise those mannerisms. I recognise the way he moves, the way he turns to saunter away towards the market with no visible limp, even though he has a deep, prominent scar on his left foot that he acquired in a climbing accident.

How do I know these things?

I can't explain, but I am convinced that I have to talk to him. He could be the key to unlocking my mind.

I push my way through the immobile figures towards the doorway, but the man is five shops away by then, striding nonchalantly through the afternoon shoppers.

'Excuse me.' I lace around a doddery group of white-haired ladies and hurry in the direction of the man as fast as my feet will allow me. There are so many obstacles: scooters; pushchairs; an orange cone marking a sunken paving slab. It's an achievement to reach the corner of the street without breaking my ankle.

I look around, trying to search him out. But he is nowhere to be seen. I put my head around the door of Superdrug; I peer through the window of Sports Direct. Standing on tiptoe, I scan each side of the road to seek out his hat.

Nothing. He's gone.

SIXTEEN

BECKA

I propose to Freddie that we should do more sociable stuff, like go out to pubs in the evening, or the theatre. Make some friends, because we don't seem to have any. He's a bit mealy-mouthed, telling me that we've always been happy with each other's company and not really the type that take turns having dinner parties with people.

'Well, let's get ourselves out there and try something different,' I say. 'We might enjoy it. Let's go and do it tonight.'

Freddie mumbles and declares himself to be an unsociable old git, reminding me that his reclusiveness stems from his childhood of stuttering, but I keep going at the subject for a while until I get him to agree to walk to the Robin Hood Inn which is only about half a mile away.

We wrap up against the wind and venture hand-in-hand to the attractive establishment advertising itself as a gastro-pub. Indoors, it's an olde-worlde indulgence of beams and wonky walls, and two-hundred-year-old wooden floors that have been worn thin by the feet of drinkers seeking solace and liquid pleasure.

The barman recommends some expensive craft ales for us

to try, and we find a table by a crackling log fire.

'Cheers!' says Freddie.

'This is nice,' I say, enjoying the convivial atmosphere that comes from being in the presence of other people.

We chat about the age of the building, the charm of the open fire and the classy clientele that filters in and out, ordering wine and cocktails and platters of ciabatta and hummus and tapenade.

'What do you think of my nails?' I extend my fingers towards him, to show off the manicure I'd had that afternoon.

'Yes, I like the colour, it suits you,' says Freddie, admiring the sparkly aqua design on my third ring finger. He touches my wedding ring. 'I should get you a new one. Something nicer.'

I'm puzzled. 'Why? What's wrong with this?'

'Well, it was only a cheap thing. I always intended to get you something better once we could afford it.'

It's a charming proposal. 'Yeah, that would be a romantic thing to do. Perhaps we could go away for a weekend and find a nice jewellers to pick something from.'

Freddie is pleased with this idea, and suggests somewhere like Chester or Lincoln or Ludlow that has quaint buildings and cobbles, where we could book a quirky hotel with a four-poster bed.

Another couple arrive at the table in an alcove, and the man takes off his leather jacket to put on the back of his chair. I'm suddenly reminded of the incident earlier in the day of the leather jacketed man whom I recognised.

'I had a weird experience this afternoon,' I tell Freddie. 'I was out shopping and I thought I saw someone that I knew. You know, from before my accident.'

Freddie, in the process of raising his glass to his lips, freezes, his beer hanging mid-air.

'What d'you mean? Who?'

'I don't know. I couldn't remember a name. It was a man in

jeans and a leather jacket with a hat on. I just knew him as soon as I saw him.'

'Really? What did you do?' A dark cloud has appeared over Freddie's face.

'I didn't get chance to talk to him. I was inside a shop and he was out in the street: I saw him through the window. But I was certain that I knew him. It was such a strange feeling.'

Freddie is rattled. 'What did he look like? How old was he?'

'Probably my age. Taller than me but not as tall as you. Medium build. Darkish hair. He was just stood drinking a coffee on the street.' I shrug. 'Do we know anyone with that description?'

It's like Freddie has stopped listening. He grinds his teeth so that his jaw juts out. He lowers his glass to the table. His nostrils flare. Eyes widen. I see his chest rise and fall with measured, deliberate breaths.

It's then that I start to wonder if I should have mentioned this sighting.

Because if I *have* been unfaithful, this could have been the man that I was unfaithful with.

We don't stay for another drink. Something has evaporated from our earlier ambience. I put on a show of stroking a black Labrador that has settled easily in front of the fire and making small talk with the people at the next table even though I know nothing about dogs. I try to return to the conversation about planning a weekend away, but Freddie tells me that he will have to check his diary before we start organising anything.

* * *

On the way home Freddie is pensive and distracted, almost walking into the path of a pizza delivery scooter.

'What's wrong?' I finally ask. 'You've been odd with me since I mentioned seeing that man I thought I recognised.'

Freddie takes a deep breath. 'Look, I just worry about you. I worry that you might end up thinking that you know someone and going to talk to them, and then some complete stranger could end up taking advantage of your vulnerability. Pretending that they used to know you for some ulterior motive.'

'Why would anyone do that?'

'There are some sick and twisted people around that would certainly see your memory loss as an opportunity. You can't trust anyone.'

I suppose I can see his point. 'Yeah, OK. If I see him again then I won't approach him. Is that what you want to hear?'

He grasps me and hugs me into his chest and presses his face into my hair. When he lets me go there are tears glistening in his eyes.

'What?' I laugh. 'Stop being soppy!'

He shakes his head and smiles, blinking away the tears. 'There's nothing wrong with being caring, is there? I nearly lost you in the flood. I'm just being protective because I don't want to lose you again.'

'You won't. I'm here and I'm not going anywhere.' I kiss him and we walk home with our arms wrapped around each other.

* * *

When I tell Freddie about how I went to Grace's to have a look at her house layout, he's intrigued by the fact that I can remember what our lounge used to look like. And even more surprised when I tell him about the woman with the rubber gloves.

'Oh God, you remember *her*?'

'Well, not really remember. But a picture of her popped into my mind while I was thinking about how the room used to look, with the yellow wallpaper and tiled fireplace.'

'That was my stepmother. Bitter-faced old cow. She's dead

now, thank goodness.'

'I sensed she didn't like me. Strange that I only had a memory of this room for a few seconds, but I could *feel* that we didn't get on.'

'She didn't like me either. And she hated me even more when she found out that my father left the house to me instead of her. Yeah, it all got a bit messy then.' Freddie goes to empty the dishwasher but keeps talking through the open hallway. 'You know, I've been thinking. About this house. About starting up the moving process again. Now you're back home and doing so well, I think it would be the perfect time to do it. We really had been talking about it for ages, and I think a fresh start could be good for us.'

'What? So soon?' His statement sparks a rush of anxiety in me.

'The thing is, we already had the house on the market and people were interested. I put things on hold while you were in hospital, but it would only require a call to the estate agent to get things going again. And now that this house is completed, it might be fun to get something else to renovate. You'd love that, wouldn't you? Putting your stamp on another property. Like a stone cottage in the countryside. That would be awesome.'

He returns with mugs of coffee and chocolate biscuits. 'What do you think?'

I'm baffled. It all feels too impulsive, too soon. I have only just started to get properly settled here after my incident. Won't it jeopardise my recovery to move away so quickly? 'How about we wait till autumn?'

'But everyone knows that springtime is the ideal time to sell. And house prices around here are doing great at the moment. We wouldn't want to miss our chance.'

He is utterly convinced by the idea to move away. I sip my drink and shrug my shoulders; he takes it as a sign that I have conceded and goes into his office to contact the estate agent.

SEVENTEEN

BECKA

I try not to overthink things, but tiny issues just niggle themselves into my brain. Lately, I have struggled to make sense of timelines. The memory of Freddie's stepmother has been in the forefront of my mind, and although I have attempted to clarify dates with him, Freddie has been quite dismissive of my need to sort out a specific history.

The thing is, Freddie's stepmother – Hilary – died before we got married. There was some kind of dispute over his father's will: money had been left to Hilary but the house had gone to Freddie, and it caused a lot of trouble. Hilary had expected to get the lot and there was an issue around her moving out of the place so that Freddie could inhabit what was rightfully his. A solicitor was involved and it got stressful on both sides. But finally, she packed up and left the place, before dying quite suddenly only a few months later.

There is no doubt in my mind that the memory I had of the woman with the rubber gloves in the yellow wallpapered room was the same person. But why would I remember being there, with her? Freddie had previously told me that he no longer lived in the family home – he had his own bedsit on the other side of town – and never visited her. She had kicked him out when he was twenty-two, and he had been independent with his work and living arrangements since then, meeting up with his father occasionally in a café in town. Then Freddie met me when he was twenty-four, some months after his father had become seriously ill and was taken into a care home.

It is all quite bamboozling. Particularly if I start to add other layers of information, like the thing that Grace told me about a fire at the house.

I should get a notebook and start writing everything down. Dates, names, events. I'm not being weird. I should double-check because I don't know if it's *my* memory playing tricks on me, or maybe Freddie is genuinely forgetful, or maybe – for whatever reason – I am being deliberately misled.

It must be the pizza that I eat too late in the evening that sets me off dreaming again. Images that are so vivid; conversations that are too real to be illusory. I am caught in it, reliving a lost moment, letting the dye of it spread its colour through my memory.

I'm in a pub, at a small round table, a glass of fizzy wine in my hand. In the middle of the table there's a bucket of ice, a nearly empty bottle sitting in it, party to what, I assume, is some kind of celebration. There's a man beside me but I can't see his face properly, only his hands that are holding his phone, typing a text while I ask him why it's so important to disrupt our time together. Something agitates me so that I swig aggressively at my wine and top it up again from the bottle. I wind my arms defensively around my body and suddenly I'm saying to the man, 'Put the fucking phone down, will you,' and then after that there's some confusion as I'm tossing in bed, kicking down at the sheets, before a voice is saying in the pub in the dream, 'I don't

love you any more. There's someone else, someone else. I don't
love you.'

My heart races and sweat breaks out on my neck and chest.
I rise to the surface of my dream and stare at the darkness while
I try to make sense of it all.

I was with a man: was it Freddie? It felt vaguely like it was
Freddie. But who was saying the words? Was it Freddie telling
me that he didn't love me any more, or was it me telling
Freddie?

My palpitations subside; the sweaty fever turns to chilli-
ness, and I pull the covers back over my body. Freddie reaches
over in his half-sleep and puts a calming hand on my thigh.

Why does it matter?

I ask myself what good it will do to keep analysing everything, to keep wanting to return to the point before my accident.
Why can't I leave it all in the past and enjoy what I have now: a
fantastic, caring husband, a lovely house, a rosy future? Maybe I
need medication to alleviate the stresses that my mind
constantly picks over. Or hypnotherapy sessions. I have an
appointment for another scan soon. Perhaps it would be best if I
talked over everything with the consultant.

When Freddie gets home, he's excited to tell me that the estate
agent has contacted him about clients who want to come and
view our house. He gets out his laptop and we sit on the sofa as
he logs into a property website.

I watch his fingers flicking around on the little pad. I could
do that, I think. I know that the doctors have recommended I
don't do it yet, but I could work out myself how to use a
computer again without having to rely on Freddie to teach me. I
will wait until the next time he is at work and try the one on the
desk in his office.

'Did you mention something about us moving to the Peak

District?' I trawl through my recent memories that I have managed to keep. 'Bakewell, wasn't it?'

'Well...' he scrolls through some photographs. 'I was thinking more about Wales. Properties are so much cheaper there. And the countryside – mountains and everything – is so lovely. Proper views but without all the tourists like you get in the Peak District.'

The pictures whizz past before I have chance to see them properly. Then he stops and clicks.

'Look, imagine that,' says Freddie, tilting the laptop towards me so that I can see a photograph of a steamy hot tub with a flamboyant sunset in the background. 'How good would it be to have a garden like that?'

'It looks beautiful.' But why do I have such a stubborn sense of attachment to this part of the country, feeling that I would be leaving something important behind if we moved away? Maybe it's the house itself and all the work I put into doing it up. I need to stop being sentimental about it and look forward to the challenge of renovating something else.

'What if I book us a few days away next weekend so that we can go and have a look? Mini break in a nice hotel and a nosy round the Welsh countryside?'

'Yeah. OK.' I determine to get behind this proposal. 'Yeah, that sounds like fun.'

He hasn't even heard my answer though, because he's already on *Booking.com* selecting dates.

A fool-proof recipe for blueberry muffins on a TV cookery programme provides me with baking inspiration. I buy ingredients and follow the instructions rigorously, ensuring that this time I don't open the oven door during the cooking period.

Finally, a cooling rack holds the satisfactory results of my efforts, and the house is filled with a happy, comforting aroma.

Hopefully, Freddie will enjoy these treats later, but in the meantime, I plan to take some over to Grace as an excuse to get into her house again.

* * *

'The door's unlocked.' The reedy shout is only just audible after I have knocked.

When I go through to the living room, I see that Grace is not alone. A lithe, blonde-haired woman in her late twenties is sitting on the sofa with some kind of small black poodle on her lap. Grace introduces her niece, Jessica, and Jessica introduces the dog, Bear.

I smile and say hello, proudly handing over the plastic tub of muffins.

'This is the woman from over the road who does the baking,' Grace tells her niece. She's forgotten my name again. 'You know, all the posh cakes. *You* bought one from her, didn't you?'

'Hi,' says Jessica, but there's the hint of apologetic amusement on her face.

'I'm Becka,' I say.

'Sorry,' says Jessica. 'I think she's confusing you with someone else. There was someone from the house opposite who made a cake for my engagement party, which was about a year and a half ago now. Cake was lovely but the relationship didn't last.'

Something feels strange inside my head, inside my belly. I look to Grace for assistance. 'Someone from over the road who baked a party cake?'

Grace nods. 'Yes, it's Becka here who does the cakes.'

'No... it definitely wasn't you. I would have remembered,' Jessica tells me. She squints and looks at the ceiling as if there's a clue painted on it. 'This is going to bug me now.'

I stare uncertainly at the tub of blueberry muffins that

Grace has placed on the coffee table. Jessica takes out her phone and starts to jab at it with her thumbs. Grace and I sit in an awkward silence, and the dog begins a fit of scratching.

'I don't mean to be anti-social' – laughs Jessica without lifting her eyes from the phone screen – 'but you know how it is when you know that you know something but you just need a bit of help?'

'Tell me about it,' says Grace, and I smile politely at her, because we're all here in the same position, aren't we? She reaches over and takes a muffin out of the tub, telling me how lovely and fluffy they feel.

'Bingo,' says Jessica, at the same time as shoving the scratching dog away from her. She leans forward to show me the phone screen.

Bling-Bling Bakes. There are photographs and a logo and a website link. She swipes at the pictures until she arrives at a huge chocolate affair decorated with red hearts, the top iced with the names in swirly lettering 'Jessica & Bradley'.

I'm confused.

'So where did you get this from?' I ask.

'A woman across the road. She had a small business doing cakes. As I said, it would be about eighteen months ago.'

'But are you sure it wasn't me? The thing is, I had an accident and lost my memory and there's a lot of stuff that I can't remember at all. It's completely gone. I know I used to do cakes because all my equipment is in the cupboard at home, with photographs and everything. And I've been living there for the past seventeen years.'

She examines my face, frowning and slowly shaking her head. 'Pretty sure it was someone else. Maybe similar age, similar size, but different hair and features. I just can't remember what she was called but I know it definitely wasn't Becka or Rebecca or anything like that. Weird name, I seem to think. Possibly foreign. I thought it might be on the website but it isn't.'

'Hmm. Well, it's intriguing, isn't it?' I raise my eyebrows at Grace who is sweeping crumbs from the front of her blouse.

The dog – Bear – jumps off the sofa to snaffle the muffin crumbs, and Jessica puts her phone away. I decide that it is a good time to leave and go home to check my – or someone else's – baking cupboard.

EIGHTEEN

BECKA

How can something so indulgent and sweet as cake be so stressful? I have been through the cupboard of baking equipment and ingredients searching for clues, for information about myself or this other mythical person who might have been here baking cakes, and can find nothing. Yes, the photograph album is still there and I have been through all the pictures again. I gaze at the picture of the engagement cake with 'Jessica & Bradley' iced on it, because it's not just on Jessica's phone, it's here in front of me, laminated and enlarged.

What does it mean?

I ask myself over and over, reminding myself of the facts that a cake was baked in this house and then photographed, probably by Freddie. My memory loss means that I don't remember baking this cake – or indeed, any cake that is featured in the album – but I have assumed that I did.

And now I have been told by the person who bought the cake that it wasn't me.

So, who *did* bake it? And who was in my house, eighteen months ago, and why hasn't Freddie mentioned them at all?

* * *

In the afternoon a man in a van comes to hammer a 'For Sale' sign into our front garden. I watch him through the living room window, and my head feels empty. It's like I only exist in a dream. How do I connect myself to this place and everything that has happened here? The vague recollections I do have seem meaningless: different wallpaper, Freddie's stepmother, the monkey puzzle tree.

Perhaps Freddie is right. Moving away to somewhere new will be the best thing for my mental health. Staying here would only torment me, with my memory offering up titbits that make no sense, seeing people that I think I recognise, while others show me photographs of cakes that I may or may not have baked.

I need to reset my head, start all over again. Whatever has gone before is irrelevant now. Playing detective will not help me.

* * *

Freddie rings me at lunchtime, to check in like he often does.

'Are you OK?' he asks me, and, 'What are you up to?' wanting to know my plans for the afternoon and making suggestions that perhaps I might like to do a bit of cutting back in the garden, some tidying of the borders ready for the prospective buyers.

It occurs to me that Freddie doesn't want me out around town. I might bump into the man again. Stop it, I tell myself. Put it all behind you, whatever has happened.

'That's a great idea,' I say.

'There's also a pile of receipts and invoices on my desk that need filing, if you'd rather be indoors. Or, you could start packing for our break,' he says. 'I can't wait. A fabulous room with a four-poster bed. And you.'

'I know. We're going to have plenty to do even before we start viewing property.'

I go into Freddie's office, picking up the disarray of paperwork to put in the correct files on the shelf.

There's a key dangling from the filing cabinet. The tall metal container is usually kept locked, and I have wondered for the last few weeks if Freddie has anything secret stashed in there.

Like what? I ask myself. Information relating to what happened before my accident? Or the answer to all the stupid cake business puzzle?

Freddie normally keeps his cameras and photography equipment in here: I've seen him putting things away when he comes in from work. But it wouldn't hurt to look what else might be there too.

My curiosity starts with the top drawer, and I examine the contents of each one in turn. Lenses, leads, different sized foldable tripods and cases. I work my way down but there's nothing that gives me any answers to my questions, and nothing amiss.

Then I reach the last drawer at the bottom.

I pull it out and stare at the thing that takes my breath away.

It's a gun.

Ludlow. A quirky, three-hundred-year-old hotel that claims to have original beams and fireplaces, creaky floors and a resident peacock in the gardens. Top-notch food and four-poster beds. An orangery in which to take afternoon tea. A modern attached annexe that has a swimming pool and spa facilities for guests' use.

Freddie has booked us in for five nights so that we can explore the area and view some potential new homes. And, he tells me, down one of the cobbled side streets, there's a quality jewellers that makes bespoke wedding rings. The cheap one that I wear, and the one that he lost in the sea at Lyme Regis some years ago can now both be replaced during our romantic break.

We sit at the island in the kitchen with glasses of white wine and the laptop, making plans for our time away next week, looking eagerly through the hotel breakfast menu that features 'Duck Egg Royale with Basil and Rocket Dressing'.

The alcohol warms me, relaxes my overthinking mind. I look at Freddie and know that he loves me and wants the best for us. Getting stressed about little things like cakes and clothes in a bin bag is pointless and won't help us move forward. Maybe it's better if I don't visit Grace any more. I only come home with questions and doubts.

And all the stress with the gun...

Well, we can laugh about it now.

It was small and heavy, black and smooth. Freddie took it out of the filing cabinet and mauled it briefly before passing it to me. I felt the weight and threat of it as Freddie explained how it had saved his life. He'd been on a wildlife shoot, freezing his balls off in Hudson Bay.

'We were in an encampment and I'd come out of my tent early one morning when this polar bear just literally strolled up. It can't have been more than twenty metres away.'

I gasp. 'You didn't shoot it?'

'No, but I would have if I'd had to. The bear just kept coming, its eyes on me all the time. I was fucking terrified. Luckily, I had this gun on me – we'd all been advised to carry one – and I shot it into the air first. The bear stopped but was still watching, so I aimed another shot which hit the ice about a metre away from its feet.'

'Oh my God.'

'A couple more seconds passed, and then it just turned

round and strolled off, cool as anything. And that was the point when I got my camera on it and bagged the best shot of all: a brilliant picture that ended up in *World Wildlife Magazine*.'

He clicked into a file on his laptop and brought up the photograph.

'Wow,' I said. My heart glowed: I was so proud of him.

He put the gun back in the bottom drawer of the filing cabinet, locked it up and slipped the key onto the keyring in his pocket.

* * *

We kiss hungrily. Wet lips, hot steamy breaths. Naked, we move against each other and I run my fingers through his hair. He is on top of me, skin on skin, a steady, easy rhythm that we're both comfortable with. I wind my feet around his and feel with my toes the deep scarring on his foot. The bed is too warm so we rip the covers back, kick them down to the bottom of the bed, and I bring my hands to his hips, then to the toned muscles of his back, to guide his pace, keep him constant because I'm getting there, closer, closer, and it's excruciating how strong the feelings are, just a few thrusts more...

I open my eyes to look at him, at his face above mine, and I see who it is, and there's not a flicker of doubt...

Suddenly I'm awake and the dream is gone. Breathless, like it was real. Skin burning, the sensation of disappointment flooding down my body as the scene ebbs away.

I focus on remembering, focus on bringing that face back into my mind. It was all so vivid. Me, having sex with someone.

But that someone wasn't Freddie.

It was the man I saw in town. The man with the leather jacket.

Oh God, who *is* he?

There's no way I can tell Freddie about this dream. It's one that will stay with me all day, maybe longer, lurking at the front of my mind, reminding me of that man's face, making me question who he is and how I know him and if I actually have had sex with him before. It will take me back to a week ago, where he stood out in the street drinking coffee before unknowingly leading me to follow him around town.

His face haunts me and I am filled with guilt. There's an ache between my legs. I *feel* like I have been unfaithful.

I hold my secret in the darkness, knowing that I will be awake now until it's light. Beside me, Freddie breathes deeply, submerged beneath the surface of sleep.

NINETEEN
BECKA

Our long weekend away is like the honeymoon that I can only imagine I had seventeen years ago. The hotel room is perfect: robes and luxury toiletries in the bathroom, fresh flowers in the windows, champagne and Belgian chocolates waiting beside the huge bed.

We pop the cork and chink glasses, laughing and flirting as we strip off our clothes to test out the four-poster.

'This is the life,' I say as Freddie feeds chocolates to me with his mouth, like a bird.

He swipes his phone screen to Bluetooth a music playlist to the room's stereo system.

'Here we go. Our song.'

I... want you back in my life...

'The other guests are going to think we're having a rave,' I say as the disco beat pumps through the speakers. 'Maybe we should choose something a bit slower, something more romantic.'

'This always makes me think of us when we were young. Cruising round in my car. Getting it on in my bedsit.'

'Oh God.' I suddenly sit up and put my hand over my mouth. 'Oh God, I've just remembered something.'

'What?' Freddie freezes, his eyes widening.

'Red satin sheets. Remember? On your bed. I can picture them now. We both thought they were the slinkiest, sexiest thing ever. But they creaked every time we moved.' I laugh, and Freddie relaxes, pretending to be offended that I am criticising his choice of bedding. 'Yes, the image just popped into my head. It must have been the song. The consultant at the hospital did say that music can trigger memories.'

Freddie grabs me and wrestles me onto my back again. 'I should have requested them on this bed, shouldn't I? We could have relived our youth.'

'Red silk might be nicer. Satin is like a cheap version.'

'You take that back. Calling my old bedding cheap.' Freddie splays my arms out and hovers above me with a smile on his face.

'Why, what are you going to do about it?' I know what he's going to do though. And it's just what I want.

Later, we go out around the town, finding a quirky tapas bar to eat in. Everything feels good, it feels like fun. We're happy and relaxed: even Freddie doesn't mind chilling out and engaging in some people-watching. There's a completely different vibe about him to a week ago when we went to the Robin Hood Inn.

'It's nice to see you not stressed,' I tell him.

'Me? Stressed? Like when?'

'Well, usually around other people. You always seem on edge when we're in a crowd. But it doesn't feel like that tonight.' I smile at him. 'It's good to be somewhere different, isn't it?'

'Yeah, it's great.' He lets out a sigh. 'Who knows, we could go back home to find that the house is sold. That would be fantastic, wouldn't it?'

The estate agent has already got four viewings booked for

while we are away. Freddie is grinning at me, an aura of contentment radiating out of him.

'What?' I ask.

'Nothing.' He shakes his head. 'I just love to see you happy, that's all.'

Our food arrives and I juggle the dishes around the table so that the breadbasket is in the middle and the garlic mushrooms can be closest to me. When I look up Freddie is still watching me, still beaming.

* * *

The next day, Freddie is behaving mysteriously. He collects a key from an estate agent and drives us out into the mountains. Winding lanes lead us to a stunning cottage that seems vaguely familiar. Then I realise: it's the one we looked at on the internet.

'What do you think?' says Freddie.

I nod my head. 'Nice.'

There are blue skies and an eager sun shining down on us, drenching the place in splendour. Dark hills and green fields provide a blissful backdrop. Freddie takes my hand and gives it a wiggle of excited anticipation, and I feel my spirit stirring in my chest. This place feels good.

He unlocks the door and we step inside.

It's an old house with character features but renovated to a fantastic standard. Flagstone floor and four-oven range in the kitchen. Oak panelled doors, inglenook fireplace. Quirky corners and subtle lighting and windows with stunning views feed our appetite for this major life change. The wraparound garden has a surprise summerhouse which is being used as an outdoor bar, and although the hot tub has a lid on it, we can easily imagine relaxing in the bubbling water and looking out towards the distant mountains.

'I love it,' I tell Freddie.

'Really?' There's an outbreak of pure joy on his face. 'Well, that's good. Because it's ours.'

'Ours? Surely we have to make an offer and have it accepted?'

'We already bought it. Before your accident. I didn't know if you'd remember.'

I stand in the garden and gaze at the house and its surroundings. Nothing is triggered in my memory, but something dips and squirms inside me. My face must show some kind of uncertainty, because Freddie wraps his arms around me and squeezes his body to mine.

'It's going to be great.'

I look again and we stroll back around the garden to where the car waits. The place is faultless. The setting is spectacular: two miles from the village and surrounded by fields, woods and mountains. No near neighbours.

Just as I approach the car I hear Freddie's phone ringing and he hangs back to answer it. I wait as he takes the brief call, seeing his face open up with delight.

'What is it?'

He tucks his phone into his pocket.

'We've just had an offer on our house. Full asking price.'

'Wow, that's brilliant.'

He takes both my hands and pulls them to his mouth to kiss them, his shining, ecstatic face reflecting my own. 'Yes, it is brilliant. Just like life with you.'

* * *

We are back in Ludlow by mid-afternoon.

'Let's have a look around the shops,' Freddie suggests. 'And then I'll take you to the jewellers that I told you about.'

So first we browse all the eccentric emporiums offering books, art, shabby chic furnishings, vintage clothing and liqueurs of the world, before eventually finding ourselves in a sparkling shop full of glass cabinets twinkling with gold, silver and all manner of precious stones.

Freddie gets me to remove my old wedding ring, and we both try on a range of new ones that can be adjusted to suit our sizes and tastes. The polite old man who serves us is helpful, patient, bringing tray after tray of rings to inspire us.

'This is gorgeous,' I say, twisting a loose band onto my finger. 'We could have matching ones.'

So Freddie tries on the same design and we entwine our fingers to see how they look, and everything in that moment feels so wonderful that the past and any secrets that it may hold doesn't feature at all in my thoughts – our new house and our future together is what it's all about.

We decide on the rings and the jeweller calculates our finger sizes. Freddie pays on his credit card and we arrange to pick them up on Monday morning before we leave to go back home.

Outside, the streets have got busier because the kids have finished school. Parents are dragging children with PE kits and book bags into the mini-markets to shop for dinner ingredients, and teenagers in dishevelled uniforms cavort boisterously on and off the pavements and between the traffic. Pent-up chatter, laughter, shouts and banter.

I cast my eyes back to the jewellers' alluring window while we wait for a gap in the traffic before crossing the road.

'Hey, Mum!'

I turn quickly and instinctively at the words.

A girl, thirteen or fourteen, dashing across the road to a woman in a work suit. 'Hey, wait for me.'

My heart is skipping. I watch as the woman turns and lets the girl catch up. The voice and words resound in my head. *Hey, Mum! Hey, Mum!*

Freddie is already at the other side of the street. With a

queasy stomach and wobbly legs I look around with uncertainty. What just happened? I don't know the woman or the girl.

She wasn't my daughter. I don't have a child. Why would I respond to the words *Hey, Mum?*

'Hey, Becka!'

Freddie gestures to me as I stand, bewildered, watching the cars pass between us.

'I'm over here.' He laughs.

A lull in the traffic lets me cross.

'You were in your own little world then,' he says.

I press a hand to my forehead. 'I just had a strange moment. Don't worry, I'm OK.'

He takes my hand, and I try to peer down the road at the mother and child, but they are both long gone.

TWENTY

BECKA

Something inside of my being has changed. A void has been discovered. I don't know how to explain it to Freddie, so I say nothing about it. I hide bouts of tearfulness in the toilet, and take paracetamol for aches and pains that strike without warning. Maybe it's anxiety. The thought of moving house, which is supposed to be one of the most stressful events in a person's life. Or maybe I'm entering the menopause and these are symptoms of my hormones changing. I don't want to talk about it with Freddie yet, because he's so analytical and we will only spend the rest of our holiday focused on how I'm feeling, when I would rather mask my angst and give us a chance to have some enjoyment.

In a restaurant, early evening on the Saturday, we are celebrating selling our house. Everything is falling into place perfectly. When we get home, we will contact a solicitor to act on the buying and selling, and get some quotes for home removals. There's a buzz about Freddie, who is gushing with enthusiastic ideas for the new house and how we could furnish the rooms. I listen and intervene politely with colour suggestions, but my attention is diverted behind him, to a table in the corner. A young couple is sitting there, and I am aware that the woman is breastfeeding her baby. She eats one-handed and the man passes a muslin cloth over the table, then she's trying subtly to move the child to her other side without exposing her breast, and the man is doing his best to seem helpful instead of just tucking in and eating his meal.

'...but the beauty of having that extra room downstairs means that we can use it as a snug, with the wood-burner of course, but a nice sofa and snuggly blankets and a TV...'

'A crackly fire will be lovely,' I say, but I am not really invested in the conversation: my heart is swelling with the sight of a baby's tiny hand clawing at the front of its mother's unbuttoned shirt.

Suddenly, my nipples begin to tingle. There's a crushing sensation in my belly. My breaths are quick and shallow as I yearn for something – a small, helpless being – that I don't know if I can have.

Freddie spins in his seat to see what I am looking at.

My face must be giving everything away, because when he turns back to me he takes my hand across the table and gives me such an expression of sympathy that I have to bite my lip to stop the tears welling up.

'Honey,' he says. 'I think we're turning into softies in our old age.'

Old age.

Forty isn't too old, is it?

I put a brave face on and pick up my fork to resume my meal. 'Did we ever properly discuss the subject of having children? I mean did we actually consider and then dismiss it? Or was it one of those topics that we just put aside to think about at some later date?'

Freddie stares into his food. He moves food around with his knife to create an empty triangle in the middle of his plate.

'I suppose we were never that interested before. We were too busy doing things for *us*.'

I glance again at the family in the corner. The mother has the baby draped over her shoulder while she rubs its back.

'I've just got a really weird feeling. Like my body is trying to tell me that time is running out, I suppose.' I shrug and try to hold my wobbling chin still.

'You want a baby?' Freddie whispers. 'Our baby?'

I exhale and sip my drink. 'Maybe it's my hormones. The last few days I've felt different. I just don't want us to have regrets later. You know?'

He chooses his words carefully. 'Do you think it's all right – I mean, is it possible – to have a baby? Could we really be parents at this point in our lives?'

I can't answer his question. I haven't had a period since my injury, so it could be likely that my body has given up on babies. Over in the corner, the woman has her face pressed into her infant's downy hair, and as I watch them both I sense the softness of the child's head, the smell that will be filling the mother's nostrils, the warmth, and the endorphins that will be flooding her body with love and protectiveness.

I want that feeling. Desperately.

* * *

Something has happened to me overnight. Alongside my hormonal display yesterday, another dream possessed me in the early hours. A powerful, evocative set of images which led me to cry in my sleep, soaking the expensive white linen of the hotel pillow.

I had a baby in my arms. The weight of it felt so real, almost as if it was *remembered*. There was a velvety plumpness to its limbs, and as it suckled my right nipple I looked down into its blue eyes and it caught the love and the bond between us, smiling as its tongue continued lapping. Drops of milk dribbled at the corner of its mouth and I stroked its cheek and whispered that it was a gorgeous little munchkin.

The dream carried on and I did nothing else but feed the baby for minutes and minutes – ages, it seemed – and that was all that happened, but it was the feeling of intense bliss and contentment that made me weep. I was a mother to a beautiful child.

But then, after a while, I felt the pressure of someone coming to sit by my side, to join me in looking at the baby, at caressing its smooth skin and making low murmuring noises to keep the infant calm.

Freddie.

From within the confines of my dream, that is who I presumed the person to be. But when I turned to look, it wasn't him.

It was the man in the leather jacket.

* * *

Dawn is only just seeping through the edges of the curtains when I lumber from the bed into the en suite to get a tissue and dry my tears. I sit on the cold toilet seat for a while in the grey-ness and take some deep breaths as I wipe my face.

What is all this? A mid-life crisis? A sudden sense of unful-fillment that is making me broody?

There is an aching in my belly and in my chest. I lean my head into my hands to try and hold back further sobs that are threatening to escape me.

Suddenly, Freddie is there in the doorway, the light cord is pulled and brightness blinds me.

'What's wrong?'

'Nothing, I'm fine.'

He squats down in front of me and puts his hands on my knees. I blow my nose and Freddie waits for more of an answer.

'Strange dream again, that's all. And I just feel a bit... out of sorts.'

He gives me a quizzical eyebrow.

'I think it was something to do with all the baby talk, you know, yesterday?'

'Honey. You know I'm with you all the way. Whatever you decide.' With a kiss on my knee, he stands up. He caresses my neck and shoulder before leaving and closing the door.

I'm OK. People have strange dreams all the time. It's no different for me, and the feelings in my body are just a phase I'm going through. I do some more inhalations and start to get some composure. And it's then that I notice...

Blood.

My period has started again. Like it's trying to tell me something.

I *am* capable of becoming a mother after all.

TWENTY-ONE
BECKA

We go to the jewellers to collect our new wedding rings. Instead of putting them on, Freddie puts the velvet-lined boxes into his coat pocket and taps his nose.

Outside, we walk through cobbled streets, imbibing the smell of fresh coffee and baked goods that drifts from the open shop doors.

'Where are you taking me?' I ask Freddie, who has my hand and is leading us purposefully to some mystery location.

He answers with a knowing smile, and we continue for another five minutes until the impressive medieval church looms into view, and I realise what he is doing.

'Here we are,' he finally replies as we arrive at the front porch, stepping through the huge door into the magnificent building.

There are other tourists inside, browsing around the architecture, kneeling in silent prayer, reading the information boards. Spring flowers are displayed beautifully around the building. A soothing holy vibe touches all our senses: the smell of snuffed-out candles and ancient fust; the shafts of coloured light through the stained-glass window; the organ music that resounds around us. We walk respectfully down the aisle to the altar, and Freddie removes the rings from his pocket, from the boxes.

'With this ring, I thee wed. I will love you and honour you, and even death will never part us.' Freddie speaks quietly as he slips the ring onto my third finger.

I take his ring to repeat the ritual, but can't remember the words, so I tell him, 'I love you and want you forever.'

We gaze at each other for a moment before sealing the deal with a kiss. There's a brief commotion and we break away to see a small gathering of people that have been watching us and have spontaneously broken into reverent applause.

'Wow,' Freddie says. 'We've done it now. Man and wife.' We entwine our newly ringed fingers and smile at our improvised congregation.

'Thank you,' I say to the people who will be returning later to their families and friends to talk about us over dinner.

I turn and whisper to Freddie. 'Don't tell them we've been married for seventeen years already; it might spoil things for them.'

He laughs and pulls me into him. 'Come on, let's go and celebrate. We need a champagne toast. It's been quite a weekend!'

* * *

'It actually felt like we got married earlier,' says Freddie, when we are back at the hotel. 'There was such a special atmosphere, and with everyone there literally clapping us on...'

'It was lovely. And the place was beautiful. I thought we would just walk out of the shop with the new rings on, but you took me by surprise.'

Freddie beams with pride and picks up the second bottle of champagne to refill our glasses. A thought suddenly strikes me...

'Where did we originally get married?'

The bottle strikes the edge of the glass and with a clatter it's off the table, shattered on the floor. The fizzy liquid pools and runs, dripping onto my lap as I try to dam the flow with a beer mat.

'Oh crap. Sorry about that.' Freddie looks sheepishly towards the efficient member of staff who is already making his way over with a cloth and a dustpan.

We shift out of our chairs and move things round on the table so that the waiter can clear up the mess, and Freddie apologises again, explaining that we may have celebrated a little too hard.

And when it's all sorted and we sit down again I have forgotten the question that I didn't get an answer to, and Freddie has started on the subject of babies and how the back bedroom with the fitted wardrobes in the new house would be ideal for a nursery, and I am luxuriating in the thought that I am sitting here bleeding which means that I should be ovulating in around fourteen days' time.

It's Tuesday afternoon when we finally arrive home. Already, the estate agents have been and put 'Sold' over the board in the garden.

Freddie unlocks the front door and stoops to gather up the pile of letters on the floor. A frown appears between his eyes as he shuffles through them.

'What is it?' I ask.

He opens the door of his office. 'Nothing, it's fine.'

He tosses the correspondence onto his desk and pulls the door shut behind him before going to collect our luggage from the car.

I stand in the doorway of the living room, taking in the

décor, the light pouring through the bay window, the ornamental fireplace.

'It's nothing compared to where we're going, is it?' Freddie plonks the bags down at the bottom of the stairs.

'Well, I was just thinking I will be quite sad to have to leave it behind. It's been a nice place for us. We've been happy here, haven't we?'

A look sweeps across Freddie's face. Embarrassment? Awkwardness? A moment of disagreement? His neck flushes red and he goes to the window to point the fob and lock the car. I cringe inwardly, realising that I cannot make statements like this when I am unable to remember what has happened with us. If I have been unfaithful.

And before I can prevent it, that other face has crept into my head again. The man with the leather jacket.

I blink him away and go to Freddie, to embrace him and tell him that I have no regrets about us making an offer on the new house, and that I can't wait for us to get there and start the next chapter of our lives, which may even include a baby within the next year.

We stand locked together for a few minutes and I breathe in his familiar scent and feel the solidity of his muscles under his jumper. I glance towards the house across the road and, predictably, the net curtain moves and Grace gives me a wave. I wonder what she will think about us leaving.

* * *

That night, when we are in bed I see our wedding canvas on the wall and I am reminded about our celebrations after the church wedding ring ritual.

'You never answered my question,' I say to Freddie. 'When you were pouring the champagne and the glass broke on the floor.'

'What question?'

'I asked you where we got married originally.'

He shrugs. 'Just the Registry Office. We only wanted a small affair and we didn't have loads of money to spend. So yeah. Just a basic service and a quiet reception in the back room of a pub. The White Swan, just out of town. It's been knocked down now.'

'It looks quite swish.' There are blue skies and trees in the background, with twinkling hanging fairy lights, like we are in some fancy gardens. My dress and Freddie's suit look stylish, expensive.

'Photographs can be deceptive,' says Freddie. 'I should know.'

He kisses me and tells me that what we did yesterday in the church felt so much more special than what was going on in the canvas over the bed; and I know that I have to believe him and trust him because something has obviously happened in the seventeen years between then and now, and the declarations of love that we made to each other yesterday were a new starting point.

Everything that has gone before must be forgotten.

TWENTY-TWO

BECKA

I hadn't planned on visiting Grace in the next few days because things have been good between me and Freddie, and all the confusing stuff seems to be on hold in my mind. It feels so much better for my mental health when I'm not overthinking everything. But when I go outside on Friday to drag the wheelie bin to the pavement, she has moved from the net curtain to the front doorstep, where she is waving and making a *coo-ee* sound.

Maybe she wants to ask about the house sale. It's only natural she would want to know.

So I pop over the road and she invites me in again for tea. There's a spring of excitement in her movements and it's obvious that she has something to tell me.

'You've been away, haven't you?'

I begin to tell her about our new property in Wales, but she's not interested in that. She wants me to know that someone came round to our house – twice – trying to get hold of us.

'What did they look like?' I ask. No one apart from tradespeople has ever visited us since I have come home from hospital.

'A young girl, teenager. I don't know: fourteen, fifteen, maybe older. You can't properly tell these days with all the make-up they wear. She had jeans on and a red top with a hood on it. Longish hair, not dead straight but not curly either: a dark brown colour. Nice skin, not spotty or anything like they get at that age. And on her back there was this little kind of rucksack thing. It was probably just a fashionable bag because you wouldn't have been able to put a coat in it.'

'Well, that's a very detailed description.' I laugh. 'If she was there to burgle the place then the police would get a great statement from you.'

'She didn't strike me as being a criminal. I saw her early evening on Friday the first visit. She knocked quite a few times on the front door and then had a wander round the back. Then when she didn't get an answer she left. But she came back on the Sunday afternoon, at quarter past two. Same clothes, same bag and everything. Knocking on the door, going round to the back garden. Then I saw her looking through the front windows. It seemed a bit odd, so I went over to ask her what she wanted.'

'Really? That's brave of you, confronting a stranger.'

'She seemed nice enough, a polite girl. She was looking for the woman who bakes cakes.'

Oh no, not all that business again!

A flash of confusion brushes Grace's expression and she scratches her head. 'It's not *you* that does the cakes, though, is it? I couldn't remember what we said last time.'

I shrug and hold up my hands in submission. The cake mystery is yet to be solved.

'Well, anyway,' Grace continues despite her setback, 'I thought – you know, with my poor memory – that I would write it down so that I could pass the message on to you.'

Proudly, she goes to extricate a used envelope from the sideboard drawer.

'Here it is. I wrote down the name of the woman she was looking for. It's *not* you, is it?'

I take the envelope from her hand. MAGDALENA it says on it. Something nudges for a second in my brain, but it's gone before I can focus on anything. I turn the envelope over but it's just printed with Grace's address.

'This is the woman who bakes cakes?' I ask.

'Yes. It's quite confusing, isn't it? But I called my niece – you know, Jessica, the one with the dog? – and she said straight away that that was the name of the woman who did her engagement cake. Magdalena. But that's *not* you, is it?'

No, it's not me. I'm Becka. Over the road, at home, there are letters from the hospital and brochures from home furnishing companies addressed to me. There are photographs of me at different stages of my life. I am definitely Becka.

But... have I had another name at some point? I begin to wonder. I stare at the name in front of me.

MAGDALENA.

Oh God, it's happening again, isn't it? The uncertainty, the brain fog, the tricks of the memory. It all feels like that moment when I was pulled from the water and taken to hospital and everyone kept asking my name and I couldn't remember.

Who am I?

I'm Becka, aren't I? I am pretty sure of that.

So, if I *am* Becka, then who is Magdalena? And why is someone looking for her?

It's two hours until Freddie is due home. I am worn out with worry, with trying to work out the puzzle of it all.

I empty everything out of the baking cupboard and go through all the equipment, the recipe books, the photograph album, but there are no further clues. All I know is that a woman called Magdalena used this house to run her cake-making business from.

But how does that fit in with me? How does that fit with the seventeen years that I have been here, married to Freddie? Did I move out for a while and Magdalena was his new partner? Or did she live here with both of us, maybe as a lodger?

I go into Freddie's office, to look through the files on the shelves but nothing relates to anyone called Magdalena. His drawers contain the usual bric-a-brac: pens, loose coins, batteries, memory sticks, the instructions for a camera lens. In the wastepaper basket is a scrunched-up piece of paper, and I remember how we arrived home on Tuesday and Freddie picked up the letters from the floor with an anxious expression on his face as if he had read something troubling.

I remove the paper and flatten it out. A handwritten note, in large, neat writing with a phone number at the bottom:

> Please can you help me? This is URGENT and linked to the case of a missing person who may have been murdered. I am looking for information about Magdalena Harper and her past whereabouts. Anything at all, however insignificant it may seem. Call anytime and leave a message if I don't answer

A sudden queasiness lurches in my stomach.

Missing person.

Murder.

A woman who used to live here.

I think of Freddie and his lovely, gentle ways and how he slid the wedding ring onto my finger only two days ago.

I think of the gun in the bottom drawer of the filing cabinet.

It must have been the girl that Grace saw who put the note through the door. Maybe Magdalena is – or was – her mother.

What connection does Magdalena have with this house? Me and Freddie have lived here for seventeen years, so surely we will both have known her. Has something serious happened to her? Has she died? And if so, has she died *here*?

I think about the guest bedroom upstairs, stripped of everything. Did she stay in there? The bin bag in the cupboard: women's clothes, make-up, the half-bottle of perfume. Were these *her* belongings and not mine?

I remember nothing about this woman. But what does Freddie know? What is he hiding?

And why didn't she take her stuff with her?

The room looms inwards and I sway on my feet. Quickly, I dash to the back door, to stand on the step and gulp the air, holding myself steady against the wall. I need to think, but I dare not think about what might have happened to this missing woman.

Could Freddie *really* have killed her?

I take in the newly landscaped garden, all done quite recently. The decking, the fresh turf that is growing beautifully, the budding borders and shrubbery. What if...?

Oh God. I stagger to the flowerbed and vomit onto the soil. Oh God, what if...?

What if it's *me*?

What if *I* have killed her?

PART TWO

TWENTY-THREE

MAGDALENA

Me and Freddie had history. We went way back to the time when his father married my mother, and I – a self-conscious fifteen-year-old with acne – had to stand outside the Registry Office and pose in an off-the-shoulder taffeta dress in coral peach that cut me in half. Freddie wasn't in the photographs. He was the one taking them, bossily snapping around as he manipulated us into positions that would look dreamy and captivating, so that he could get some event experience and build his portfolio.

It was an unusual coupling. Our parents had met through some kind of history club. Freddie's dad had been a quiet and modest man, always well turned out in a shirt and tie; and I suppose that's what my mother found attractive in him since he had no interest in religion of any sort. There was also the fact that she had been widowed for over ten years and struggled to manage the family budget, so their friendship had blossomed more quickly when she saw the comfortable detached property and bank balance of Freddie's father.

My mother and I had been living in a rented two-bedroom terrace in a grotty area of town. It was the sixth of its kind. Flit-

ting from one short-term tenancy to the next was the norm, and
it was probably more to do with this than my mother's spiritual
views that we never attached ourselves to material possessions
and keepsakes. So it had felt thrilling to be putting down roots
in a spacious, charming house that didn't have neighbours
whose dogs and arguments and sex you could hear through the
walls.

A new place to live. Another new school where I would
have to put on a brave face and try to make new friends.

It had become clear within a matter of weeks that my
mother and Freddie would not make good housemates. Everything they did irritated the hell out of each other. His car on the
drive; her Bibles and Jesus pictures on public display; his lack of
punctuality to the table for dinner; her insistence that prayers
were said before every meal; his atrocious taste in music – how
can you possibly *like* that awful banging row? – and the volume
he played it; her hosting of church gatherings in the front room
where devotions would be chanted so that it made the house
feel like something out of a horror film.

My mother had wanted him out from the start. She niggled
at him, on and on, about growing up, taking responsibility, not
treating the place like a hotel. He'd always been OK with me,
and we'd had an unspoken agreement that we wouldn't snitch
on each other for anything, particularly things like the booze
and cigarettes he would buy for me.

Freddie's father had tried his best to keep the peace
between everyone, but during the space of one weekend an
argument over the disappearance of some communion wafers
that had been brought home for the Tuesday prayer group just
sent everything spiralling towards a big family split. It came to a
head with my mother screaming 'it's him or me – someone's got
to go', and I'd had that familiar sinking feeling of anticipating
packing up my stuff ready to move house again.

But it wasn't to be. There had been an icy discussion

between Freddie and his father, which ended with a bout of door-slamming and the throwing of a kitchen chair. My mother had waited until Freddie's car had screeched out of the drive before emptying his wardrobe and drawers, throwing all his possessions out of his bedroom window and onto the back lawn.

Maybe it had been something to do with all this conflict that caused Freddie's father's stroke, the first one that led to the discovery of his brain tumour. I didn't know. But there were still socks and underpants and T-shirts bowing the heads of the delphiniums, and shirts spread-eagling the grass as the ambulance crew had made their way out of the back door with him on the stretcher.

During the days afterwards, the house felt more *normal* with just my mother and me in it, as if it had been her plan all along. While Freddie's father lingered in Ward C4 of the Royal Hospital, my mother revelled in entertaining her church friends and creating a permanent worship room, hanging a crucifix on the back wall and a huge picture of Jesus with outstretched arms over the mantelpiece, ready to catch anyone at risk of falling into the fire.

Freddie got a bedsit in town and continued his job as a photographer for the local newspaper. I kept in touch with him. My mother never knew. He had a sporty car and I would ride around with him, his dance music blasting through the speakers. Freddie had the money to buy stuff for me; he was kind and funny and generous.

I was in my last year at school when I introduced Becka to him. They hit it off straight away. In some ways it was too much, too intense. Obsessive.

Freddie changed overnight. He didn't need me any more; there was only one passenger seat in the car and she had claimed it.

Becka. She was the same age as me, in the same Art class. I had befriended her at the beginning of the year, although it mainly felt like she just humoured me and didn't really want to let me get close. She could be two-faced at times and always had an attitude of superiority. Even though I took her to my house on occasions, it always felt like there was a motive behind her visits, a snigger behind a hand as she stepped through into the hall.

So. *Her* and Freddie.

Deep down, I was jealous. I was the one who'd always been his confidante, the one who rode shotgun, the one who gave support and advice because Freddie wasn't always socially confident. It felt like he had deserted me, been stolen away from under my nose.

In Art class I tried to continue the friendship with Becka, but it seemed that now she had what she wanted she wasn't interested in me any more. She spread rumours about my mother, laughing at her 'religious lunacy'. She moved her work onto a different table, away from mine, so that she could chat with some of the more popular girls, trying to impress them with talk of her new boyfriend and his car.

The opportunity for me to break up their relationship came when Freddie's dad died and Freddie had been called to the care home. He should have been meeting Becka but wasn't able to get a message to let her know what had happened.

At school the next day, I heard as she confided to her new friends in Art that Freddie had not turned up to see her the previous evening. She had waited and waited and even gone to the car park near his house where he kept his car, but there had been no sign of him. She was upset that he had stood her up, frantically speculating about what he might have been doing instead.

I listened with glee, knowing that the perfect opening had arrived. Sauntering over to Becka's group, I admitted with a solemn face that I had overheard their conversation and felt I ought to let her know that Freddie had found someone else. I didn't mention the death of his father.

'I'm sorry to be the bearer of bad news,' I said, with a fake-sad expression. I could tell that Becka was unbelieving at first, but when I described the new girlfriend – someone he worked with that had luscious blonde hair and a fantastic curvy figure – she became devastated.

Inwardly, I was bursting with delight, even though I realised what I'd done wasn't right, knowing that Freddie was grieving his father and needed Becka more than ever.

Maybe Becka sensed my joy, my spite. She may have seen the glint in my eye as I told her how promiscuous Freddie was, how she shouldn't have trusted him.

I didn't anticipate how she would repay me.

Because she lashed out in such a hurtful way, spreading more rumours about my mother, and then – oh God, it makes me want to cry again at the thought of it – stealing and destroying my complete art portfolio that needed to be handed in at the end of the week.

My dreams of university, of being an artist or a designer, were all gone.

The day following the incident, when all my pieces of art had been dragged, slimy and pulpy from that stinking pond, I spent an hour sobbing my heart out in the school toilets. Eventually, I wiped my eyes and went to the sixth form common room, where I dragged Becka to her feet with the collar of her shirt and vowed to get revenge one day.

'Keep checking behind you,' I told her. 'Because you won't know when or where or how I will do it. Just be assured that it *will* happen.'

TWENTY-FOUR

MAGDALENA

The autumn after I failed my Art exam – failed my life – was when everything else went wrong.

Since the death of Freddie's father, there had been a tirade of solicitors' letters through the door. Each new one would set my mother off, and she would place the offending correspondence on the mantelpiece while she prayed and handed the matter over to God, believing that somehow it would get sorted out without any further involvement from her.

She wouldn't accept that we had to leave the house, that we had to literally hand it back over to Freddie because that was what his father had specified in his will.

I knew that Freddie would do something. There had been a sullen, voluminous feeling in the pit of my stomach that had started when he turned up to demand that we leave his property and find somewhere else to live. He'd been seen with Becka again. Despite my best efforts, they had been like magnets, pulled back to resume their relationship, and this had revitalised his need to evict us. He wanted the house for *her*.

Freddie had been threatening, even attracting the attention of the neighbours, which was something that heaped huge embarrassment onto my mother. Aftershocks came in the form of further letters from the solicitor.

I continued to hope that we could negotiate a resolution so that we could all live happily ever after. I missed Freddie. He hadn't just been my stepbrother; he'd been my only real friend. Now, he didn't want to know me any more.

My mother was still in denial about everything, unwilling to either challenge the will or find us another house to live in. This stalemate situation smouldered with tension for all of us. Something needed to change. Someone had to make the first move.

It was Bank Holiday carnival night when it happened. After a busy shift at the sandwich factory, where I worked, I stepped off the bus and smelt the air, heard the cracks and fizzes, and saw the coloured sparkles in the sky. Music, fairground rides and fireworks had drawn the usual crowds to the local park around the corner.

As I turned the corner of the street towards our house, I saw the blue flashes of the fire brigade and smelled the acrid burning stench that was nothing to do with fun and celebration. A gathering of onlookers gazed upwards, open-mouthed, to my mother's bedroom window, where a ladder stretched to the broken glass. Smoke poured out of the gap as a fireman leaned in with a hose to direct a jet of water.

I ran.

More sirens and blue lights. An ambulance screeched to a halt beside me.

'Oh God, where's my mother? Is she in there?' I screamed at a fireman unravelling a hose. The front door was open and flames were visible.

'She's out, love. Don't worry, she's out.' The next-door neighbour appeared and pulled me by the hand to where I could see over the wall into the garden. There she was, flat out on the lawn under the monkey puzzle tree with a paramedic kneeling beside her.

'Is she dead?' I pushed through the spectators at the gate and ran to her side as the first aider was manipulating her into the recovery position.

'Mum, are you all right?' I squatted down, but was unable to get a reply as the ambulance crew arrived with a stretcher.

A police officer ushered me out of the way. 'She'll be fine. Just leave them to sort her out.' He began moving nosy neighbours to the other side of the road, away from the sparks and smoke.

'Come along now.' I was shepherded off the grass and onto the pavement.

'That's my mother,' I yelled as I was forced back behind the wall. 'It's my actual house that's burning down.'

I watched in horror as the windows blackened and shattered, and the flames spilled out. All our possessions were gone.

And we were homeless again.

TWENTY-FIVE

MAGDALENA

I don't know the details of how it all played out with Freddie and Becka, but the fire was the end of them. Freddie got arrested on suspicion of arson, and was questioned and released, then questioned some more.

Eventually the police were satisfied that he had been at the carnival at the time of the fire, and let him go without charge. The cause of the fire was put down to a stray rocket from the firework display.

It wasn't the happy ending Freddie wanted, though. Rumour had it that Becka's father somehow got involved in the situation and made threats to him. There was no way he wanted his darling daughter hanging around with a suspected arsonist. Next thing, Becka was on her way to Glasgow School of Art to do her degree, and Freddie had disappeared to a new photography job, leaving his inherited burnt-out shell of a house behind.

I only saw Becka one last time before we all went our separate ways. She was waiting in the queue of the coffee van that trades in the marketplace on a Saturday. Alone, she looked coy and vulnerable, a smudge of make-up below her right eye, and lank tendrils of hair freed from her ponytail slapping her face in the breeze. An antelope away from the herd. She stood weighing the cash in her hand, checking over her left shoulder as if looking for someone. Vibrant pink T-shirt, frayed shorts and bare legs with flip-flops. Her tan had faded as if she had spent too much of the summer indoors, and I noticed that she had a plump blister on the side of her right big toe.

Anger bubbled like acid inside me at the sight of her. I watched her for a few seconds more, attempting to calm myself so that I could turn and leave, but the rage grew at the mere thought of her existence, at the thought of everything – and particularly the most recent thing – that she had done to ruin my life.

She didn't see me. I uttered a silent curse on her and convinced my livid urges that it would be better to bide my time. And then I walked away.

My mother spent ten days in hospital after the fire, her lungs badly damaged by the heat and smoke inhalation. A colleague from work was kind enough to lend me clothes and let me sleep on her sofa because I had nowhere to live. Everything in the house had been destroyed. Steel fences were erected around the fire-damaged building, and forensic investigators sifted through stuff for a while before boarding up all the doors and windows and leaving it to the elements. We weren't allowed back, but then again, it didn't belong to us anyway. A social worker helped us to find yet another shabby rented terrace – on the opposite side of town this time – so that my mother would have somewhere to go when she left hospital.

We were given some basic second-hand furniture by a charity, and the church rallied round for donations of kitchen equipment. It looked like some of the donors saw it as an opportunity to declutter their cupboards, and we were bombarded with boxes of battered saucepans, mismatched cutlery and chipped crockery, most of which went in the bin.

So, back in the environs of drug dealers and backyards with yapping pit bulls and revving motorbikes, we resided in the tiny damp rooms sandwiched between warring families. Prayer meetings were no longer held at our house; my mother wouldn't have had the energy to leave her bed and make the journey downstairs anyway.

She had left hospital wheezing and reluctant, connected to an oxygen tank that she was dependent on. Health professionals came and went, stomping up and down the uncarpeted stairs while trying to avoid ripping their shoes on the redundant gripper rods, taking blood, giving medication and advice as my mother slowly faded away.

By the time Advent arrived she was gone, taken by a malicious bout of pneumonia. The church rallied round again, this time with a requiem mass and a tray of potted beef sandwiches. It was only after I had thanked the priest for the church's generosity that I found out I was due no inheritance: the money left to her by Freddie's father had all gone. Guilty that she'd had unpaid tithes, and raring to get her advance ticket to heaven, my mother had given it all to the Church.

I didn't earn enough then to get my own place. My elusive Auntie Kaye took pity on me and let me live in her house for the next three years. In Liverpool.

She had a well-paid job in the office of a hotel chain, and used her contacts to get me employment as a commis chef in one of the best restaurants in the city. The hours were long and the work was hard, but my artistic flair soon got me promoted to pastry chef.

I was twenty-one years old. But despite my life finally being on a good track I was unable to make a success of myself. I was easily distracted and lacked motivation. Time and money fizzled away with nothing much to show for it. Over the next eighteen years or so my attention span deteriorated in everything I did. Jobs, friends and lovers never lasted more than a few months. I flitted from one workplace to another – bars, bakeries, factories and bistros – and from one relationship to another, often overlapping them. Shy younger men that needed bringing out of their shells; gullible old men with brimming bank accounts; adventurous tattooed women that were philosophical and usually anti-establishment. They provided free temporary accommodation – of varying standards – and I was in and out of their houses with my belongings in bin bags.

I never really noticed the slow and gradual return journey that I was unintentionally making over the years. My route took me from Liverpool to Manchester before skirting around the underside of the Peak District, through twenty-two different places I called home for a while, until I was only a stone's throw from the blackened, derelict home that I had left at the age of eighteen.

Of course, anyone would be curious. What normal person wouldn't want to revisit a place that had been such a turning point in their life?

It was most likely that the house would belong to someone else now: perhaps an investor had bought the fire-damaged property and renovated it to make a fortune. It didn't matter who was residing in it, though.

Surely a look wouldn't hurt me, would it?

TWENTY-SIX

BECKA

Freddie is two hours late getting home from work. Punishing gridlock sealed up the motorway after a lorry shed a hazardous load over all three lanes. The thought of Magdalena has wormed its way into every part of me during that time, but I know better than to confront Freddie immediately when he steps, frazzled and hungry, into the hall. I need to be subtle, luring out the information like it's a shy brown trout.

I reheat the chicken casserole in the microwave and watch as he downs lager straight from the can to ease his stress.

'I'm not going to miss the M1. It will be a change to get stuck behind tractors on single-track lanes when we finally get away from here.' He speaks as if we've been trying to get rid of the place for years.

We eat in the kitchen, and I commiserate over his hellish journey. There's small talk about his day photographing the interior of a car and having to get a glint of reflection on the steering wheel absolutely perfect, then about my day packing up and labelling boxes ready for our move.

I pour us both glasses of chilled Sauvignon Blanc and we do

the ritual of clinking them together for nothing more celebratory than the fact that we are here, eating dinner.

He smiles at me, but his expression looks forced, as if he's noticed that I am not quite right. He comments on the food, praising the sauce: its consistency, its creaminess, the delicate flavour of tarragon. Waiting. Disarming me. Postponing what could be a difficult or unpredictable conversation.

'We need to talk,' I say by way of an introduction, recognising that he is waiting in the wings for the main performance.

'OK, babe.' He rubs the back of his fingers lightly up and down my arm. 'Is something wrong?'

I take a deep breath and move my arm away from his touch.

'I just wondered. You know, before I had my accident and us deciding to go to Wales? Why did we want to go there? Were we running away from something?'

'Running away? Of course not. We loved the house and wanted a new challenge. That's all it was.'

'But... I don't know. There's more to it than just... houses. Sometimes it's as if you're keeping things back, as if you're not telling me the proper story. Like there's a whole layer of my life hidden, covered up, and you don't want me to know about it. But... Well, I keep discovering things.'

Freddie's face has turned white. He drops his knife and it clatters onto the tiled floor. Bending to pick it up, I see how his hand trembles.

Something has been exposed, a nerve to an icy blast of air. I need to keep going with this, even though I'm afraid of what I might unveil.

'Are you trying to protect me?' I ask, but I cannot bring myself to be direct and specific. I can't mention her name – Magdalena – because that would make everything too real. Vagueness is all I can muster up. 'Has something terrible happened and you're frightened that I will be taken away from you?'

There is no colour to him. Grey skin, a twitch in his lips, a panicked stare, quick shallow breaths. He reaches for my hand and squeezes hard, even though I'm still gripping my fork that is speared with a piece of potato.

'Talk to me,' I say. 'I'm scared.'

'Do you love me?'

'Yes. Yes, of course I do.'

'And do you trust me?'

I pause. 'Well. Like I say, it feels as if you're not being straight about what has happened in the past. And it's not fair when I can't remember, it feels deceptive.'

'But do you trust that I have your best interests in my mind all the time? That I would never be unfaithful or put you in danger or do anything to make you unhappy? Do you trust that I will absolutely love you until we die?'

'I know you're a good man. Everything you've done since my accident has been amazing and our relationship feels... I don't know... faultless. Sometimes it's even too good to be true.' I laugh, because I'm not sure where I'm going with all this now. 'It's just... what happened before my accident? It always feels like you want to avoid telling me.'

'Don't,' he says, rising from his stool and moving over to envelop me with his strong arms. 'Don't go there. Let's keep it all behind us.'

'But has there been a crime committed? I mean, something serious that the police would get involved in?'

He gulps. 'What sort of crime are you suspecting?'

I can't possibly say the word *murder* out loud. It makes me feel ill just thinking of it. But I need to say something. 'For example, a missing person investigation?'

'Yes.' The merest whisper, mumbled into my neck. 'But it wasn't intentional. It wasn't premeditated or anything.'

He pulls away to arm's length to look at me and our eyes are jammed, stuck in the same sick groove. Trying to read each other's minds, each other's stories. The thing is though, mine is blank. Magdalena is just a name, an invisible person. At this point in time, she means nothing to me. The issue is, do I keep her buried – my thoughts go immediately to the lush green turf in the back garden – or do I get Freddie to uncover her?

'And that's why you're protecting me?'

'Yes.'

'And that's why we're running away?'

Freddie kisses my forehead. 'We're not running away, as such. We're moving on. Don't start thinking that we're fugitives and we can't live normal lives. It's not like that at all. We can have a great life together, but it's probably best for us to be away from here. Like I said, you have to trust me, trust that I'm doing the right thing for us.'

'Is it something to do with someone called Magdalena?' There's a wobble in my voice as I dare to finally say her name.

'Oh fuck.' Freddie covers his face with his hands. 'What have you heard about her?'

'She lived here, didn't she? She had a cake business here, didn't she?'

Freddie blows out a long breath through his mouth. He won't look at me. Seconds tick by and we listen to a lawn being mowed somewhere down the street. Then he looks up. 'Yes. She lived here for a while. And ran a cake business.'

'Won't you tell me what happened?'

Freddie rubs his hands through his hair and sits back on his stool. 'It wouldn't help. Really, you're better off not knowing, not remembering. Because if the police...'

I understand. If I'm questioned I can genuinely say that I cannot remember. And the hospital would be able to verify that.

'OK.'

'Trust me,' he says again. 'It's for the best.'

I force my shoulders down and relax my neck, picking up my cutlery to resume our meal.

He's watching me.

I put the speared potato into my mouth, and he blows me a kiss.

He's right: I do have to trust him.

Whatever awful thing it is that I have done, I cannot return to it.

Ever.

TWENTY-SEVEN

MAGDALENA

It was a stifling white-hot day, perfect for wearing sunglasses, when I took a bus back to my old stomping ground. Weirdly, everything felt smaller, as if I were Alice eating the mushroom that made me grow. The width of the road, the bus shelter at the end, the monkey puzzle tree in the garden that I had always remembered as being colossal. I sauntered – loitered, really – on the opposite side of the road to get a good view.

There was a sporty-looking black car in the smart, block-paved driveway. Only a year old, chrome wheels gleaming, well maintained. Could it be Freddie's?

The house looked fantastic. New double-glazed windows and front door all in gunmetal grey, tidy lawned garden edged with variegated shrubs, brick-built garage at the side that hadn't been there before. I was impressed. Even without the fire damage, the previous incarnation of the house was nothing compared to this.

I crossed over and pretended to adjust my shoe by the wall, sneaking a peek through the impressive bay window. No sign of anyone inside. I made my way to the end of the drive and listened. On a day like this someone could be in the back garden, enjoying the sun. No sound of voices though. No music.

Before I realised, my feet had taken me down the drive, to the side of the house. The old kitchen door had been blocked up and there was a gate to the rear garden. Part patio that looked like it needed jet-washing, and part lawn. The straggly borders required attention. I vaguely remembered it looking the same when I was there. Perhaps whoever had the house hadn't got onto the rear landscaping yet. I pressed myself over the wrought iron so that I could see further. Ah, that explained it: a massive extension with bi-fold glass panels; a balcony above, accessed through French doors in what used to be my mother's double-aspect bedroom. Nicely done, all of it. The sort of place I would love to live in. I had almost come close to it with a retired guy called Bernard, but he had driven me mad with boredom and a yappy chihuahua that always shat indoors because he hadn't trained it properly.

Suddenly, there was movement. One of the glass doors slid open and a man walked barefoot onto the mossy patio, a phone to his ear. Cropped hair with a smattering of grey, decent tan, nice body.

'So, if you email the contract over in the next couple of days then I will certainly prioritise it...' He wandered onto the patchy lawn and turned.

Fuck, he'd seen me. Startled, I moved away from the gate, but then I looked again.

Our eyes clicked.

Freddie. My long-lost stepbrother.

He held a hand up to keep me frozen there, and quickly ended his call.

'Hey.' He grinned and came towards me. 'What a surprise. It's been a while.'

'I'm flattered that you still recognise me.' The afternoon heat was so intense that my face was melting, sweating under my sunglasses. I pulled them up from my eyes and slotted them on top of my head. Thankfully, I'd always taken Auntie Kaye's advice that it was worth buying quality make-up; and the occasional beauty treatment – a filler here and there – had been valuable investments.

'Looking good for your age.' He laughed.

'Get lost, dickhead. Whatever age I am, I'll always be younger than you.' It was like I had been transported through a time portal to twenty years ago. I reached over the gate and punched him on the arm.

'D'you want to come in? Have a coffee?'

'Yeah. That would be great.' It was not how I'd expected the day to go, but I was always up for seizing an opportunity and seeing where it would take me.

He opened the gate for me and ushered me inside, where he wowed me with how it had been reconfigured. I didn't say, but I was so envious. Here was my shy and awkward stepbrother who had made some kind of high-flying career for himself, and transformed a completely wrecked house into a fantastic-looking abode. And there was the sports car, too. What did I currently have to show for myself from the past twenty years? A part-time job in a crappy pub kitchen and about four bin bags worth of possessions in the wardrobe of someone else – Jean-Luigi – whose weird sexual preferences and a picky gluten-free diet were the early warning signs that I really needed to be moving on.

I followed Freddie around each room. It was hard to tell if he shared the place with anyone else. A wife, partner, kids even. There were no photographs of anyone on the walls and no framed prints of anyone on the sideboard or the desk in his office. Just classy art. Huge canvases. Glass-fronted pencil-and-watercolours. Abstract paraphernalia. Black and white photographs of things like a magnified portion of an oak leaf. It was a far cry from the days of the Jesus picture and religious icons. Everything was mysterious and pristine. Stuff to keep you guessing.

'Looks like you've done well for yourself.'

'I still do the photography. Just had some lucky breaks, which means that I work freelance now and charge a decent fee. Gone are the days of the *Peak Gazette*.'

Although I was his stepsister I felt there were some subjects that were out of bounds. Including Becka. And his father's will. But I sincerely wanted us to rebuild our relationship and so I let the conversation flow widely around these obstacles without touching.

'So. Tell me about you.'

'Oh God.' Where to start. I was reluctant to run through my inventory of under-achievements.

'You were mad into art, weren't you? How did that go? Rubbing shoulders with Tracey Emin now?'

Bad move, mentioning the art. He'd obviously forgotten how it had all ended with my abandoned exam and the fallout with Becka. I could have gone off on one and reminded him, but I bit my tongue.

'Nah. My line of work is more food related. I suppose, in a way it's quite arty. Gourmet meals, posh cakes, that sort of thing.' I could tell he wasn't very impressed. Probably thought I was putting some spin on working in a greasy spoon. To prove a point, I took my phone out and scrolled to a photo album. 'Here. Some of the celebration bakes I've done.'

He zoomed in on the three-tier wedding cake with lace-effect icing and hand-made edible roses. Swiped to another showcase heart-shaped gateaux decorated with gold-leaf and chocolate ganache. Took his time moving the picture around, examining my handiwork.

'They're pretty impressive.'

My chest ballooned. It was like the olden days, getting praised by my big stepbrother.

'I do a lot of wedding photography,' he said. 'Not just general stuff but high-end clients. Pop stars, bankers, television personalities, that sort of thing. People with money. A *lot* of money. And I get work through an agent that deals with the upper-echelon wedding organisers, you know? So if you like I could put you a word in. You could make a fortune creating something like this for the type of events I do.'

I was stunned. Freddie seemed genuinely keen to help me out.

'Really? That would be awesome. I don't know what to say.'

The thing is, though, I did have loads to say. And so did he.

We sat in his brand-new kitchen for over three hours – the ambient air conditioning was much nicer than the heat and glare outside – drinking wine and discussing business plans. He had some kind of smart speaker system fitted, and so he put on that awful Ibiza-type of rave music that him and Becka used to listen to years ago.

'Aren't you too old for all this sort of stuff?' I laughed as I watched his body twitch to the beat, but he told me that the songs were timeless classics, music you never grow out of.

Maybe it was a deliberate trigger for me to make comment about Becka, but I just couldn't bring myself at that point. It would require time and more wine – possibly even spirits – to broach that topic. So instead, I abridged and bullet-pointed the best of my relationships and the past excitement of city life, leaving out the lamentable losers and slum accommodation I had been forced to shack up in. It seemed to be a positive reflective exercise in itself and Freddie politely listened as I decanted my life into the space between us.

Freddie never mentioned Becka. Never mentioned any previous or present relationships. He could have been married for all I knew, and I kept wanting to bring up the subject but he seemed to prefer to talk about me than about himself, and every time I got close to asking about a significant other there would be a subtle diversion with a drink top-up and an anecdote about the Polish builders who dug out the foundations for his extension.

When the wine was gone, we moved on to shots of vodka and I was finally able to open up and pour my heart out about my failing current relationship with Jean-Luigi.

By the time I left Freddie's house, light-headed and slightly unsteady on my feet, we had arranged to meet up again. As I waved and got into the taxi, I just knew our lunch date for the following Saturday would be the perfect opportunity to engage my poor-old-me-I'm-virtually-homeless-and-have-nowhere-else-to-go mode. It had worked on countless other occasions, when I'd been able to pull a bloke and a house in one perfect move.

This time, though, I just needed a place to live.

TWENTY-EIGHT

BECKA

Magdalena shoves her way into my dreams, I don't know how. She breaks in: a faceless, ageless being, and we argue in the garden before pushing each other around. Then her daughter is there, a teenager in a red hoodie with a little rucksack on her back, crying 'leave my mother alone, she's a missing person'. I fidget under the duvet and kick out my legs, trying to keep Magdalena away from me, and in the background of it all Freddie is there, digging a hole through the grass and dandelions, telling me that he will protect me, he will cover it all over so that the police won't get involved, and then I am in a car and there's water everywhere and I'm screaming as it lurches and heaves with the rush of the river, and it's going under with me inside it and I'm kicking so much that my boots come off.

'Hey, hey, babe, easy now, calm down.'

Freddie is holding me still and I am gasping as I rise to the surface of my dream. My face and neck and hair are wet through and I am confused, half-wondering if he has just pulled me from the car.

'Shh. It's OK.' He switches on the bedside lamp and pulls

back the duvet to examine his leg. 'You've got a lethal left foot. Look, you scratched me with your toenail when you kicked out.'

I push up into a sitting position and check the weal on his shin.

'Sorry.' I grimace. 'Another one of my nightmares. Trying to get out of a car that was sinking in a river. Kicked off my boots in the process.'

He holds my face and kisses my sweaty forehead and shushes me again.

I wriggle away from him and get out of bed to fetch a towel from the en suite so that I can dry my fearful sweat off.

'I have a hospital appointment next week. Remember? I think I might ask the consultant if it's worth having hypnotherapy or something, to try and get to the bottom of these drowning nightmares. I don't know, it might help me to remember what happened so that I can exorcise my demons.'

Freddie is quick to react to my suggestion. 'Hypnotherapy is a load of mumbo-jumbo. I can tell you what's happening here, and I'm no psychologist, but it's obvious. You had an accident where you nearly drowned and now that fear of water is at the back of your mind and plays out in dreams. That's all it is. It's not necessarily memories. And trying to uncover any so-called *memories* might not be a good idea. People end up having breakdowns afterwards, when unresolved family stuff gets dragged up. It's a mental health disaster. The only thing hypnotherapy has good results with is stopping smoking.'

'People have breakdowns?'

'Yes. I've worked with people: one guy in particular who went for hypnotherapy after his mother died and rather than being useful, it raked over a long-standing feud with his siblings. He ended up trying to take his own life.'

'God. Who'd have thought that?'

'I know. Horrendous. So I'd rather *you* didn't explore that avenue.' Freddie pats my side of the bed and straightens my pillows for me to return to. 'What I think is that you'll be fine once we've moved house. I think you'll leave behind everything that's stressful and it will be like starting afresh with a blank page. And then we can think about a baby, too, can't we?'

He's right. I smile feebly at him and try to focus on the baby topic instead of wondering what else we will be leaving behind.

The girl returns. Not just in my dreams, but back to our house a week later, to knock on the front door. She is just as Grace described: jeans, red top, long brown hair, small rucksack.

I am upstairs when I hear the rap, and as visitors are rare, I go to peer through the bedroom window. There she is, below me, waiting patiently at the front step.

She turns and takes a step towards the bay window. I am startled by the sight of her, already familiar with what she looks like because of the knowledge that she has been here before, that she has appeared in my dreams.

I stand back from the curtains, my heart pounding. I can't let her see me. Is the door locked? Might she try to get in? Oh God, what shall I do? I look towards Grace's house, to see the tremor of her nets.

Then the girl is back at the door again, knocking louder. She crouches to shout through the letter box. 'Hello? Is anyone in?'

I am frozen in fear. Why has she come back? What does she know?

'Hello? Anyone home?'

The girl's tone scrapes at something in my brain, in my memory. I put my hands over my ears to block out the voice, to block out the rattle of the letter box. Should I ring Freddie? What if he arrives home while she is still on the drive?

I peek from behind the curtain to see her move around to the side of the house. Quickly, I head into the spare room to watch from the window there, to follow her path as she opens

the gate into the back garden. Then I creep back to the
bedroom, to check her whereabouts from the French doors.
She's in my blind spot. I can't see her unless I go out onto the
balcony. She must be looking through the bi-fold doors into the
kitchen.

More knocking. Her knuckles must be raw from hammering
on the glass.

Please, please, just go away. Leave us alone.

I hear the clank of the gate shutting. She must be going. But
no, it's another few minutes before I hear the snap of the letter
box and then – from the front window – see her ambling away
up the drive. Out on the pavement she stands for a few seconds
with hands on her hips, and I dip back behind the curtain as she
stares at the house. I creep onto the landing and see that she has
put another note through the door. Maybe I shouldn't go down
yet. She might come back and look through the letter box and
see me. I will wait until she has definitely gone.

Back in the bedroom I see her: she is still on the pavement
watching the house.

But then the next thing – oh God, what's happening now,
no it can't be – Grace has opened her front door and is calling to
the girl. The girl turns and sees her, crosses the road and jogs up
the drive to speak to her. They chat for a few minutes and then
something important or shocking must have been said because
the girl looks surprised and puts her hands to her face, staring
back towards my house again. Grace is nodding, pointing, and
the girl bends over as if she is out of breath.

I can't bear to watch, but I can't peel my eyes away from the
scene. They must be talking about me, about what I've done.
Grace has told her that Magdalena was here.

Then the girl is crying, wiping her eyes. I can see sobs
jerking her chest. Grace reaches to put an arm around the girl
and then the girl throws her arms around her neck in a grateful
hug.

My whole body is shaking. What will they do? Go to the police? Get them to come here and dig up the lawn?

The girl pulls away and looks towards me again. Then, with a final nod of the head to Grace – who's standing there with such an expression of pride on her face – she's back down the drive, over the road and at my front door again.

Please, go away. I can't take much more of this.

She's pounding, really thrashing at it. It sounds as if she's even kicking it.

Please, please don't try the door handle. I remember now that I didn't lock it after Freddie left for work. She could so easily be inside, up the stairs, cornering me here in the bedroom.

The letter box clacks again. What if she catches the handle accidentally? I imagine the door just swinging open into the hall, and have to stifle a whimper of fear that breaks out of my mouth.

But thankfully she doesn't. It seems like she is done here. She runs back up the drive and then she's gone. Away, down the road in the direction of the town.

My shaky legs collapse and I sit heavily on the edge of the bed. I can't handle being in this house any more. I don't need the stress; my sanity is at breaking point. Quaffing big breaths of air into my lungs, I try to relax. Stop thinking about her. Stop worrying if she will go to the police.

Stop.

I go and swig cold water direct from the tap in the en suite.

Eventually, my legs are able to carry me downstairs. The folded square of paper is still lying on the doormat in the hall, and has now been accompanied by another one. With a weight of dread I pick both of them up and unfold them.

PLEASE! I need any information about Magdalena. I know that she was at this address. This is very URGENT now. RING ME ASAP.

And the other note:

*MUM! This is your daughter Charlotte. RING ME PLEASE
AND LET ME KNOW YOU ARE STILL ALIVE!*

The same phone number is written clearly at the bottom of each page. I fold the notes together and stash them with the previous one at the back of my underwear drawer.

Freddie is right.

We need to get away from here. And we need to go soon.

TWENTY-NINE

MAGDALENA

It took only ten days to engineer the end of my relationship with Jean-Luigi, pack up my bin bags and move across to the other side of town and into Freddie's biggest guest room. Which was delightful and bizarre in the fact that it had been my old bedroom over twenty years ago.

As I arrived to receive a set of keys and the house rules, he was packing up his car with cases and holdalls.

'Trip to India,' he informed me. 'Photography for a wildlife publication. We're looking at quite a lengthy visit because the shots are going to be pitched for a prestigious award.'

I noticed the word 'we' and wondered if he was taking a partner or wife along on the journey. Getting a good look into the boot of his car, I saw a holdall that hadn't been fully zipped up, and glanced something inside that looked silky, salmon-coloured. Was it Becka's? Was he still reluctant to talk about her after what had happened years ago?

'Ah, no wonder you were keen to let me stay. House-sitting services.' I laughed at Freddie's prickly expression. I didn't give a shit though. He owed me.

· · ·

I had the run of the house to myself. He'd locked the door to his office, the master bedroom was out of bounds, and there was a strict policy of not bringing back lovers. Apart from that, I was free to use the rest of the place as I wanted.

I examined the cupboards and drawers, as any normal person would, to find out more about Freddie and his personal life. Did he live alone? Had he been married at any point? I had my doubts even though there were signs, hints of Becka around. A pencil-and-watercolour creation on the far wall of the hallway looked suspiciously like her style and was signed in the left-hand corner with a 'B'. In the downstairs cloakroom there was a scarf hanging up which I'm sure she used to wear years ago at school. I sniffed it, and although age lingered in the fibres, the smell of perfume was distinctively hers. It's funny how your senses get triggered, and your memory can drop you straight back into a much earlier time of your life: one deep breath and I was straight there, a seventeen-year-old, razzing around with Becka and Freddie in his precious VW.

The sideboard drawer held an A5 framed photograph of the both of them, youthful and carefree and madly in love. *Oh God*, I remembered, as again my perceptions were activated, *it was me who took that actual picture*. Maybe it had previously been displayed before being demoted to a drawer when the room was redecorated. Or maybe they were no longer together. I would have to wait until Freddie's return from India to find out.

He messaged me quite early into his absence to let me know that he would be away for at least two months, possibly three. It was great news. The space and the modern rooms and the fact that I had the place to myself meant that I could properly start my business. I reorganised the utility room cupboards for my baking equipment, set up a dedicated Facebook page and website, and trawled around a number of wedding fairs with business cards and free tasters. When the orders started to pour in, it really felt like my life was turning around. I forgot about Freddie; I forgot about Becka. While I was alone here, I could dream that the house was mine.

I dedicated every possible moment to working hard and making money. It was as if I had finally grown up, just in time to make a success of myself. Watching my bank balance grow gave me confidence and a new spring in my step. Being able to live here, rent-free, was such a bonus: I felt no shame about it. Basically, I was doing Freddie a favour looking after the place.

It was about ten weeks after he first left that Freddie messaged me to say that he would be back for a flying visit on the following Thursday.

Flying visit? Would that be two hours, two days, a week? Would he be alone or bringing a significant other? I didn't know what to expect but I vacuumed all the carpets, cleaned the windows, baked a cake and bleached the toilets in readiness. Prepared a taut expression and some snide comments for if he had Becka with him.

He came alone.

'It's just me,' he said, as if someone accompanying him wouldn't have been out of the question.

I fed him red velvet cake and coffee, and filled him in briefly on the positives of my new business. He only stayed the one night and declined my offer of sorting his laundry. For most of the afternoon he was speaking on his phone or banging out emails in his office. After swapping clothing in and out of his luggage and driving somewhere to get his camera accessories, he returned with pizza for us to share, and we spent the remainder of the evening reminiscing about his old red car and his crappy bedsit near the carpet warehouse, and his first photography job taking blurry pictures of potholed roads and cross-eyed dogs.

'I've come a long way since then,' he said. 'I was photographing Bengal tigers last week.'

We laughed and it felt like the old times when we sat in his car at the McDonald's drive-thru. Things felt warm again between us, and as the climate seemed fair, I dared to ask a question.

'I wasn't prying or anything, but I noticed an old picture of you and Becka in the drawer. Is she still The One?' I gave a wink to lighten up the awkward moment.

'She's always been The One. Always will be.'

There was my answer. 'So, like... do you take her with you?'

Freddie put a hand over his heart. 'I always take her everywhere. Can't live without her.' He folded up the pizza box and went to take it out to the bin. 'I think I'm going to head up to bed,' he said when he returned. 'I've got an early start which means it's unlikely you'll see me tomorrow. Goodnight.'

I watched as he took the stairs two at a time.

So, it was *her*. Still Becka. They must have got back together then.

Did she actually *know* that I was here, living in her house?

What would happen, I wondered, when she returned and found me in the spare room, running my business and living my life?

I smiled to myself, remembering how I had threatened her with revenge for messing up my life. Nothing had changed. I still hated her. And the bizarre chance of me being here just made it easier to settle that score.

THIRTY

BECKA

I ring the property solicitor to find out how things are going with the sale and the purchase. Speeding up the process is now my number one priority. We can't hang around here any longer than is necessary.

'Everything is good with your buyers, but with regards to the new house you need to check the document I sent,' he says. 'I can't proceed with the purchase property until you sign and approve the searches.'

'It's OK,' I tell him. 'Just go ahead with everything. It's important that we move really quickly now.'

'That's all well and good, but we can't progress at our end until you go through the online document and click the boxes to sign and approve, so that we can take things to the next stage. If you check your emails...'

'It's my husband you've been emailing.'

'Yes, that's right. The document was sent two days ago but I can see that it hasn't been opened yet. Maybe he needs to check that it's not gone into his spam folder.'

'I know he's been busy with work, and I'll get him to check his spam, but is there anything I can do to rush things along?'

The solicitor reiterates that the online document needs to be checked and the approval boxes ticked, and I find myself getting frustrated.

'OK,' I say, finally. 'We'll get it sorted today so that you can continue with whatever needs doing. It's urgent. We really do need to be completing as soon as possible.'

I sit in Freddie's office chair, gyrating from side to side and wanting everything done now. I try ringing his number three times but it goes to voicemail each time.

So I turn my attention to his computer. Maybe there's something I could do. I have written instructions on how to get into his emails and print off receipts and invoices to file away in his system. So, I confidently log in to examine the spam folder, scrolling through to find the document from the solicitor.

There it is. I click on the email and read through the contents. It tells me that a picture is attached, but there is nothing. Should I ring the solicitor again? Or do pictures go into a separate folder? I don't want to appear stupid so I return to the desktop and click on a folder labelled 'Pictures'. It brings up more folders: each one a photograph album. Weddings, wildlife, and commercial shoots of things like furniture and cars and a range of artisan gins.

There's an album at the bottom that sets my heart thumping. I hover my cursor over the title.

Magdalena.

Should I click?

There. I've done it. It's open, showing thumbnails of highly decorated cakes. No surprises. No picture of her face. I scroll through and enlarge some of the cakes. They are exactly the same as the laminated ones in the utility cupboard. Disappointed, I look through again just in case there is something that I have missed, some clue as to what has happened. But no. There's nothing.

I sit back in the office chair, confused, before remembering that I am supposed to be looking for a picture of the property that the solicitor has sent. Where might that be saved? I click around randomly in the pictures folder and find myself in the album entitled 'Weddings'. There is one dated a year back labelled 'Charlotte and Rupert'. The name Charlotte rings an alarm bell with the girl this morning and the note she put through the door. I can't help myself. Greedy for information, I click through the first couple of pictures.

Relief. I exhale.

The name is just a coincidence. It's nothing to do with the teenager at the door. It's just a collection of photographs from a couple's extravagant wedding. Although... on closer inspection I feel like I somehow recognise something about them. The venue. The blueness of the sky. Their wedding clothes. The shape of their bodies.

Was I at the wedding? Is this my memory being triggered?

I click to the next one.

Fuck. Fuck!

What is this?

Gripping the arms of the chair, I wheel back from the desk and stare at the picture. It can't be.

I race upstairs to the bedroom, to stand in front of our wedding canvas that adorns the wall. How can this be? The photograph captures pure happiness: me in white looking seductively over my shoulder as Freddie laughs at an exuberant surge of champagne fizz from the bottle in his hand. I unhook it from the wall and take it downstairs, to place beside the photograph on the computer screen.

It's identical in almost every way. The setting, the clothing, the champagne bottle bubbling over.

The only things that are different are the faces.

THIRTY-ONE

MAGDALENA

Freddie was away working for another five weeks. He returned, tanned and leaner, while I was out at a wedding fair.

When I got home his car was in the driveway. His bags were in the hall. His office door was open and he was tapping away on his computer. No sign of anyone else.

'On your own?' I asked, making him jump.

'Yep. Just me.' He turned round for a moment and gave a quick smile before returning to his email.

I got the impression that he didn't want me to delve. Maybe they'd had an argument. Maybe there was somewhere else that Becka stayed: her parents' house, a second home? So I shuffled out of the way to go and prepare some food.

Later, after he'd eaten half of the spaghetti carbonara that I'd made while he worked in his office, he joined me for a glass of wine in the lounge. I asked about his trip and he launched into an in-depth description of his work and the complications of trying to track and photograph animals in the wild.

I told him how my business was growing, and tried to steer the conversation towards some kind of agreement that we could put in place so that I could pay a portion of the bills and have certainty that this wasn't just a temporary arrangement, because I realised how much I liked it here and how it was the perfect location for my work. But Freddie waved away any talk of formality with assurances that I could stay for as long as I liked. He was grateful that I would look after the place while he had to spend so much time working abroad.

Invigorated by his kind gesture, I thought that maybe it was time to bring up the subject of Becka.

'So, when do I get to see her again?' I asked. 'Because we're all going to have to get along, aren't we?'

'See who?' His puzzled expression was genuine.

'Becka. Who else?'

A bemused smile and a wrinkled brow. 'What do you mean?'

'She lives here, doesn't she? I thought you said you took her with you on your photography trips?'

Freddie laughed heartily. 'Did I really give you that impression?'

'That's what you told me!'

'It was metaphorical. I take her everywhere in my mind, my heart. I know it's crazy, but I've never got over her, never been able to find anyone who could match up to her.'

I smiled carefully. 'You're sounding a bit weird.'

Freddie shrugged. 'That's just how it is. I'm a romantic.'

'Have you not seen her since...' Since what? I didn't want to venture into unmentionable territory.

'I haven't seen her since we all went our separate ways. After all the' – he gestured his hands and eyes around the living room walls and ceiling, because he obviously didn't want to speak of the fire either – 'you know, everything that happened; her father got involved and made some nasty threats to keep us apart. I heard she went to Glasgow to study Art. And although I've tried endlessly, I've never been able to track her down on social media. Maybe she got married and moved away.'

'But you must have had other relationships?'

'Yeah. Two or three. Nothing that amounted to anything. I've never had anyone actually move in with me on a permanent basis. I don't know... my head just always goes back to her. I can't help it. She was always The One. I feel like I have to keep searching for her.'

'Oh God, you're sounding like some lovestruck character out of a Victorian novel.'

Freddie shrugged and held his hands out.

'So, what will you do when you find her?' I asked. 'What if she's happily married with kids?'

'I don't know. It just feels like... I have to find out what she's doing now. In case there's still hope for us. It's something I keep clinging to, thinking that she's out there, still thinking about me, too. We were soulmates. We made a pact that we would always be together, whatever happened.' He stared dreamily into the distance, lost in the past.

I shook my head and pulled a face that said it was time he moved on. It had been over twenty years. He needed to get a life.

Freddie wagged a finger at me as if he'd been reading my mind. 'Don't judge me. It's not as if your life's perfect, is it? You never know, though, one day it could all just come right. For both of us. I could find Becka again and she might be single or divorced or whatever, and ready to resume what we had before, and you could meet the man of your dreams, the one that ticks all the boxes for a proper long-term relationship.'

'Yeah. You're right.' I conceded with a nod as I topped up our glasses.

Neither of us knew then, just how things would turn out, how our ideals would drive us in the way that they did.

Neither of us knew then, just how close to perfection we would get before it all went so badly wrong.

THIRTY-TWO

BECKA

I know what this means. I don't need anyone to explain to me. This picture – the one of me and Freddie on the canvas – is fake. Our youthful faces have been cleverly superimposed onto the bodies of a happy couple celebrating their wedding.

Why? What would make him do something like that?

Suddenly, there's a noise. The slam of a car door outside.

I freeze in horror, as if I have been caught committing a crime. My hand on the mouse, eyes on the screen. The front door opens and shuts.

'Hey, I'm home,' Freddie calls. A jolly tone, unaware of my discovery.

Footsteps on the parquet floor. Then he's there, behind me, seeing what I'm seeing: the two pictures side-by-side. The right one and the wrong one.

'What...' He stands there, arms hanging uselessly beside him. 'Oh God, I don't know...'

I swing round on the office chair.

'What's going on?' I whisper as the canvas slips from its position propped up on the desk, and clatters flat down.

'It's not what you think.' He reaches out to touch the side of my face. There is such pain in his eyes.

I flinch away from his caress. My heart is hammering so hard that I feel faint. 'What do I think? I don't know what I'm supposed to be thinking. You tell me.'

'Let's just go and sit and talk sensibly about this.' He grasps my hand to lead me away from his office, away from the telltale images.

'You don't realise how much stress I've been through today,' I say with a panicked half-sob in my throat as we go through to the kitchen, where he pulls out the breakfast bar stools for us to sit on.

He faffs about getting glasses from the cabinet to fill with water and put on the worktop in front of us. Delaying tactics. Trying to suss out how to explain away his bizarre deception.

'Why have you made a fake picture of us?'

He gulps down most of the water before looking at me earnestly. 'Becka. You know that we're in a bit of a fragile position at the moment, don't you?'

I nod, remembering the girl at the door earlier, looking for her mother. Her *dead* mother. One of us killed her. Was it really me?

'Well, it just seemed like... when you had your accident and your memory was deleted, it felt like I could rewrite history. Make some of it better than it was.'

I swig my water to try and calm my nerves. 'Why would you need to do that?'

'We didn't have the best start. We had a crap wedding and no photographer. So I just wanted to make things nice for you to come home to. I wanted it to seem like we'd had a lovely life without the hard times. That's all it is.'

'But how does that have anything to do with our *fragile position* as you call it?'

He drops his head into his hands. 'Look. I just wanted to

make everything seem normal. Just a normal couple who are happily married, moving house, getting on with life. Forgetting about everything that went before. I didn't want you to have the stress of knowing about the bad things. But it's starting to feel like it's all catching up with us now.'

'Catching up with us?'

He pulls at his hair and exhales loudly. 'I love you so much. I'm just trying to protect you from everything, protect us from... I don't know... all the threats out there that could destroy our happiness.'

'Do you mean the situation with Magdalena?' Suddenly, I decide that I can't be vague any more. I have to spill it out, because one way or another I have to know if it really was me who was the murderer. 'That I killed her?'

There's a brief pause, a quick catch of breath. 'Don't... It's not like... Oh God.' He stares at the worktop for a while before continuing. 'Look, you've got to trust me, you've got to stick with me. OK, so the wedding photo thing was a bit stupid, but everything else that you're trying to work out and think that I'm keeping from you... just go along with me. It will be OK. Yes, you killed her, but I'm covering your back and what's happened can all be left behind with the house move. We can start again and it will all be fine. Trust me. Just promise that you'll trust me and let me deal with it all.'

A veil of blackness sweeps past my face. I can't breathe, yet I can hear and feel some kind of guttural sound erupting from my throat.

'How could I? How *could* I kill someone?' I splutter the words out and my body is suddenly trembling, my heart is crashing erratically as images flash through my head: blood, knives, the gun in the filing cabinet, a poor lifeless woman sprawled on the floor, a grave dug in the lawn. What happened? How did it get to that? How *violent* was it?

Freddie reaches for me and I slap his hand away.

'Don't tell me I killed someone,' I scream at him. 'Don't say that.'

Frenzied, I jump up off the stool and he tries to grab me.

'Becka. Becka, please calm down.' His voice is too soft and serene and completely wrong for this situation, and I flail at him as he hangs on to my sleeve.

'I can't have killed her. Why would I? Why?' My high-pitched tone doesn't sound like me anymore. I'm someone else now. I'm a murderer.

My foot stumbles against the leg of the stool as Freddie pulls me, and I lash out at his face feeling my nails scour his skin like the peel of a ripe pear.

'Babe. Please.' There are two gashes down his cheek. Beads of scarlet swell and tremble nervously.

I push against him as he tries to hold me, tries to calm my pained sobs.

'What did I do to her?' I cry. 'Tell me!' I don't want to know the answer though, because then it would be stuck inside my head, the scenes playing on repeat. How could I have done something so bad? Surely it must have been accidental. I wouldn't have done anything deliberately, would I? Oh God, I can't bear the thought of it all.

'Babe,' he says again and there's a look fixed on his face: sympathy, pity, some kind of intense expression designed to ease my manic mind. But the blood on his face tells me what I am capable of.

'Sorry,' I whisper. 'I'm so sorry. I didn't mean to hurt you.'

Reluctantly, I let him take my hands and he massages the rigidity out of them, and the tremors that are rippling through me gradually begin to subside.

'Deep breaths,' he says. 'In. And out. In... Out...'

The pictures fade from my mind, until all I can see is Freddie in front of me. I look at him, at his congealing wounds, and he looks at me and we sit like that for a while, just staring at each other, trying to read what's in each other's head.

'Stop thinking about it all,' says Freddie as if he's telepathic. 'We've got to move on. Everything will be OK. It will.'

I groan and exhale and try to put it out of my mind, try to think about the house with the hot tub instead. I sip more water and close my eyes. Focus on my breathing so that my racing heart will slow. I tell myself that he really does love me – it's obvious in everything – and I metaphorically need to let myself fall back into him like a blind trust exercise.

Freddie gets his phone out and puts some music on. Dance stuff, but chilled, more subtle. The volume and repetitive rhythm washes into me, gives my head a menial focus.

Eventually he rises from the kitchen stool and takes my hand, pulls me up with him. We embrace and stand there holding each other for what might be ten, fifteen minutes or more, saying nothing. He's warm and safe and I can't bring myself to move away from him.

Finally, Freddie says, 'You know what we need to do?'

'What?'

'We need to go and make a baby.'

Really? But then again, what else *can* we do in this moment that will make everything better? I think about the breast-feeding mother in the pub and how I so yearned what she had there with her, and my body tingles with the craving of wanting a baby so badly that I let him lead me upstairs where we undress quickly, desperately, beside the bed.

It seems like the earlier revelation has triggered a compulsion in us both. We are quick and greedy and selfish, almost as if the sex act is a means of cleansing, like a hot and stinging shower.

When it's over I lie breathlessly, letting the last of my tears run over my temples and into my hair. I know I need to give myself up to Freddie and trust him with this, because I cannot sort out this situation alone. If I were to get pregnant then we could soon be away from here, focusing on our child – oh God, let it be a daughter, please, a gorgeous blue-eyed little girl – and leaving all the unremembered bad stuff in the past.

* * *

Afterwards, after it felt like something really *did* happen – our DNA merging into the first cells of a foetus – we fall asleep in each other's arms. The adrenaline, the shock of everything has exhausted me.

And I'm straight into another dream. Not a nightmare this time, but a beautiful scene where I feel such love and have a child – a daughter – on my knee and I'm brushing her long hair until it's sleek and shiny and then I'm kissing her cheek and twining her hair into two cute plaits with pink ribbons on the end and I'm cuddling her and I'm inflated with so much joy in my heart...

And then the girl says '*Mummy*' and turns to look at me, but it's the face of the girl that was kicking at the door this morning, and my feelings of love and joy suddenly turn into dread and confusion, and I thrash around in bed until Freddie wakes me again.

THIRTY-THREE

BECKA

I return to the hospital for a check-up. Freddie drives me there and stays in the waiting room.

'I don't miss this place,' he says as he sits in the chair that he spent so many nights sleeping in while I was in the ICU.

After my brain scan I get a brief consultation with a doctor that I have not seen previously. He asks about my co-ordination and my speech and my memories that haven't yet returned, and I tell him as much as I can, mentioning that we will be moving house very soon. It's suggested that I register with a new GP as soon as possible and change my address so that I can get my results once the scans have been analysed. He mentions that hypnotherapy might be useful, and I smile and tell him that I'm OK, thanks.

Freddie sorts out the issue with the solicitors. It's a simple document that needs signing. No problems. Within days the process is moving at speed. We are told that the completion date is only two weeks away; and Freddie has booked a removal lorry to transport our belongings to the new house.

I spend most of my time sorting and packing boxes upstairs. The front door is locked and I don't put the radio on. We are so close to getting away from all the stress, and the last thing I need right now is the teenage girl returning to catch me out.

But on the Wednesday I catch a glimpse of her again from the bedroom window. This time she's in a school uniform with her hair tied back. It's almost five o'clock and she strolls tenaciously down the drive to rap forcefully on the door. I stop what I am doing: any accidental noise like an ornament being dropped would reveal my presence in the house. The letter box clacks. I wait.

'Mum!' she shouts. 'Mum, are you there?'

I imagine her squatting, putting her mouth to the gap.

'Mum, please.' She's crying now, actually sobbing out the word 'Mum' as she bangs on the door. 'Please answer the door. I need to know that you're alive.'

I wait with my breath held. Eventually she stands and spends a few seconds wiping her eyes.

Then it's the usual routine that I have now come to expect. Round the back and through the gate to knock on the bi-fold doors and look into the kitchen. The whole palaver takes around ten minutes before she's out on the pavement and moving off along the road.

I can relax again.

I step closer to the window, remembering my most recent dream, remembering the same voice that said '*Mummy*', remembering how I plaited her lavish length of hair...

Suddenly Grace's front door opens and she's calling out, making her way down her path to talk to the girl again. Irritated with her unnecessary involvement, I retreat but keep them both in my sights. The girl takes something out of her bag – a picture or a card – and shows it to Grace, who makes a sad face and puts a hand to her heart. They talk for a few minutes more before hugging again – what is all that about? – and then they go their separate ways with Grace holding on to the thing that was in the girl's bag.

I creep to the top of the stairs and look down into the hall-way. Thankfully there are no notes this time.

But for how long do I have to keep hiding? Every day, avoiding the transparency of the windows, reluctant to use the kitchen for fear of the girl appearing in the back garden. Twelve days, I tell myself. That's all it is. Then I can live normally and go for walks and there will be no ghost of Magdalena, and we can be miles and miles away without leaving a forwarding address.

It's Thursday evening, with an early June sky blazing crimson and black over the back garden, the sort of colours I would love to capture with my paints if I were brave enough to be in the garden for any length of time without being terrorised by the teenage girl. Freddie is in his office, sorting and packing his files and equipment. In the kitchen there are stacks of boxes filled with crockery and utensils, and I am limited with my meal choices now most of the store-cupboard ingredients are no longer available to use.

It's getting late for our evening meal so I decide to make a Caesar salad with pre-cooked chicken that is close to its use-by. The comforting pump of dance music seeps from Freddie's office, and I feel safe with him in the house. My guard is down and I am absorbed in my task of ripping up lettuce, so I don't hear the click of the back gate.

There's a rap on the glass of the bi-fold doors that makes me jump back from the worktop. A face pressed close. My heart flutters and a knife is knocked to clatter and spin on the floor tiles.

'Grace! You scared me. We don't normally get visitors to the back of the house.' I pull the glass panel away and stand in the space.

There's no smile. She eyes me candidly, bearing important news.

'I had to come. I didn't know what else to do and it's been weighing on my mind.' She has something in her hand held close to her chest. 'There's a girl been coming round trying to find you. Four or five times now. She's desperate, but you never answer the door.'

My chest flutters. My mouth goes dry. The sky suddenly darkens with a black cloud washing over all the red.

'I often don't hear people knocking if I'm busy upstairs,' I say.

Grace grabs my arm, pinches her claw-like fingers around it. 'This girl isn't just *people knocking*.' She shows me the photograph that was held in her other hand. 'Look.'

I take the picture from her and flick my eyes over it and... What? No! I don't understand. It can't be real. Is it a trick?

There's me and the girl, our arms around each other on a golden beach with rippling turquoise water in the background, and we're laughing like we're having the time of our lives. Something inside me feels as if it is crumbling, breaking away like cliffs being eroded by the sea. I sense the smell of her hair in my nostrils: a fresh citrusy nip that comes from the Faith in Nature shampoo she uses, and it's immediately there in the front of my mind, a picture of it on the edge of the bath.

All these auras crowd in on me and I swoon so that I have to grab the edge of the worktop. What is happening?

'Look,' says Grace again. 'It's you, isn't it?'

It definitely is *me*. And the girl. But how can that be? Is it another faked picture like the canvas in the bedroom?

I turn the photograph over to see writing, the same writing as the notes I've been getting.

Me and Mum. Our Italian holiday.

'I don't understand,' I say, feebly, as the stability drains out of my limbs, and my body dips erratically at the knees.

'The girl came here looking for Magdalena,' says Grace.

I shiver at the name.

'She thinks that Magdalena was involved in the disappearance of her mother. But what confused me was that we were talking about the cakes, and I couldn't remember if that was you or her...'

'What?' My scalp prickles. Has Grace found out about my crime?

'Becka? Becka?' I jump as I hear Freddie in his office, calling me. And then something in my head changes as I try to make sense of what Grace is saying...

'And then the girl gave me this photograph of her mum and I said I would keep an eye out for her. But then it just came to me only half an hour ago: you know how mixed up I get with all the names.' She takes a little break to chuckle at her foolishness, and I'm thinking *hurry, hurry, Freddie could appear any time soon*, and I'm wondering why I suddenly feel so scared of him, and then Grace is speaking again. '...that this is a picture of *you*, isn't it? Becka. And I know that you've had problems with your memory and maybe you had forgotten about the girl or lost touch with her. So I worked out that, well, it must be that *you're* her mother.'

'What?' I whisper as the room swirls around me and I hear the office door clicking open. Freddie's footsteps in the hall.

'That girl, Charlotte. She's your *daughter*. You can see the likeness, can't you?'

I lurch then, but it's OK because Freddie is right behind me, ready for me to tumble into his arms.

'It's all right, babe,' he's saying. 'I'm here.'

And I have no idea what happens with Grace or the photograph or the sudden burst of rain that without warning throws itself down and through the bi-fold doors onto the kitchen floor.

Because everything goes black.

THIRTY-FOUR

MAGDALENA

My life was the best it had ever been. So easily attainable, it was as if success had been handed to me since my reunion with Freddie. For well over a year we cohabited platonically and professionally. During that time – and all thanks to Freddie – I was commissioned by a number of rich and famous people to supply cakes for their events, as well as locals who had found me through my website and word of mouth. The old lady across the road, Grace, became my ambassador in the vicinity, and I often popped over with samples and offcuts which she would relish. I bought myself a car – not quite the convertible sports car that my long-term sights were set on – but something decent that I wasn't embarrassed to visit clients in.

It was on a Saturday afternoon in early October when the crucial turning point arrived. A single chance event that wouldn't have happened had I not had a last-minute order for a wedding cake. A nervous young girl on the phone wanting just a small, two-tier cake for the following Friday. Her aunt had promised to make it, she said, but then changed her mind. Would I be able to put their names on it in some kind of gold writing? Verity and Ben. But it would probably be best if I put Ben and Verity. His name first.

I didn't need the work, but something in the girl's bleak tone clawed open the rare soft spot buried deep inside me. A rushed wedding at the Registry Office with only thirty guests. Maybe she was pregnant. Or dying.

So I quoted low and suggested a semi-naked sponge cake with a buttercream skim decorated simply with fresh flowers. The top would have their names in swirly gold leaf. Verity sounded close to tears as she thanked me and gave me the delivery address. I didn't even ask for a deposit.

The nerve that this telephone call touched in me was left tender and open for the next couple of hours as I imagined this girl and her prospective husband. I'd never had an order before for a *two*-tier cake. Why had the aunt changed her mind about baking for her? Had something gone horribly wrong in the family?

Wrenched from my pondering, I suddenly remembered that I was supposed to pick up an order from the cake supplies shop in town. There were items that I needed so that I could finish decorating the vintage-themed bakes that were required for delivery tomorrow.

Shit, how could I have forgotten! The shop would be closed in twenty minutes and I had to get through town and parked up.

I rang them and with a grovelling tone told them that I was on my way. 'Please don't close before I arrive. I'll definitely be there, hopefully in the next ten minutes if the traffic is good.'

* * *

The roads were a nightmare; the Spireites must have been playing a home game. I pulled into the main town centre car park at twenty-five past five and dumped my car in a space. Over by the ticket machine there was a cluster of people, and I wondered whether to just leave my car for the ten-minute dash to the cake supplies shop and risk a parking ticket. Better not. It was a strategy I'd employed a few weeks ago, but I'd returned to find a summons stuck to my windscreen.

I jogged to the machine where four people were trying to instruct someone else how to use it.

'Is there a problem?' I asked the man at the back of the queue.

'I don't know,' he replied. Helpfully.

I looked around. A couple were walking through the car park, the man carrying a bag that clinked with wine bottles. He pulled out his keys and zapped one of the parked cars so that its indicators blinked. Here was my chance.

'Excuse me!' I ran over as they opened the boot and put the carrier bag in.

But I don't think they heard me. No one turned around. The woman had her back to me, just about to open the passenger door, as I approached and asked politely if they had any time left on their ticket.

The man responded first. I clocked his good looks and his physique and the clothes that he wore as he peeled the ticket off his windscreen. Fitness type, outdoorsy, probably a mountain-biker or fell-runner, that sort of thing. Our eyes met and I couldn't help the subtle smile and the hair-fondling thing I automatically do when I see a bloke I like the look of.

'There's half an hour left on here.'

He held out the ticket and I had to go back round to his side of the car to collect it. That's when I looked over to see his partner.

No.

It couldn't be.

It was.

It was *her*. I stared for too long. She stared back. It was as if both of us had been struck dumb.

'Are you who I think you are?' I said, finally.

She didn't respond. Anyone else might have thought at that point that they'd been mistaken, they'd got the wrong person, but I knew. It was definitely *her*.

'Becka, it is you, isn't it?'

There was an awkward silence. In the space of six or seven seconds it felt as if the atmosphere had moved in to crush the three of us as we stood around the car, assessing each other. It was obvious that Becka was uncomfortable, struggling to acknowledge that she knew me. But finally, she pursed her lips and shaped them into something that might pass for a smile.

'Mags. I haven't seen you for ages.'

PART THREE

THIRTY-FIVE

TOBY

It started by chance. Well, didn't most things, though? Just an afternoon out with his wife – a *date day* as people called it – to try and keep life fun and interesting. It was all too easy to fall into a rut after marrying young, when each year was just one endless cycle of routines.

Toby drove them into town and parked up behind the old theatre, where they got out to meander along roads that were narrow and shops that were tiny and eclectic. A group of teenage girls, fresh-faced and plump, swung Primark bags as they barged along the strip of pavement.

'Excuse *me*,' Becka said as one of them knocked her shoulder in passing.

The girl didn't reply; didn't even look back.

Becka tutted loudly and shook her head.

'They're only kids.' Toby laughed. 'You were like that once.'

Becka rolled her eyes. 'You make me feel ancient.'

'Well, now you're forty...' he reminded her.

She knew what was coming next.

'...and I'm still in my thirties.'

There were eight months between them, Becka being the

elder. They had been married for sixteen years, after meeting at a fundraising event organised by Toby's aunt. And with the bonus of a beautiful daughter – Charlotte, who was fifteen – life was comfortable. They had a nice house, two cars and a decent inheritance from Becka's late father. They had cottage holidays, OK sex, occasional quiz nights at the pub. His work as a Logistics Manager for a big warehouse was steady and paid reasonable wages, and although he often wished for something better, he couldn't really complain.

And Becka. She still had a great figure and wasn't that much fleshier now than the day they had met. She had always been fun and arty, with a laid-back approach and a generous nature, but lately they had both wandered down their own routes a little more, disagreed about things where once they would have compromised, and looked for opportunities to indulge their tastes and amusements individually. Toby loved adventure and adrenalin and The Great Outdoors, while Becka preferred the calm, relaxing environment of a quality spa. They'd had a couple of separate breaks recently. It wasn't really anything to worry about, but... Well, a *date day* now and then would likely solve anything that might go amiss.

The wind gusted and slapped a crisp packet along the kerbside. A smoky dusk was starting to usher the autumn light away, and Toby realised that it was only four weeks until the clocks went back. The end of his nose startled with cold.

'Cheese,' Becka announced, pulling him into a delicatessen. 'Let's get something nice.'

Toby savoured the warmth and provocative smells, while she moved back and forth along the glass counter like the shuttle in a loom, choosing a sliver of ewe's cheese, creamy Roquefort, and a small tub of glistening queen olives.

'Ten sixty-six,' said the ruddy woman squashed into a Victorian-style pinafore. Toby got his bank card out to tap on the machine.

'Battle of Hastings,' said Becka as they left the shop.

Toby looked puzzled.

'Ten sixty-six: Battle of Hastings,' she explained. 'It's the only thing I can remember from school history.'

'Random,' he said, holding her into the side of the path as a scrap truck rattled past.

They browsed in a second-hand bookshop for a while but didn't buy anything. They paid over the odds for two bottles of Merlot in a quirky, Tudor-beamed off-licence ('I'm sure I've seen these in Tesco for a fiver each,' Toby remarked). They stopped off after Becka suggested that they go for a coffee, and found a shabby chic emporium of gingham and flaking paint where, ironically, she had a pot of tea and Toby had hot chocolate topped with marshmallows.

They walked aimlessly around more streets before returning to the car park. It was getting dark and a group of people were clustered around the ticket machine having some sort of confab. Toby unlocked the car and put their purchases in the boot.

The woman seemed to come from nowhere. Becka was just about to open the passenger door when she was tapped on the shoulder.

'Have you got any time left on your ticket? It's just that I'm only going to be ten minutes and there's a problem with the pay and display thing.'

Toby reached into the windscreen and peeled it off.

'There's half an hour left on here,' he said, holding it out.

Becka stared at the woman. The woman stared back at Becka.

'Are you who I think you are?' she asked.

The woman had a distinctive way of speaking through her teeth. She stood there, scrunching and gathering her hair to lift and subtly show off the curve of her bare neck. It was like an involuntary habit, a mating gesture. She was attractive, mid-thirties maybe – it was hard to tell – with a confident stance, naturally full and pouting lips, and heavily mascaraed eyes. Weighty silver hoops swung in her earlobes.

It was obviously one of those situations where someone that his wife used to know and hadn't seen for years expected instant recognition, but Becka was just standing there embarrassed, trawling through her brain for the correct name. That's what Toby thought.

But he was wrong.

Becka told him later it wasn't like that. She knew immediately who the woman was. Seeing her again without warning after all that time had just left her speechless for a moment.

'Becka,' the woman said, squinting at her. 'It *is* you, isn't it?'

There was a pause then, as if something should have happened. Something like a clattering of starlings escalating into the air, or a crack of thunder or a car screeching uncontrollably towards them so that they had to jump apart. Some kind of warning. But nothing happened.

Becka wrung her face into a tight smile.

'Mags,' she said. 'I haven't seen you for ages.'

A slice of time wedged itself between the three of them, so that no one moved and no one said anything and Becka examined the top button of her coat, and Toby had to switch his eyes to the group at the ticket machine when the woman turned her intense gaze towards him.

'Is this your significant other?' Mags asked, nodding at Toby; and he wondered if she was eyeing him up.

So Becka introduced them, mentioning that they'd been married for sixteen years, with a teenage daughter.

'Well, well,' Mags commented, with a wry squirm on her lips.

'How about you?'

'Still young, free and single,' she remarked, quickly, with a toss of her hair. Then, 'Do you live locally?'

Becka glanced quickly at Toby before answering, 'Oh, not far. Just the other side of town really.'

'Well, we ought to meet up,' she said brightly. 'Have a drink and catch-up. Give me your mobile number and I'll text you.'

'Oh, I've left my phone at home, and I can never remember my own number.' Becka laughed. It was true though. She always had to ask Toby what it was.

Toby's eyes met Mags's again as he stamped his feet to keep them warm.

'How about yours instead?' There was something in her look towards him, something obviously appealing, because Toby – who wouldn't normally bother doing this kind of exchanging numbers thing – got his phone out and started opening up his contacts.

She told him her number and he rang it and Mags's phone buzzed a couple of times until she said, 'Got it, thanks,' and then they smiled at each other. Then a car on the corner beeped its horn – accidentally by the look of it, after they had all turned together to stare – and Mags reached out to squeeze Becka's shoulder.

'Great then, I'll track you down and we'll have a girly get-together. And thanks for this.' She waved the parking ticket and disappeared.

* * *

'Mags isn't a name I've heard you mention before,' Toby said as he reversed out of the parking space. 'Short for Margaret?'

A shadow flitted quickly over Becka's face. Then she blinked as she looked through the window and watched Mags looking back at her from the other side of the car park.

'Her name's actually Magdalena. Her mum was religious. Extremely so: a really odd woman. Everyone said she had a stigmata but I don't know how true it was. I met her on a couple of occasions but she always had rubber gloves on.' Becka laughed.

'Were you close?'

'God, no. Although *she* got it into her head that she was my best friend, even though our friendship only lasted for a few months at most. Looking back, I wasn't very nice to her really. We fell out and she got quite weird and threatening with me. But, I suppose... well I did stuff that I've regretted since. Having a teenage daughter makes you think differently about things, doesn't it? Because I wouldn't like the thought of someone treating Charlotte in the way that I behaved with Mags. But no, we were never close. We sat together in a few classes, that's all. Art and history I think.'

'Battle of Hastings,' Toby quipped.

'Ten sixty-six,' she replied instinctively, her mind elsewhere.

THIRTY-SIX

TOBY

It was on the following Monday that Toby received a text message.

> *Hi, you gave me your parking ticket the other day. I'm Becka's friend, remember? Would you ask her if she can ring me so that I can arrange drinks or something. Cheers, Mags x*

He was on his lunch break at work. There was no point getting in touch with Becka immediately, and he reminded himself that he would tell her later. But by the time he had finished a busy afternoon of work, he picked up his phone to find four missed calls and a voicemail from Mags's number. Annoyed at her impatience – he had fully intended to pass her message on to Becka when he got home – he considered ignoring everything and deleting the contact details. But something stopped him. Something drew him to click on the voicemail.

'Please, help me. Please, I don't know what to do. I'm at the side of the dual carriageway near the big Tesco with a flat tyre

and there's a weird bloke outside who keeps trying to get in my car.'

There was a hammering sound amidst the rush of traffic noise. Toby felt his chest tighten as he puzzled over what he was hearing.

'Please. My phone is broken, I don't know what's happened. This is the only number it will ring. I can't get hold of anyone else. Whoever's number it is, please help.'

There was the sound again, like a metal car roof being pummelled. Then a scream and some unrecognisable panicked gabble.

'Get away, you freak! I'm calling the police. Just fuck off and leave me alone. Oh God, please, please if you hear this come and help me.'

The message ended and Toby stood, stunned. Was it some kind of joke? He clicked to listen to the message again. It didn't appear to be a hoax and the fear in Mags's voice was apparent. Toby tried calling her back once, twice, three times. Each time the number failed. He wondered whether to call the police, but he didn't know her specific location or even what type of car she was in.

And although he had never considered himself a superhero type of guy, and Mags was almost a complete stranger to him, he knew that he had to go to her assistance. Luckily, it was on the way home.

* * *

It was still light as Toby drove out of town and joined the rush-hour traffic. He got stuck for a while at the main roundabout, but once on the dual carriageway the stream of vehicles travelled steadily towards the commuter villages and new-build estates. There was no hard shoulder, but he could see the wide strip of grass verge that edged the road. It was only minutes later before the expansive banner of the Tesco superstore reached his sightline. He slowed to forty, then to thirty, spotting in the distance the hazard lights flashing beside the moving lines of traffic.

Toby checked his mirrors and indicated in plenty of time, braking and pulling onto the ground at the back of the stationary car. From behind, he could see a woman's head in the driving seat. He switched off the engine and waited a few seconds, expecting to see someone else – the freaky bloke who had been pestering her – in the vicinity. But no. There was no one.

He slid awkwardly across the gearstick and over the passenger seat to exit the car safely away from the road and approached the immobilised vehicle. A flat tyre at the front was evident.

'Hey, are you all right?' He rapped his knuckles on the window.

Mags shrieked and held a hand over her mouth. Then she slumped in recognition and relief as she saw him, pressing the unlock button, and saying, 'Oh, thank God, it's you, I didn't know what to do.'

Toby opened the door and stuck his head inside. 'What happened?'

'Shit... oh God.' She scrunched her fingers around her forehead and took a deep breath. 'There was this man hanging around trying to get in the car. I think he might have gone down the embankment now. Looked like he was a druggie, or homeless or something. I thought he was going to rob me.'

Toby took some paces away from the car, checking over a small barrier to where the ground dropped away, down to a cluster of scrubby bushes. 'I can't see anyone.'

He got into the car, pulling the door partially shut. 'You probably need to call out the breakdown services. It's not a good idea to try and change a wheel yourself on a road like this. And I've got no idea where to start with that sort of thing.'

Mags waggled her phone at him. 'Yeah, I know. Brilliant time for my phone to die, isn't it? I've got no idea why you were the only person I could call.'

Toby took her phone and turned it in his hands, pressing the dysfunctional buttons. 'Strange.' He handed it back and got his own out.

Mags put a hand on his knee. 'Thank you so much. You saved me. I could have been stuck here or I could have been attacked, and I don't even know you but you came to my rescue.'

He looked at her. She squeezed his leg a little. There was some kind of magnetism in her eyes, some kind of sexual bewitching quality in the tone of her voice, some kind of fascination with her half-open lips that gleamed with lipstick or gloss or her own saliva. Voluptuous eyelids. A thin tangle of hair that trailed down, guiding his view to where there was an extra button undone on her blouse enabling a nick of cleavage to be displayed.

A spell. That's what it seemed like, because he'd never looked at anyone else before and felt such an instant stirring. Her hand burned on his leg. The sweetness of her perfume got into his lungs, down into his stomach, his groin.

He tore his eyes away, fixed them back on the screen of his phone. 'Which breakdown company are you with?'

'Let me,' she said, taking the phone out of his hands.

He watched her fingers slide seductively over the screen, imagined them on him...

'I'm just going to check that all your hazard lights are working properly. I can't remember if they were on when I pulled up.'

He got out of the car and walked back to his own, to put a hand on the roof and gulp the air. What on earth was happening to him? Legs like jelly, his insides inflamed. It was just like when he was thirteen and had a major crush on his teacher.

* * *

Toby went back and waited in the car with Magdalena until the breakdown van arrived. And during that time – fifty-two minutes exactly – they talked about their backgrounds and childhoods, their careers and aspirations, their pet hates, their favourite cities, and funniest films. They had so much in common. A love of the outdoors and embracing extreme challenges that took you over rocks and dangerous inclines to unspoilt summits where you could look out at the curvature of the earth. A loathing of religions and superstitions and things like horoscopes and psychic mediums. A desire to own a cat, specifically a Maine Coon. 'We should get one and call it a name like Gary,' said Magdalena. They burst out laughing. 'Or Pauline,' said Toby. They howled at the suggestions until tears ran down their faces.

When the tyre had been changed and the breakdown man had handed over the paperwork, Toby realised that he had fallen in love. Madly, stupidly in love like he had never felt before.

He drove home beaming like a child at Christmas, with Mags's face in his head, her voice in his ears. Churning, jittery feelings in his stomach distracted him so that he ended up missing a turning; his feet were fidgety on the pedals and he kept braking unnecessarily until the car behind him beeped a long aggressive honk. It was madness. He really didn't know what had come over him.

Arriving home, he parked up and rubbed forcefully at his head to banish his adulterous thoughts.

Get a grip, he told himself. You're not fifteen, for God's sake.

Inside, Becka greeted him with a face like thunder.

'What?' he said.

'You were supposed to pick Charlotte up from hockey. Don't you ever answer your bloody phone? *I* couldn't get her because I was stuck in the dentist's waiting room for my appointment, so in the end I had to ring my mother to go and get her and she'd been standing outside school *on her own* all this time.'

'What? You never rang! You know I would have answered.' He took his phone out and jabbed at the side. 'Shit.'

'Yeah, about twenty missed calls and a dozen furious texts.' Becka flicked her finger at the phone in his hand and strode out of the room.

'It was switched off. I must have done it accidentally,' he shouted after her even though there was no point in trying to explain. The damage had been done. What could he say anyway? That Magdalena had used it and turned it off afterwards? He waited for his mobile to fire up, listening to the incoming pings of the unanswered messages.

Suddenly the screen flashed up, making him gasp out loud. A new picture stared at him: Magdalena pouting her sexy lips in a half-smile, left eye frozen in a conspiratorial wink, with a straggle of hair brushing her right cheekbone. She must have taken a selfie with his phone and set it to be his screensaver after making the call to the breakdown company.

Oh God, he thought. If Becka sees...

But adrenaline was coursing through him, flushing his face, pummelling his heart, and he realised that it wasn't just fear, it was arousal. He rammed his phone into his pocket. He would need to delete the picture, but he didn't want to delete the picture...

'Are you ignoring me or what?' Becka was in the doorway, hands on hips.

Red-faced, Toby floundered, making a meal of taking his coat off. 'No. I told you. I don't know, it might be a problem with my phone. It's done that before, switching itself off.'

'I don't mean that. I've just asked you twice if you want fajitas or stir-fry and you can't be bothered to answer me.'

'Either, I don't mind.' There was going to be one of those nights of stony silence in front of the television that seemed to occur more regularly nowadays than they used to.

'Fajitas,' declared Charlotte as she appeared, fresh from her shower. She mock-punched Toby on the arm. 'Thanks for forgetting about me today, Dad. I had to stand outside school in my kit covered in actual mud, looking like an idiot, for hours.'

'I know, I know.' Toby put his hands up. 'I'm sorry, sweetheart, I think my phone has gone dodgy and switched itself off. I didn't leave you there on purpose.'

Charlotte held out her hand. 'Let me look at it. You've probably got a suspect app that you need to delete. I'll sort it for you.'

'It's fine.' Toby grasped the phone in his pocket, feeling suddenly faint. 'Anyway, I need to go and get changed. It's been a long day and I need a chill out.'

He took the stairs two at a time to the bathroom where he locked himself in.

Oh God, what the fuck, Magdalena. What have you done to me? Her photo seduced him all over again as he sat on the toilet, and he held the screen to his forehead for a few seconds before pressing delete.

THIRTY-SEVEN

TOBY

Toby held off texting Magdalena for four days. It would have been easier to spend four days standing in the seething flames of hell. He couldn't stop thinking about her. He checked his phone repeatedly with every ping, fearful yet hopeful that it would be her. Deep inside, he felt that she was waiting for him to contact her. It was like there was some telepathic connection between them, and he imagined her reclining in a foamy bath drinking chilled white wine and saying his name through those red pouty lips, a picture that haunted him until, exactly ninety-seven hours after he had watched her car pull out of that lay-by on the dual carriageway, he sent her a message:

> *Random question, but have you been drinking wine in the bath?*

Less than a minute later, the reply came through:

> *Chardonnay.*

Even though they had both declared themselves to be disbelievers of anything slightly supernatural, Toby took this as a valid sign, a confirmation that they were meant to be together, failing to consider that a long-term marriage and daughter would impede their union.

And, strangely enough, Magdalena made no further mention of contacting Becka for reunion drinks.

They met discreetly in vegan cafés and motorway services, the unlikeliest of places where friends and family would go. Under the blanket of dusk they groped and French-kissed like pubescent teenagers, alternating cars. It was obvious that Toby couldn't take her back to his house, but Magdalena's housing situation wasn't ideal either. She was lodging temporarily with her stepbrother, whose offices and facilities she could run her events planning company from, with his own freelance work overlapping and complementing hers so that they could often share contracts. He was a helpful guy business-wise, she told Toby, but his strict rules meant that she couldn't take anyone back there.

They needed to find somewhere else.

So Toby dared to pretend to Becka that he had to work an occasional night shift due to an inquiry into a health and safety complaint. And within the anonymity of an eighty-roomed Travelodge just off the southbound M1, he met up with Magdalena and they spent full nights enjoying each other in every way possible. The bags under his eyes were testament to his lack of sleep.

It was only a matter of weeks before Toby realised that he was trapped in his marriage. He had begun to consider his future and how he and Magdalena could take their relationship forward without having to meet secretly. He was no longer in love with Becka: something within him had died and couldn't be revived. Their *date days* fizzled out, and Becka had even stopped suggesting they bother. It seemed like her mind was elsewhere, too. He stopped calling her *darling* and *sweetheart* and conversations became humourless and perfunctory. Neither of them initiated sex any more, so it no longer happened, and any pleasure that he used to take in watching her dress in the mornings was gone. It was as if he had begun to be physically repulsed by her. The decline, once set in, was swift, and it astounded him. Surely it was inevitable that a break-up of their relationship would follow.

Toby had to think logically. Financial planning. How he could make it work with Magdalena.

The thing was, Becka had assets from family inheritances but Toby only had his name on the mortgage. And Magdalena had nothing to speak of. No property or significant savings: she got by on the income from her events business.

The thought that Toby could walk away from his family and make a new life with Magdalena was impossible. He would need to pay maintenance for Charlotte, maybe university costs at some point.

He discussed it all with Magdalena during one of their hotel all-nighters.

'When you say that Becka has assets, what do you mean? What sort of value?' Mags sat on the bed, cross-legged, facing him as they tried to see a way out of their predicament.

'Well, she has a lot of jewellery that was left to her by a grandmother. Nothing that she would ever wear, but you know, sentimental stuff. Valuable stuff, a lot of gold. Some of it was on *Antiques Roadshow* once, and they said it would fetch around thirty grand.'

'Nice, but not really a life-changing amount though,' said Magdalena.

'She has a load of cash, too, from her dad. He ran a used car business, and she worked as a secretary for him since she left uni—'

'What, she never did anything with her art?'

Toby laughed. 'No. Complete waste of a degree if you ask me.'

The bitterness that Magdalena felt made her shiver. That bitch deprived her of the chance to do art *properly*, and then just squandered her own opportunity. It wasn't fair.

'Anyway,' Toby continued, 'her dad used to hand over loads of money to her, so he could avoid paying tax. I always thought he was a slimy fellow. And then as he got older he would just slip cash – like, envelopes of ten- and twenty-pound notes – into her handbag when he popped round. For safekeeping and emergencies, he said. But Becka thought it was because he was worried about his health, and how all the money might be taken into consideration if he had to go into a nursing home. So it's all locked in a safe behind a secret panel in the utility room, and we've been working our way through it.'

'Wow,' said Magdalena. 'It's a bit *Breaking Bad*.'

Toby shrugged. 'I've no idea how much is in there. Hundreds. Thousands. Tens of thousands. I really don't know. She takes some out now and then for us to put petrol in the car or do a big shop or pay for a posh meal or take on holiday. It always feels like money-laundering.'

'I suppose it is in a way. Is her dad still alive?'

'No, he died about four months ago. I don't think her mum even knows about all the cash. She was always insistent that he did things properly, always afraid that even minor irregularities would catch up with him.'

'So who has the key to this safe?' Magdalena winked at him.

Toby laughed and shrugged. 'It's a code number thing. Four digits.'

'I bet you could guess it.'

'Hmm. Maybe. I could probably just look over her shoulder

the next time she opens it. It's not like she's particularly careful – well, possibly around Charlotte – but then again if I needed money for anything she'd just give it to me. There's a level of trust with it all, I suppose.'

'So you could just take the money and run.' Magdalena's eyes sparkled with enticement.

Toby threw his head back, laughing. 'Yeah, like I could really get away with that and she wouldn't notice.'

'Ah well,' said Magdalena in mock-acquiescence, 'we'll just have to murder her then. I never liked her anyway.'

Toby pushed her over on the bed and they made a show of playful wrestling until their desires got the better of them and they stripped the clothing from each other and made love again.

THIRTY-EIGHT

TOBY

Christmas came and went and was uneventful, with Becka's mother visiting more times than Toby would have liked, and taking over his favourite armchair and remote control. He sneaked away during the interminable festive period for snatched moments with Magdalena: a couple of hours here and there when he could get away with it. Walks in woods that had to be accessed over stone walls. A gig for a band they'd never heard of in a darkened jazz bar in Nottingham. Takeaway coffees in a lay-by just off the A1. It seemed like forever before they could properly get back to what was their normal.

Only a few days into the new year, Becka was behaving strangely. The way she spoke to him; the questions she asked him about his work and about where he was really going when he said he needed to pop out and get petrol for the car; the way she took to checking his pockets under the pretence of looking for a receipt so that she could return a newly purchased but temperamental air fryer to the electrical store. Toby started to worry that she suspected his affair. He had to be more careful about covering his tracks.

But then only a week later, it seemed like all was right

again. Perhaps his guilty mind had imagined things. Becka announced that she had taken the initiative and booked a weekend away for them. Nothing too fancy, nothing too far away, just a cosy self-catering cottage in a picturesque little village beside the River Trent. Decent pub a stone's throw down the road and plenty of footpaths for them to get out walking. Charlotte wasn't bothered about going as she had a hockey match on the Saturday, so she would stay with her grandmother instead.

'It's what we need,' Becka insisted. 'Some time away for ourselves. The weekend after next. It feels like we've drifted apart just lately and let work take over. When was the last time we had a date day? When was the last time we even went out for a drink in a pub? It must be at least three or four months ago.'

'I'm not sure about my work schedule...' Toby began, but Becka was quick to silence him.

'Don't worry, I checked on the calendar before booking. It's a free weekend.'

They kept a family calendar in the kitchen to keep track of work, school and social events. Although nowadays the social events were non-existent. Charlotte's sporting fixtures were in red felt-tip. And Toby had been using it recently to forewarn of his nights with Magdalena, under the guise of 'H&S investigation'.

Toby didn't want to go. But he couldn't think of an excuse not to. He saw it like a chore, an unpleasant job to do on behalf of the family. Because everything Becka did at the moment irritated him. The way she held her cutlery. How she always stacked the dishwasher wrong. The saccharine voice she put on when she spoke to her mother on the phone.

Three nights. And all the days in between.

An unbearable amount of time that he would be forced to spend in her presence.

Unable to look forward to the weekend, his mind began to tease him, offering speculative scenes in which he saw himself getting drunk and confessing to Becka about his affair with Magdalena. Stress built, day by day, at the thought of being cooped up in an unknown cottage with a wife he no longer loved. At the expectation to have fun and heart-to-hearts and make plans for the future like they used to on such breaks away from home. At the knowledge that he would be craving Magdalena like a hardened addict.

The weather forecast for the weekend wasn't great. Showers with periods of heavy rain at times. When he mentioned this to Becka she told him to stop being so negative and get into the holiday spirit. Yes, it might be wet but the temperatures didn't look too bad. There was no such thing as bad weather if you took the right clothing: he was supposed to be an outdoorsy person, wasn't he? Anyway, if the rain got torrential then they would just have to spend more time in the pub, wouldn't they?

He felt sick as he watched Becka folding fleeces and water-proof jackets into their shared holdall. Thick socks, underwear, washbags and toiletries. She packed them in and pulled the zip across. Dutifully, he carried the bag downstairs, into the utility room to put with their waiting pairs of walking boots.

'Let's splash some cash,' she joked. 'We can eat in the pub and order the most expensive wine.'

She slid the microwave oven along the worktop to access the secret panel in the wall behind it.

'Six hundred?'

'That should be plenty,' said Toby, watching her putting in the four digits. One-one-one-two. It was hardly the safest, most original number.

She counted from a wad of twenty-pound notes and put the remainder back in the safe. The panel closed, the microwave pushed back against it: no one would ever have known it was there.

'Sorted.' She smiled and tucked the cash into the inside pocket of the holdall. 'Friday here we come.'

He managed to catch an hour with Magdalena after work the next evening.

'You don't have to go,' she told him. 'She can't force you.'

But Magdalena didn't know what it was like to juggle two lives. Toby shrugged and rolled his eyes to demonstrate the extent of his reluctance. 'It won't be for long. We'll get something sorted soon.'

'You might fall in love with her all over again and come back and dump me.'

'Don't be silly. I would never do that. This, us' – Toby waved his hand between them – 'we were meant to be. It was all decided in the realms of the phone gods when your message for a superhero to come to your aid would only send to *my* voicemail.'

There was a glint in her eyes as Magdalena looked up at him. 'You really believed that?'

'What?'

She started to laugh. 'You thought that my phone had actually broken and I couldn't contact anyone else?'

Toby's eyes widened. 'It was a set-up? To get me to meet you?'

Laughter had Magdalena holding her side. She wiped a tear away so that her mascara wouldn't run. 'Obviously. Although the flat tyre wasn't deliberate. That was real and accidental, and a brilliant excuse to ring you. But if that hadn't happened, I would have found some other reason.'

Toby's mouth hung open. 'You little minx.'

She shrugged. 'Yeah. I fancied you from that first moment in the car park. And I noticed that you fancied me, too.'

Toby smiled knowingly. He shook his head in mock disbelief.

'So anyway. Don't go away with her. Stay with me, even if you have to spill the beans about everything. It's going to come out at some point.' She tried to reach out, but Toby leaned his elbows on his knees and put his face in his hands.

'I can't. I just can't. Not yet.'

There was a pause, and Magdalena went silent, her eyes steely on his. Then she took her phone out and started looking at her emails. Swiping and tapping. Deleting the junk. Pretending to take an excessive interest in an invoice for work-related materials.

Toby realised that she was sulking.

'Hey,' he said, snaking an arm around her shoulder and fingering the soft skin beneath her ear. 'Don't fall out with me. It's not as if I want to go away with her. I'd much rather be doing this with you.'

'Yeah. Course you would.' Her voice was tight. Eyes still on her phone screen.

'A wet fucking January weekend at the side of the River Trent, with someone that I have really started to despise? Come on, it's hardly Barbados.'

She looked up at him. Went into bitch mode. 'Well, make sure she doesn't trip and fall in the water then. That would be a terrible shame, wouldn't it?'

Toby snorted out loud. 'Ha! The perfect crime. She's actually a crap swimmer, you know?'

'There you go then. One push could solve all our problems.'

He fiddled leisurely with the hem of her skirt, moving his hand up to stroke her thigh. 'I found out the code number for the safe the other day.'

She pricked up her ears, interested. 'Really? You're kidding me. What? What is it?'

'If I told you I'd have to kill you.'

He smothered his mouth onto hers and reached across to recline her seat. She had already started to unbutton her blouse.

THIRTY-NINE

TOBY

A year ago, if he had gone with Becka to the little cottage by the river he would have enjoyed it immensely. Biking, walking, enjoying the range of ales in the pub. He would have taken his binoculars and appreciated the wildlife, cleared out the space in his head of all the work clutter and stressful minutiae of life that took up too much of his worry time: the way the neighbours had trimmed his side of the hedge without asking; the expensive cycling magazine subscription he had taken out without checking the terms and was now locked into for two years; and the mysterious patch of recurring damp in the downstairs cloak-room that had even started growing actual mushrooms.

But now...

He sat miserably with his phone that could only get an intermittent signal in the tiny kitchen-cum-living room. Rain chucked itself lividly at the windows, impeding the view of the river. How could this be described as a *cottage*? It was hardly more than a shed. Without wi-fi too. He'd had words with Becka about booking somewhere as crap as this, but she'd got her glass-half-full head on and had been pretending it was fun and cosy and an *experience* since they arrived two hours ago.

Fucking experience.

'We could just get togged up in our waterproofs and go for a stroll anyway,' Becka suggested. 'What the hell, it's only a bit of water. It won't kill us.'

Toby shook his head and looked at her as if she was stupid. 'I'm going nowhere in this.'

'Spoilsport.'

She busied herself around, thumbing through the small bookshelf of visitors' discarded novels, admiring the selection of herbal teas that had been left in the welcome pack and browsing the file of tourist information leaflets.

Toby went through to the bedroom to put a thicker jumper on. Another area of the shed where he was unable to get onto the internet. He half-wondered whether to just tell Becka about Magdalena and be done with all the months of deception. At least he'd have a decent excuse to go home. But he knew deep down that he couldn't do it. Sometimes he felt as if he would be waiting forever for the right moment.

He sat on the bed and let his head drop into his hands. The situation was excruciating. Something had to happen.

Something had to happen soon.

* * *

The weather was set in. A storm from America – some exotic name beginning with a J – trying to blow itself out.

Toby suggested that they should go home. What was the point of staying, in this? You couldn't call it a holiday; it was an endurance test. But Becka was stubborn, still insisting that it would pass, that they were over the worst of it now. She had something special planned for him on the Sunday: a canoe expedition. She knew how much he loved outdoor pursuits and so she'd booked a session with a local water sports company. An extreme experience on a challenging section of the river with lots of hidden currents to negotiate. An exciting afternoon for Toby who wasn't a seasoned kayaker but always liked the idea of trying something new.

He was touched, somewhat, by her thoughtfulness. At least, he thought, if he couldn't go home then he would be able to have fun on the river. Becka could stay in the cabin, reading or watching TV and they could enjoy themselves separately. Their break might be endurable after all.

They slept tortuously, intermittently that first night. Roof tiles hammered in the wind, threatening to be picked off with every gust. The windowpanes felt like they were actually moving at the back of the building, and there was a fitful knocking sound throughout the night whose origins couldn't be identified.

In the early hours Becka reached out to him, snaking her hand up his thigh. Middle-of-the-night sex was a rare occurrence, and the blackness of the room and the rain on the roof could have added to the gripping nature of it, but Toby pushed her hand away and turned over.

'Come on,' she said, pressing up to him, nibbling at his neck. 'We could make this fun.'

'Yeah, it will be great fun until the roof blows off.'

'What happened to your sense of adventure? We always used to take opportunities like this. You know, back in the old days. We don't even have Charlotte here with us to worry about overhearing things...'

'No one could overhear *anything* in this. I wish I'd brought earplugs.'

The wind changed direction for a few seconds, howling down the chimney. Outside, it sounded as if the rain had turned to hail, pelting the glass like pebbles.

Becka caressed his chest, but he was tense and unreachable. Eventually she turned over and left him alone.

FORTY

TOBY

Water had pooled on the windowsill in the kitchen the next morning. It continued to drip in from a gap at the top of the window. Toby said that the frame had obviously been done wrong, even though he knew nothing himself about building.

'It feels like it's slowing a bit,' said Becka as she took bacon, mushrooms and eggs from the fridge.

Toby snorted. He peered towards the outside through a moving film of water that ran down like some kind of garden feature. Out on the road a small trampoline bobbed around, and a sopping red mitten tried to cling to the edge of where the pavement had been. The river had risen visibly during the night and had started to lap onto the wide grass verge with every gust of wind. Maybe it was high tide at the moment. He didn't know if that made any difference.

He checked his phone. No signal. No internet. It was half past nine. The day that waited in front of him sneered mockingly. He pulled an Ordnance Survey map of the area down from the bookshelf and wondered what time the pub would be open.

Breakfast was over all too soon, and there was a limit to the amount of coffee that Toby was capable of drinking. He admired Becka for putting on a false show of cheerfulness and felt guilty about appearing so negative.

So they pored over the map and some local guide books for a while, pointing out landmarks and interesting features of the area despite knowing that they wouldn't be visiting. They switched on the television to check the weather forecast again, but the double black raindrops remained firmly on the map.

'We could drive out somewhere?' Becka suggested, and they amicably discussed the advantages and pitfalls of a journey into Lincoln, where they would still have to take on the elements once the car was parked. And shopping had never been Toby's favourite pastime.

Resignedly, they concluded that chilling out at the cottage was the only sensible option. There were books to read and a small DVD library. Toby scoured the visitors' file again and found that the pub opened at midday.

* * *

They held off until twenty past twelve, when they braced themselves to hurtle in their cagoules through the lashing rain to the pub, where they found a table in the back room by a cosy log fire. Toby logged in to the pub wi-fi, messaging Magdalena as he went to the bar.

People came in and ordered steak pies and chicken tikka and salmon hollandaise, and the flagstone floor ran with wet footprints. A member of staff came and mopped up periodically, so that the kitchen staff wouldn't slip. The barman plugged an iPod into a stereo system and an inappropriate selection of disco songs filled the spaces between everyone's conversations.

Becka began to sing along embarrassingly. 'Rah rah, ah-ah-ah.'

Toby flashed her a look to stop it.

'Hey, don't you recognise it? Mine and Charlotte's karaoke song?'

Toby shrugged, dismissing the good times they'd all had on their family holiday last year, when Becka and Charlotte had won the karaoke competition. It wasn't as if old memories could keep his marriage alive for much longer.

He checked his phone again and found that a network signal had appeared.

'Won't be long,' he said as he pocketed his mobile and made his way to the toilet, where he locked himself in a cubicle and dialled Magdalena. 'Hey, babe, I'm missing you.'

She made out she was with friends, having fun and a boozy catch-up, but there was no noise in the background and Toby suspected that she was lying in an effort to make him jealous. He played on his grim situation, describing his accommodation as a *bleak wooden chalet* and apologising for the lack of wi-fi and signal the previous evening.

'It wouldn't be bleak if I was there,' said Magdalena. 'I'd be able to cheer you up.'

Toby smiled at the thought of them both, segregated from the world, in the tiny cabin. 'I know. But I'm just going to have to grin and bear it with the help of plenty of alcohol. Keep me posted. You can message me and I'll respond when I have a signal.'

Back at the table, Toby chugged halfway through his pint.

Becka's phone suddenly pinged.

'Oh no.' Disappointment washed across her face as she read the message. 'They've cancelled your canoe trip. Treacherous conditions apparently.'

'No shit, Sherlock,' said Toby. He slumped, sighing, back in his chair. The best bit of their weekend break had been snatched away. 'That's such a shame. You know, we'd be better off going home.'

'Don't be boring. At least we're in here looking at different scenery. If we were at home I'd probably be doing the ironing. A change is as good as a rest, so they say.'

She could be so stubborn sometimes.

Toby's phone vibrated in his hand and he looked at a new message from Magdalena.

Come back! You can sit in a pub with me instead! Xxx

We're monitoring the weather he typed in reply. *If it gets much worse I'm going to put my foot down. Could be back by evening. Xxx*

'Who are you messaging?' Becka leaned over, and Toby quickly clicked the screen off.

'No one.'

'Anyone would think you've got a bit on the side.'

Toby flushed. He couldn't tell if she was being sarcastic or not. 'It's bloody warm in here.' He rolled up his sleeves, then put his phone face down on the table. Mistake. If it pinged then Becka might pick it up and check. He moved his pint around and fiddled with the beer mats before retrieving his phone to slip into his coat pocket.

By half past two he was on his third beer of the day, and Becka was still eking out her first glass of wine. There was a newspaper abandoned on the adjacent table, so Toby went to claim it, to relieve the tedium as the rain continued in torrents outside. Becka was entertaining herself with *Candy Crush* or some kind of crap game on her phone.

How bad did everything have to get before something happened?

They sat in their own silences while people moved around them: a woman came to stoke up the fire with logs; a waiter to remove plates and empty glasses; an elderly couple to sit at and appraise three different tables for the most comfortable and bright positioning before settling at the one beside the bar.

'Are you getting peckish yet?' Becka said later, scanning the menu. 'Looks like they serve all day. We don't need to wait until the evening session.'

Toby shrugged. 'What are you thinking? Not a big meal. Something light would be fine for me.'

They decided on a sharing platter of chicken wings, spicy wedges, battered prawns and onion rings with a selection of dips. It filled up a little more time, choosing the food, waiting to be served, eating at a leisurely pace. But by the time they had finished there was still no let-up in the weather.

'So you think we should just stay here for the rest of the evening?' Toby's speech had started to slur. 'We could still go home. You'd probably be all right to drive: you've only had a glass of wine.'

'Large glass,' Becka reminded him.

'Just tell me... what is the point of being here?'

'You've forgotten, haven't you?'

'What?' Toby combed his memory. Their wedding anniversary was in August; Becka's birthday was in June.

'It's actually twenty years this weekend since we met. Your Auntie Anne's fundraising thing that she did for the children's hospice? We were eyeing each other up over the tombola.' Becka laughed, her face shining. She was still good-looking, just no longer attractive to Toby.

'How do you expect *me* to remember that?'

Becka pulled a face. 'Why not? *I* did.'

Toby felt that he was being railroaded into a session of pointless reminiscing.

'We should celebrate properly,' said Becka, pushing her chair back to stand up. 'I'm going to the bar.'

She took her purse and left the table, and someone came to clear up their platter and the remains of the meal. An opportunity offered itself to message Magdalena again, and Toby returned to the action on his phone. The pub suddenly got busier as if a coach party had turned up, and a noisy group engaged themselves in pushing two tables together and gathering up spare chairs. Toby shuffled himself in as people nudged behind him. He had to stop someone from taking Becka's seat even though, with her coat draped over it, it was obviously being used.

She returned, eventually, with a bottle of Prosecco in a bucket of ice, and two glasses hanging from her hand.

'You wouldn't believe what it's like in the other side of the bar,' she said. 'Absolute bedlam. There's water everywhere: it's come in under the front door. The staff are trying to sweep it out but it's coming in faster than they can deal with it. They've got sandbags and towels everywhere, and there are still people trying to eat meals at the end of the room. That's why it took so long to get served. It looks like everyone's moving through here where it's a bit drier.'

She put the glasses on the table and took the bottle of fizz out of the bucket. 'Do you want to do the honours?'

'I'll leave it to you. It's not like I'm a fan of that stuff anyway.'

Becka bobbed out her tongue. 'What a misery guts you are. Come on, we're celebrating, we deserve it. Twenty years is a long time.'

'Too long.'

He didn't think that he'd said it out loud, but he must have. Becka froze with the bottle in her hands, glaring at him.

'So, is that what you really think?'

'I was joking. Chill out.'

'Joking? After being so negative about coming away? After being so wrapped up in *work*' – her fingers scratched inverted commas around the word – 'that I've hardly seen you for the last few months? A comment like that – *too long* – makes me think that you're speaking your mind because that's how you really feel.'

Becka angrily popped the cork out of the bottle. It frothed and spilled onto her lap, and she moved quickly to pour it in a glass, where it rose and flowed over the side like lava.

Toby watched, inhaling carefully. She hadn't poured a drink for him, so he continued with his beer. He put his phone face down on his left thigh, out of her reach.

'What's gone wrong with us?' Her look was wistful, giving away a tremble at the side of her lips.

Toby shrugged. 'Nothing.'

She picked up her glass, downed the cold liquid in one and refilled. The fire spat an aimless ember onto the hearth, and Becka watched as the orange died to black. Toby returned to his phone.

Talk moved from the bar to the adjacent table like a Mexican wave, saying that the pub would have to close early because of the weather. The evening bookings were being cancelled, the kitchen was closing. Two of the staff had moved their vehicles out of the car park and up to higher ground. A flood alert had gone out for the area. Becka swigged the Prosecco as she listened to the rumours, seeing the staff bustle in and out with mops and buckets.

'Do you *want* some of this or what?' She held the bottle over the spare glass.

Toby looked up. 'No thanks. I'll stick with the pale ale.'

'Suit yourself.'

It didn't seem possible that the rain could get any worse, but water was lashing down the windows even more ferociously. The fire hissed as it dashed down the chimney onto the logs. Staff were slopping full buckets of water backwards and forwards. The barman checked his wristwatch and rubbed a hand over his stoic face.

Becka got up and traipsed through all the clean-up activity in the other room to go to the toilet, and Toby was still typing a message when she arrived back at their table. She sat and watched his thumbs jabbing, his fingers curled around the gadget to prevent prying eyes.

'Why is it so important to disrupt our time together?' she asked him, picking up her glass again to gulp savagely. The bottle on the ice was almost empty. 'I'm not just talking about you sitting there on your phone, but I'm also thinking about the nights that you have to work on this so-called health and safety inquiry.'

Toby froze. He couldn't meet her glare. She *knew* something.

'So, tell me more about the health and safety thing.'

'You know I can't. It's confidential.'

There was a long pause and he foolishly thought he'd got away with it. He swigged his beer. Looked out towards the rain again. Meanwhile, her eyes were burning into him.

'Don't. Lie. To me.'

He looked up. 'What?'

'I rang your work to double-check dates on the calendar when I was in the process of booking this. No one seemed to know anything about a health and safety inquiry. No one knew anything about you working nights.'

'Well, as I said, it's confidential, so most people don't know it's happening—'

'Don't lie to me. I know there's something going on. It's not just the nights thing, it's all the other stuff...'

'What other stuff?'

'Just... I don't know. You're different. I know there's someone else. I can just tell.' Becka wound her arms defensively around her body.

Toby's shoulders dropped in defeat. He didn't know whether to deny it or own up. But then a vibration on his phone made him glance fleetingly towards his messages again.

Suddenly Becka vented, 'Put the fucking phone down, will you? Do you really have to be such a selfish bastard?'

A woman from the next table turned to stare at them so that the rest of her group followed her gaze, and then everyone in the pub seemed to go quiet for a second. Toby looked up in embarrassment at her outburst, his fingers frozen over his mobile, and that was when Becka seized her opportunity. She grabbed the phone, but Toby instinctively, fearfully, jumped up and pulled it back out of her grasp. Too late, though, the screen brightened, the name displayed for her to see.

'Magdalena?' She tried to reach the phone again, but he turned away. 'Magdalena? What on earth are you doing messaging *her*?'

The deception was over. Toby didn't know how to excuse himself; he didn't know how to explain himself.

'Look, it's complicated...' he began as Becka latched her fingers onto the sleeve of his jumper to try and pull him back around to face her.

'*What's* complicated?' Her eyes widened, darkened, as the realisation spread like an inkblot.

Toby tucked the offending phone back into his coat pocket with a shaky hand. 'I never meant to hurt you. It was just something that got carried away. And then. And then...'

Becka's face collapsed. The Prosecco glass tipped momentarily in her hand, sloshing its contents onto her leg.

Toby continued. 'It's just that... I don't love you any more. There's someone else. So. Well... I don't love you.' There. He'd said it. And now it could never be unsaid.

Their futures would never be the same again.

FORTY-ONE

TOBY

'You bastard.' She turned her face to look into the crackling fire because she didn't want his eyes on her. A tear slipped down her cheek, and she nudged the back of her hand under her nose to dam the unavoidable rush. 'Her. Why *her*? I mean I guessed that something was going on with *someone*... all the signs were there. But *her*?'

'I never meant to. It was purely accidental, honestly.'

'You've been conned. She doesn't love *you*. She's done this to get at *me*. This is something that stems from a long time ago.'

'What do you mean?'

'We had a fall out, years back. She always swore she'd get revenge. And now look. This' – Becka waved her hand at the distance between their chairs – 'This is how she's finally done it.'

'Come on,' said Toby. 'It wasn't planned. It was all accidental, like I said...'

'So what happens now? What about Charlotte? The house?' Becka's voice had risen in tone and volume.

'Look. I don't know. It's a mess. I didn't want us to be in a mess and I don't really know how to sort it out but... I mean, I think the only thing—'

Suddenly, the barman was at the table, reaching for the ice bucket. 'Guys, you need to go. Sorry to kick you out, but we've got a weather situation here.'

Toby looked around at the scuffle of customers tipping drinks down their throats, scraping back their chairs, hefting on their heavy waterproofs for the cruel outdoors. It was only just past five o'clock, but a sham of a night had settled in, black and scornful, behind the rain.

'We'd better go.' He pushed the remains of his drink to the middle of the table, and rose to kit himself out against the vile storm.

Becka remained, the muscles of her jaw clenching and unclenching. Persistent, the barman leaned in and picked up the Prosecco bottle and glasses.

'Come on, I'm afraid drinking time's over. There's a severe flood warning and the village has been advised to evacuate. The river will be hitting high tide in the next hour.'

Toby held Becka's coat out as, dazed and speechless, she stood and wriggled her arms in without further protest. They followed the rest of the banished customers onto the main road beside the hurling body of water where it swilled and lapped around their ankles. Stunned with the drink and the cold, they held on to their hoods and paddled gingerly along the path.

'Fuck, I didn't realise it was this bad.' Toby switched on his phone torch and grabbed Becka's arm, and they sloshed through the freezing water, through the darkness, into the battering onslaught of wind and rain towards their accommodation, unable to differentiate between the road and the edge of the pavement.

'Get off me.' Becka shook his hand away.

'I'm just trying to help you.'

'Fuck off with your help.'

Toby winced at her words. His heart and his coat were sodden, cumbersome. How was he to deal with this toxic combination of disasters?

'So when you said you were working nights, you were with *her*, weren't you?' She bellowed out her question that the storm was trying to quell, stumbling and shivering behind Toby. 'Well, you're going to regret this. You are so going to regret it.'

'Shut up and concentrate on getting through this water. It's bloody dangerous, I'm not kidding.' A wave surged and crashed against their calves, knocking them off guard.

'You've been fucking lying to me for weeks, haven't you? And what's Charlotte going to think of you? Her own dad, with that bitch.' She screamed the words out between chattering teeth, getting no answers, no response from Toby, until finally they were back at their cottage, bursting through the door to an inch of water all over the floor and the lights flickering menacingly.

'Tell me! Stop being such a coward and answer my fucking questions.' Becka's anger was renewed with the warmth of the kitchen.

'Just leave it for now. We've got to get out.' Toby threw the door key down onto the table. 'We need to pack our stuff and get away. Just shove it in bags as quick as you can, and I'll go and bring the car to the front door.'

'How can you drive? You're drunk.'

Toby mentally totted up his trips to the bar. Five full pints. And then another, the remains of which he had left behind in the pub. So nearly six. 'Well, what have you had?'

'You know what I've had.'

'It's probably best if you drive,' he said to Becka.

'Oh, so it's OK if I get pulled up and breathalysed then? It's OK for me to lose *my* licence?'

Fuck, what were they supposed to do? The water was visibly rising around their feet as they stood and argued. If they didn't do something they would be caught in the tide of the river.

'Let's just grab our stuff and go.'

Within minutes, bags were crammed with their clothes and toiletries, and, inadvertently leaving behind the smoked salmon and bagels in the fridge that had been meant for the next morning's breakfast, they waded out to the car.

'What a complete fiasco.' Toby threw their gear into the boot and passed the keys to Becka.

'Are you talking about this trip or our marriage?' Becka slammed the driver's door and pulled the seat belt across.

'Can we just get on the road, please? I know I've messed up and we've got stuff to deal with – we will talk, we *will*, at home – but at the moment we have to focus on making it out of here alive.' Toby realised how precarious their current situation was. What if the car ended up in the river? What if, what if...?

There was a devil on his shoulder, whispering into his ear, reminding him of Magdalena's sarcasm last week: *Make sure Becka doesn't trip and fall in the water. That would be a terrible shame...*

The engine started and Becka reversed carefully out of the space. With the windscreen wipers slapping frantically at the rain, she edged onto the main road that ran beside the river. The water trammelled the car to a careful crawl, and Toby felt the power of it under his feet as it pounded the underside of the footwell.

'Slow down.' Toby sat forward in his seat, one defensive hand on the dashboard, as Becka gripped the steering wheel like a clamp.

The windscreen wipers thrashed uselessly at the torrent of water outside. It was impossible to see more than a few metres in front of them.

Suddenly a slew of water bombarded them from the side.

The car lurched and lifted and Becka screamed. Then, with a brief splutter, the engine died.

Toby realised that the car had been dragged off the road and was wedged on the grass bank. Another swell would sweep it straight into the river. Outside, water swirled past treacherously, churning into the footwell.

He turned to look out of the back window, at the tide of the river down the road, overspilling, chasing, running towards them like a huge black demon.

There were only seconds left…

FORTY-TWO

TOBY

It had all happened so fast. He could hardly believe it.

But then he found himself soaked and breathless, clawing at a wall, horror pummelling in his chest and rising up from his stomach, forcing him to bend over and grip his thighs as he vomited into the gushing water.

Suddenly, there was someone beside him, pulling at his coat sleeve.

'Mate, come on, you need to get out of this. The tide's rising.' A bearded bloke togged up in hardcore waterproofs dragged him along the length of the building, round to a side street, then another parking area, where the slight incline of the road meant they could get out of the water.

'It's under. The car. It's taken the car. Under. It went down.' Toby stuttered the words. He knew that he made no sense: a combination of the shock, the cold and the alcohol had taken him into a surreal dystopian world.

On the forecourt of a disused petrol station there was a pack of people hauling sandbags off the back of a truck. A car engine was running and a large dinghy was being inflated beside it. A man with a megaphone was giving instructions on taking people to seek refuge in a local community centre. Someone was unpacking life jackets from a battered Land Rover.

Toby stood, dazed, letting the rain pelt him, until a woman with a large flask of soup came and offered him a polystyrene cup half full of watery chicken broth.

'Have you come to help?' she asked. 'I think they probably need more volunteers to distribute the sandbags.'

'My car,' he said. 'It went in the river.' He pointed in a vague direction.

'Oh God, no,' the woman replied. 'Have you reported it? Although... hang on, they've arrived finally. You're probably best speaking to them.'

A fire engine pulled into the area, followed by a shrieking police car.

'My wife was in it,' Toby said to the woman, but she had already turned her back, was already pouring out soup for the fireman that was grimacing and jumping down from the truck into the heinous downpour.

There was a military operation going on around him with a babble of phone calls, instructions to emergency services and the distribution of equipment. Toby stood, soaked and shivering, replaying that final moment in his mind.

What should he do?

What *could* he do?

He splashed down the side street again to see the place where the car had gone under, until he heard people shouting at him to get out, to come away from the rising river.

There were firemen with heavy-duty torches and ropes wound around their shoulders kicking through the water towards him, and he stepped back as they ran past, followed by two blokes in life jackets carrying the dinghy.

'Couple in a car have gone in,' one of them said to Toby. 'Keep yourself out of the way.'

Then they were gone, sloshing into the depth of water to

float the boat and search out survivors. Toby returned to the centre of activity, to find that another fire engine had turned up and another dinghy was ready to go.

Toby collared one of the policemen. 'Do I need to give a statement or something?'

'What for?'

'My wife was in a car that got swept away.'

'They've just gone out to look for the car. Best thing you can do is go and wait under that canopy. I think someone has hot drinks somewhere.'

'But I'm OK. I got out. They told me it was a couple, but it's not. It's just her.' Toby realised that he was slurring his words again.

The policeman put a hand on his shoulder. 'Leave them to it, they know what they're doing. Look, go and have a seat in the back of our patrol car. Warm you up a bit.'

Toby sat in the police vehicle with more of the tepid soup. Reality was somewhere miles away. He remembered Charlotte, but it was as if she belonged in a different universe: he couldn't connect to the thought of her. His head felt like it was full of concrete. The car was warm and stuffy, with steamy windows, and as Toby's chills subsided he felt himself dozing into semi-consciousness as rain continued to drum on the roof.

Suddenly, outside, the activity ramped up. An ambulance screamed onto the busy forecourt. There was shouting, people running with blankets, torch beams flashing around, and the barking of a dog. Toby opened the door of the patrol vehicle.

'What's going on?' he said to the man who was still unloading sandbags.

'Sounds like they've recovered someone from the car that went in.'

More sirens, more blue lights.

Another ambulance.

Vehicles blocking the road. Spotlights being rigged up.

Stretchers being wheeled down towards the water, getting drenched in the process.

Toby's legs could hardly hold him up as he saw the edge of a dinghy, watched a body being lifted onto a stretcher, heard a shout and the words, '*Oh my Christ, the poor woman,*' being shouted into the storm.

He threw up again, beside the rear wheel of the police car, and remembered his last meal with Becka. The platter of chicken wings and dips and wedges. The Prosecco to celebrate their twenty years together. The confession that he made just before they left the pub. How he didn't love her any more.

Because he loved Magdalena. He'd not known up until this point how it all might work out, how he could possibly afford to leave the family home, and what to do about Charlotte, because he hadn't been able to see a way of doing it.

But now...

He looked at the stretcher being wheeled up to the ambulance, the body on it covered head to toe.

Here was his answer.

FORTY-THREE

TOBY

Sometimes, though, things aren't what they seem.

Toby went and huddled under the old petrol station canopy, and rang Magdalena. Told her what had happened with the flood and the car and Becka.

'Shit. Really?' Her voice was restrained. 'Shit. I know we had a bit of banter about getting rid of her, but still... You've done it?'

Toby was still stuttering. It was the shock. 'It wasn't me! It wasn't really deliberate. Well, not at all. The car. Well, the water, the flooded river. It just came out of nowhere.'

'So, *you're* OK then?'

'Well, yes.' It sounded dodgy, didn't it? It seemed suspicious that he was alive and Becka had drowned. He didn't want Magdalena to think that he had *murdered* Becka, that he was a man who was capable of murder. Because even though he didn't love or want Becka any more, and he had joked with Magdalena about pushing her into the river, he wouldn't really have chosen this outcome.

Or... would he?

'Do you need me to come and get you or something?'

The thought of being in Magdalena's car, out of the rain, out of the way of all this emergency commotion, with her holding him and telling him that it wasn't his fault: his eyes welled up and he felt small and vulnerable.

'Yes. Please, yes. But I don't know if I have to speak to the police or go with them to give a statement. Let me find out. I'll ring you later.'

'Keep your chin up. It's all going to work out fine.'

He smiled weakly and agreed, tucking his phone back into his coat. It could all work out very well indeed for both of them, for the future of their relationship. He couldn't have planned it any better. A suitable send-off, an acceptable period of mourning, a claim to the insurance company, and he would have a tidy sum of money and a mortgage-free house to introduce Magdalena into. No custody or maintenance battles: Charlotte would get a stepmother and they would all live happily ever after.

* * *

At the back of one of the ambulances the stretcher had been loaded in, and a paramedic was talking to one of the policemen. Toby made his way towards them.

But then the doors were quickly slammed shut and the paramedic went to get in the passenger side. The engine was started and pulled respectfully onto the road. No sirens. No blue lights. The emergency was over.

'Hang on,' Toby said, breaking into a half-run. Shouldn't he have been informed about where her body was being taken, about what he needed to do? Surely there were procedures, things to do with death certificates, forms to fill in?

'Can I have a word?' Toby called to the policeman who seemed to have become embroiled in some extended hubbub further down the side street.

The policeman put a hand up to keep him at bay, as another team of firemen dragged the second dinghy around the corner. Then, yet another stretcher was wheeled from the other waiting ambulance, there was more shouting, more splashing from the urgent booted feet down the road, and Toby watched in horror as another person was lifted out and attended to.

'Still breathing!'

The dramatic news spread through the emergency workers and the volunteers, back to Toby.

Fuck. What was going on? Another person pulled out of the water? What if the previous one in the ambulance *hadn't* been Becka? What if this was her and she was still alive?

Toby pushed his way through the water, through the gathering of people. He had to see. He had to know.

'Please, folks, keep out of the way. We have a job to do here.' The policeman shepherded Toby and the volunteer with the soup flask away from the stretcher.

'I need to know if it's my wife,' Toby shouted, pushing back against him.

'It's not your wife. It's an elderly gentleman. So, please, move along.'

'Did she go in the other ambulance? I need to know where they have taken her.'

The policeman kept his calm, kept them moving along the street. 'Sir, the lady in the other ambulance was this gentleman's wife. Their car got washed off the road.'

'What?' Toby wiped a hand over his drenched and dripping face. His whole body was soaked down to his underwear. It was like being stuck in a nightmare; he didn't understand what was going on around him. They had been searching for Becka, hadn't they? 'My wife, Becka, was in a car that went into the river. A Honda Civic. Have you found it? Have you found *her*?'

The policeman looked confused. He took Toby back to his

car where they sat while Toby gave a statement. The policeman got on his radio to the people involved in the search.

'Silver Honda with a forty-year-old female in, swept away... when?'

'About an hour ago. Maybe longer.' Toby couldn't remember.

'We're on it. So sorry about that, mate. I really can't apologise enough. Mixed messages earlier. We've had reports of at least five cars pulled into the river tonight, and apart from the old couple earlier, thankfully no one in them. It's been a mad evening.'

So Becka was missing. Surely, though, the way the car had tipped and gulped the river in, the speed of it submerging, the ferociousness of the tide, the temperature of the water: everything pointed to Becka being drowned.

Toby couldn't see how she could possibly make it out alive.

* * *

He waited for hours. In the back of the police vehicle. Out, under the canopy. Traipsing down the side street to glimpse the terrifying expanse of water that had claimed so many cars.

The rain stopped around midnight, the storm finally blowing itself out to the east. Then there was a kerfuffle in the early hours when one of the dinghies returned, and Toby held his breath, not quite knowing what to wish for. But it wasn't Becka. It was the lifeless body of the red setter dog that had been in the car with the old couple.

Toby closed his eyes and exhaled. Took his phone out to update Magdalena again.

FORTY-FOUR

TOBY

By the time dawn broke – a wishy-washy thin light with a tease
of blue – the water had receded a little as the tide had gone out.
The fire engines had moved down to the main road where wet
and weary workers were doing something with pumps and
hoses.

Toby felt spaced-out, light-headed, as if he had taken drugs.
His feet were damp and spongy. The morning brought a
different landscape to the one he had seen all weekend, and he
stared out at the edge of the riverbank, to where he could see at
least three car roofs bulging out of the muddy water as a family
of ducks swam past. Everything was bizarre. Apocalyptic
almost.

He'd had to speak to Charlotte, and Becka's mother,
Maureen, during the night, letting them know about the
ongoing situation. Frantic with worry, they had both been
messaging constantly, and Toby's nerves were frazzled with
having to keep them – and Magdalena – informed. All he
wanted was to get into a hot shower and go to bed. He was fed
up of drinking lukewarm tea, and the woman with the fucking
soup...

He rubbed his eyes to try and keep himself alert. Maybe he should go home. Wait for news there...

'Hey!' A different policeman held his hand up to get Toby's attention. He was talking into the device attached to his shoulder as he approached. 'Bit of news.'

'OK.' Toby's head pounded. Any news, good or bad: he just wanted it said out loud. He was desperate to get away from all this watery limbo land.

'Your car's been found. Washed up over a mile away upriver and caught on the bend. The tide must have dragged it. They're saying the passenger door was partly open, but no sign of your wife.'

'OK. So where...?'

The policeman gripped a hand onto Toby's shoulder. 'Search and rescue are still out there. It's not great news, but it's not the worst news.'

Exhaustion was painted onto Toby's face. He didn't know how much longer he'd be able to keep on his legs.

'You don't need to be here,' the policeman told him. 'Can we contact someone to pick you up? Or give you a lift somewhere? Are you local?'

'No, not local.' Toby took his phone out. 'I've got someone who can collect me. I'd hang around but...'

'You must be shattered. Go and get your head down. There's nothing you can do here, and we'll keep you posted on any developments.'

* * *

An hour later, Magdalena pulled up outside the pub where Becka and Toby had been drinking only a day earlier.

'You look absolutely knackered,' she told Toby as he climbed into the car.

His physical appearance wasn't the only problem. He stank horrendously, of damp and sweat and emotional fatigue.

They travelled in near-silence to Toby's house, to where Maureen – having a spare key in case of emergencies – waited with Charlotte. Magdalena dropped him off near the end of the road and left quickly. It wasn't the right moment for her to meet his daughter. The enormity of the situation was too much for everyone to comprehend, and they all needed their own shock spaces.

Charlotte received the news with defiance, resolutely believing that her mother would have survived, dragged out along the riverbank somewhere or taken in by kind strangers who had no means to contact them. Maureen was not so hopeful, her face and gait slumped with defeat as she made endless cups of tea that were left to go cold. Toby didn't know what to think: after a solid five hours' sleep, he woke with a juxtaposed blanket of guilt and relief and exhilaration wrapped around him.

Mid-afternoon brought news to Toby that a size six woman's ankle boot had been found in the water close to where the car had entered the river. Toby identified the photograph that was sent over: yes, it was Becka's, it was one of the pair she had been wearing that night.

By the next evening the search and rescue operation had been called off. It had got to the point where there was virtually no hope of finding Becka alive. Divers had checked the area around where the car had gone in, and up to and beyond where the car had been found. The most logical explanation was that she had been washed north by the tide, possibly even as far as the Humber Estuary and into the North Sea.

Maureen cried and decided that it was the right time for her to go back home.

'You never think that you'll be burying your own child,' she said, packing her slippers into a carrier bag.

Toby didn't like to mention that there was no actual body to bury. He closed the curtains and sat with Charlotte huddled around him while the television played a programme counting down the best music videos of the 1980s.

'I need to go out and stock up on essentials,' Toby said to Charlotte, who was under her duvet on the sofa.

It was four days since he had returned from the weekend break without Becka. So much had happened in that time, had impacted on their lives, even though it felt like the clock had stopped. Insurance claims needed to be made: for retrieving their car from the water; for their damaged belongings; for Becka's mobile phone.

'Why didn't you save her?' Charlotte asked accusingly.

'Darling, it was a split-second decision. I only just got out in time and I thought your mum was right behind me. I didn't expect the car to be swept away so quickly.' Toby had been expecting questions and accusations. He had prepared himself.

'You could have held on to her, pulled her out. Not just left her there to drown.' The pain in her voice brought tears to Toby's eyes.

'I tried to get back to her. You don't know how much I tried. I did everything I possibly could, believe me.'

Charlotte glared at him. The depth, the examination contained in her stare. He had to look away.

Magdalena met up with him in the supermarket café.

'How are you doing?' she asked carefully.

'Yeah, not bad. It just feels so weird. But hopeful, you know? The acting is taking its toll though. I ought to get an Oscar.'

'What about Charlotte? How is she taking it all?'

Toby shrugged. 'Just how I expected. She's grieving, angry, thinking that I could have done more to stop it happening. It will take a while for her to settle.'

'Strange, isn't it?' said Magdalena. 'How it all happened.'

'Don't you start on me as well. It was an accident. I was drunk and only just managed to get myself out of the way.'

'Sorry.' Magdalena held her hands up to him. 'That's not what I meant. I mean – I know it sounds harsh to say it – but it could all work out good for us.'

'It could.' Toby smiled and let his body relax. The future was waiting for them. 'Just think, six months' time, how it will be.'

'Six months' time.' Magdalena nodded her head. 'I can't wait.'

FORTY-FIVE

BECKA

I'm in bed but I don't want to open my eyes. The blackness feels safe. I can hide behind my eyelids and pretend that I'm asleep while I think, while I try to understand everything that happened earlier: Grace with the photograph, telling me that I have a daughter who has been looking for me. Freddie catching me as I passed out from shock, as Grace scuttled away into the sudden burst of rain. Did Grace still have the picture or was it left behind for Freddie to see?

He carried me up to bed and tucked me in. It's likely that he will still be here, watching over me, waiting for me to wake up so that he can trick me with some kind of excuse.

There are things that make more sense now. Dreams of the blue-eyed baby, the girl with the plaits, the gut feeling that I got when I heard someone shout '*Mum!*'

I am already a mother.

I have a daughter.

My own flesh and blood; my own child. The thought that she exists makes me want to cry. I can't do that, though. I have to be strong, I have to work out what on earth is going on. Because, suddenly, being here feels very dangerous.

Why would Freddie not want me to know that I have a daughter? Why? After all the recent discussions we've had about babies.

It must be that he's not her father.

But even so: lots of stepfamilies exist harmoniously without lies and deception. There must be something more sinister to it all. What else? I think about the recent discovery of the fake wedding photograph and how that fits into the situation...

And then it hits me. It's obvious. I can't believe I've been so bloody stupid all this time.

Freddie is not my husband.

He has abducted me.

I trusted him when he took me home from hospital. I came here and found a wardrobe full of clothes that were supposedly mine, yet they didn't fit me properly and looked as if they were new. Even the ones I retrieved from the bin bag in the cupboard seemed wrong, somehow.

Yet he had photographs of me. But they were pictures from when we were much, much younger; he never showed me anything recent, anything from the past ten years.

He pretended that we'd had a life together, that we'd been married for seventeen years before my accident. He filled me in on my history: my parents, my childhood. How does he know so much about me? Although... what if it's not true? What if everything that I have believed has been lies?

And then there's the death of Magdalena. How does she fit into all this? Did I really kill her? Or has Freddie been lying about that too, just to keep me here?

Nothing makes sense.

If I have been abducted, then where did I come from? I have a daughter somewhere else – do I have other family? Another husband?

I have so many questions in my head but I can't ask Freddie. What do I do?

Who can I ask?
Who can I *trust*?

* * *

I hear Freddie moving quietly around the bedroom, opening and shutting drawers, tugging the curtains across. Then he's in the en suite, pottering, rearranging toiletries, rinsing out the bath.

It's a struggle to keep my eyelids closed: they quiver, desperate to spring open. My foot itches but I cannot move; I need to remain in this fake sleep for my own safety.

The door to the en suite closes softly. Then I feel Freddie's shadow over me, watching me, his breath sweeping my eyelashes. A warm hand on my forehead as he strokes my hair, waiting for me to wake up.

The way that he cares for me has become terrifying. It's no longer love: it's a deadly obsession.

I cannot give myself away. Not yet, because I don't know what to do, or how to resolve this. He needs to think that I am still compliant, unsuspecting, happy to be his wife. I need to think. I need to find someone who will help me.

Then I remember.

The notes in my underwear drawer. The telephone number that is urging me to respond, to get in touch with her. That is who I need to help me.

My daughter.

FORTY-SIX

MAGDALENA

We had reached that point in our dating where we had to tell his daughter, Charlotte. Trying to maintain a level of secrecy had become unsustainable, and Toby and I were both sure that she suspected we were involved in a full-blown relationship due to the amount of time I was spending in the house. Although Toby had intended to have a grieving period of at least six months for the sake of family decency, by mid-April it was obvious that everything needed to be brought into the open.

Charlotte was fifteen years old and trapped in a phase that saw her unpredictable behaviour escalate over the most tenuous things: the consistency of gravy; the wrong sort of fabric conditioner purchased from the supermarket; curtains not being opened in a certain way; adverts for life insurance on television. Toby was undoubtedly struggling with her but her anger was understandable; the grief and puberty combination didn't make for a good cocktail. These outbursts were largely stifled in my presence though, and instead I became a recipient of the silent treatment.

I took a gift for her, a set of different flavoured lip balms, with a sparkly bow wrapped around the box.

'That's so thoughtful,' said Toby, when I presented it over the table.

He had chosen a family friendly pub for us to have a meal – nothing posh – that had plenty of vegetarian options, as Charlotte had recently declared her meat-free status.

I took off my jacket and put it on the back of the chair. 'It feels like spring is upon us now, doesn't it? It's a lot warmer out there than it was two weeks ago.'

Charlotte glanced towards the gift. No small talk, no grateful thanks. Her lips were firmly sealed.

'Anyone want a drink?' I asked in a falsely jolly voice, but Toby and Charlotte already had glasses of Coke in front of them. I reached into my bag for my purse, to go and get myself a drink, but Toby gestured for me to sit down with them instead.

'Charlotte, we have something to tell you,' he said with a brief hand flourish towards me.

'What?' she said, tearing her eyes away from her phone for at least half a second.

I decided that it wasn't my place to tell her. Toby had probably practised a speech. The gift box loitered unopened between us.

Toby looked expectantly at me and rolled his eyes before reaching over to pinch the corner of Charlotte's phone between his finger and thumb.

'Charlotte. Phone? Remember?'

This was some kind of code for her to turn over the device and lay it beside her glass. She blinked and folded her arms. It was obvious that I had ruined her afternoon.

'Shall we choose the food first?' Toby smiled and dished out the menus.

In a phoney show of solidarity, I made the same menu choice as Charlotte – creamy broccoli pasta – instantly regretting my decision as soon as the food was delivered and I saw Toby's lamb shank with redcurrant jus. We had already wasted a lot of time discussing what were supposedly the best Netflix offerings of the past month, and so I picked up my cutlery and signalled with an expression of eyebrows to Toby that he ought to be reaching the tricky subject of our relationship.

It somehow felt as if this was a formal interview for the job of stepmother, even though I had been involved with the family since the tragic incident that had left Toby a widower. For three months, in the guise of a police family liaison officer, which Toby and I had come up with, I had comforted them, made countless cups of tea, and taken offerings of donuts and cakes and hearty casseroles. I had got involved in writing statements for Toby's insurance companies, had liaised with Charlotte's school to beg for project extensions due to extenuating circumstances, had discussed ways with her maternal grandmother that the family could hold a memorial service in the local church. I had mowed the front lawn, cleaned out the fridge, washed the contents of the laundry basket right down to the lingering odd socks at the bottom. I had dealt with a large amount of the day-to-day stuff, ensuring that Toby remembered to pay the credit card bill and sign Charlotte's homework book.

I had hoped that Charlotte would have had some feelings for me by now, some element of gratitude or friendship after I had already spent so much time in her company, comforting and counselling her. In some ways I had already taken on the mother role, particularly with the household chores and all the cooking. She loved my cakes, even though she never admitted it. She liked the way that I folded her T-shirts with the logo outwards and the sleeves in, the same as they were done in TK Maxx, and although she wouldn't have considered mentioning it or saying *thank you*, I could tell by the way she smoothed and placed them in her drawers that I had got it right, even if I hadn't yet got her respect.

'We brought you here to tell you something,' Toby announced to Charlotte.

'OK.' Charlotte didn't look up from her bowl of pasta.

'It's about me and Magdalena.'

There was no reply from Charlotte. The expression on her face didn't change.

'You've probably noticed that Magdalena has spent a lot of time with us over the past months, and that's been a good thing, a really helpful thing after what happened.' Toby left a pause for Charlotte to say something, but again she chose not to. 'And during that time, we've become very close to each other. I don't know if you've noticed?' Toby fiddled to prise the meat from its bone with his inadequate cutlery, and I felt compelled to speak at that point, because Toby was talking to her as if she was an eight-year-old, and I had already spotted the early signs – flared nostrils, clenched jaw – that she wasn't happy.

'Charlotte, me and your dad have fallen in love. You might think that it shouldn't have happened so soon after your mum's death, but we've all had to muddle along, and during that process we've found that we enjoy being in each other's company. It's just one of those things that we can't control, and obviously we were worried about what you would think, but we intend to absolutely do our best for you, for us all to be a family. I'm not trying to replace your mother, but I would appreciate you giving me a chance to make your dad happy again after what he's been through.'

Toby had finally stripped the lamb away and smiled admiringly at my speech before spearing a chunk onto his fork. He waited for Charlotte to react, but she continued to dig and dissect her meal without meeting anyone's eyes.

I would have left it for a while so that she could have some time to think, but Toby was straight onto her, nudging for a response.

'Just think of it as good news,' he said to her. 'We wanted to get it all out in the open with you so you didn't think we were hiding anything. And you like Magdalena, don't you? You're going to get on like a house on fire, aren't you?'

I watched her turn her head away from him to look over her shoulder, at a family eating near the bar: father, mother, two children in their early teens. She stared and chewed on her lip and I almost thought of pointing out that they could be a step-family too. Who could tell whether parents were biological or not? After all, they could have seen *us* and thought we were just an average mum and dad with teenage child out for a meal.

I touched her gently on the arm. 'Are you OK, Charlotte?'

She turned back towards us and her eyes were brimming. She shrugged and pushed her bowl away without a word. I ate a couple more forkfuls before doing the same.

I didn't have children of my own. There was no medical reason; but it had never seemed the right time. And I didn't particularly warm to babies. All that hassle, with sleepless nights and dreadful nappies and not being able to put yourself first. Someone had once said to me that it would be perfect if I found myself a ready-made family well past the baby stage that I could just step into. It was a way of having it all.

And she was absolutely right. I knew that it wouldn't be easy with Charlotte, but I was prepared to work at it, and it was still early days. Toby thought that by Christmas everything would be much better. He suggested we all go on a cruise or a winter sun package at October half term, so that Charlotte would feel as if most of the year's adversities were behind her and good times were on their way. We had a number of options to look through and it would be a positive thing for the three of us to get round the laptop together to choose and plan a family holiday.

* * *

'That went reasonably well, don't you think?' Toby said afterwards, when we were back home and Charlotte was holed safely in her bedroom with phone and wi-fi.

'I suppose we got away without it all turning into a scene or an argument.'

'She's a teenager. That's what they're like anyway, regardless of what sort of news you're breaking to them.'

'I know, but still, it must have been difficult. And she's bound to have some apprehension about how the new arrangement will work.'

We opened a bottle of wine and talked about the proposed holiday, talked about treating Charlotte to a bedroom makeover, perhaps with new furniture, like one of those dressing tables that have a light-up mirror.

'Do you think there's anything to worry about?' Toby said suddenly. A fretful ridge deepened between his eyes. 'I don't just mean Charlotte. But, you know, about *everything*?'

'Like what?' I said lightly, but I knew what he was thinking. It was the unspoken thing that waited in the corner of the room and watched us while we tore breathlessly at each other's bodies; it was the subject of a phone call from an unknown number; it was the unfamiliar car across the road; the Facebook request from a stranger with no mutual friends; the feeling of being watched in a busy pub.

It was the fear that her body still hadn't been found yet.

It was the fear that she was somewhere out there, watching, waiting.

It was the fear that she wasn't dead after all.

FORTY-SEVEN

MAGDALENA

The way that Charlotte looked at me sometimes. It jolted me, made my heart stop. She was so much like her mother had been around that age. The first sight of her took me right back to those times with Becka, with Freddie, and the way we all thought we were so cool and invincible.

But those icy blue eyes, though. It was like she could see right through me.

I tried my hardest with her: well, hadn't I always, right from day one?

The day that she caught me there, in the house, with her father. Early February it must have been, around three weeks after the river incident. It wasn't as if we were in bed or anything, but just sitting comfortably in the kitchen with a cuppa on the table and a plate of extra gooey chocolate brownies that I had made and brought with me: simply doing that was enough to summon her dad into the living room. I listened behind the door as she asked him a string of questions.

'Who's she?'

'What's she doing here?'

'Why is she sitting there looking normal?'

'How long does she need to be here for?'

'Why is she dressed wrong?'

Toby had his work cut out trying to think quickly of a logical reason for my presence. He told her that my name was Mags and that I was a Family Liaison Officer. I didn't need to wear a uniform and I was just talking through the procedure for a missing person. I would be supporting the family by communicating information about the case and giving advice. I would be around for as long as it was necessary during the investigation and this might mean sometimes being there overnight.

I thought the 'overnight' bit was daring, but Charlotte initially accepted her father's explanation. It didn't prevent her from keeping me at arm's length, though, and she continued to treat me as if I were invisible.

Toby told me about the theories that she kept testing on him: 'Surely the police would have found her other boot. If they looked for it, then it might give more clues to where she might be'; 'Someone with a boat might have rescued her and taken her to another part of the country'; 'She might have climbed out of the river but run away for a while because she was fed up with her home life.'

He tried to be gentle with her, but he couldn't let her keep speculating because it would give her false hope. Charlotte was a teenager that had a life to continue, exams to revise for, friends to have fun with. A missing mother couldn't carry on disrupting her daughter's existence for longer than necessary.

'Charlotte, sweetheart, we have to be realistic here. Every day that passes means it is less likely that she will be found alive. It has been over three weeks now. I saw the car with her inside go into the water and I'm the one that has to deal with those horrible memories. Her bag with her phone and bank cards was also in the car, so she has no access to money and no way of communicating with anyone. The problem with that river is that it is a massive body of tidal water. Which basically means that your mum could be anywhere, even washed out to sea. I know it's a hard thing to hear, but the longer this goes on, we do have to think about preparing for the worst-case scenario.'

For the first fortnight Charlotte refused to leave the house, but was then persuaded by her father to resume her school life. Reluctantly, and only by being taxied by her father, she went back to her studies. Exams loomed and she needed to work hard.

So, I partially moved in with them. Bit by bit, I transferred my belongings from the tiny studio flat that had been my home since my major fall out with Freddie. A travelling acquaintance had let me unofficially take over the rental of their damp, poky rooms for up to two months, and my time would soon be up. I used the cupboards and drawers in Toby's spare room to hang my clothes and stash my meagre accumulation of possessions. I texted Freddie to arrange to pick up my remaining belongings, but he replied that there was nothing left: he had taken everything to the tip. Furious, I rang to give him a piece of my mind but he threatened to tell the police everything if I ever contacted him again or returned to his house. Then he immediately blocked me.

He had cut me off completely. My business links were broken, my emergency refuge no longer available, our friendship dead and buried.

There was no going back now.

Four months after her mother's disappearance, it finally felt like we were getting somewhere, Charlotte and me. After some persuasion from her father, she reluctantly agreed to let me take her shopping one Saturday, and I helped her to choose new jeans, trainers, some tops and T-shirts and a trendy little rucksack bag. We went together for coffee and cookies where I tried my hardest to prise out information about school, about her friends. I felt positive that I had been upgraded from the silent treatment to the monosyllabic phase. People in the shops looked at us assuming she was my daughter, I'm sure of it, and I noticed in myself a lightness, a new type of joy that I could only think of as pride. And during the day out, her mother didn't get mentioned once.

Getting her to talk and come out of her shell, though, had its disadvantages. Only two weeks later, she came in from school and, while holding a tumbler under the running cold tap, asked quietly where my badge was.

'Badge?'

'You work for the police, don't you? I thought all police force employees had to wear a badge.'

I had to think quickly. 'Oh shit, have I forgotten to put it on again?' I tapped myself around the neck where the lanyard should have been.

'You *never* wear one though.'

'I do, I always do. Sometimes it's tucked under my jumper because it can be so annoying at times. Accidentally going in my dinner. I'm forever getting gravy on it!' A high-pitched laugh made me seem hysterical, and I felt a flush redden my cheeks. 'It's a good job you reminded me: I'll have to put it on before I go to that meeting at the station later.'

I pretended to go and look for it upstairs, but when I returned to the kitchen she was still there, watching. I made a show of rummaging through the contents of my handbag on the table. 'No. I must have left it in my desk drawer at work.'

'But don't you need to swipe things with your badge to get in and out of places?'

'Yes, but... Don't worry, there will be someone on reception who can buzz me through to the incident rooms.' Fuck, where did that come from? Incident rooms? I was getting too deep into all this mess.

She didn't make eye contact, but I noticed the tiny shake of her head before she allowed the topic to lapse and finally retired to her room.

Panicked, I locked myself into the downstairs toilet with my laptop, and after much googling and acquainting myself with Photoshop, created my own Family Liaison Officer badge using my passport photograph. I ordered a lanyard and plastic holder on next day delivery and breathed a sigh of relief, flushing the toilet behind me.

FORTY-EIGHT

MAGDALENA

So I had to wear a bloody fake badge and pretend to go to work.

'This is not what I signed up for,' I told Toby. 'Your *quick thinking* meant that I'm constantly tripping myself up with lies.'

'Look, just keep at it for a few more weeks, then we can pretend that you've packed your job in and left the police force. Change of career or something.'

I grudgingly agreed, and a façade was created over dinner of mentioning how I was fed up with work and wanted to set up a business. Toby joined in, saying that I should do baking as a profession. We fed each other lines in order to foreshadow the writing of my resignation, and Charlotte remained silent at the table.

Eating and listening, eating and watching. It seemed like my posturing was forever under her surveillance.

Over the next fortnight I made an extra effort with Charlotte, cooking her favourite food, and trying to make time to ask her about school and what she wanted from the future. I encouraged her to bring her friends around; I encouraged her to go out and have fun. She did neither.

Sometimes, out of the blue, she would ask random questions

about me, and so I would tell her about my time in Liverpool or Manchester and the music scene there and the restaurants that I had worked in. Most of the time, though, she would hide away in her bedroom with the comfort of her laptop.

'You have such lovely long hair,' I remarked to her one evening as she emerged from the shower. 'How about I plait it for you?'

She looked at me as if my intentions were despicable and disappeared into her room without even bothering to reply or make an excuse. I looked towards Toby, hoping that he had noticed how badly his daughter had treated me, but he just shrugged and said, 'I think she might have grown out of plaits now.'

Wounded, I went upstairs and quietly opened Charlotte's bedroom, intending to instigate some kind of heart-to-heart.

She had earphones in and didn't hear me. I leaned into the doorway and watched her for a few seconds, tapping away on her laptop. Homework, I assumed.

Although I made no sound, no movement, she suddenly turned and our eyes met. She snapped her laptop shut, broke our gaze and yanked out her EarPods.

'Are you OK, Charlotte?' I asked softly.

'Yes, I'm fine.' She examined her thumb, ripping a shred of skin away and squeezing until a drop of blood appeared.

'It might actually be nice if we both made the effort to get on,' I said.

She twitched her nostrils and bent to suck the blood from her thumb.

'What do you think?' I took a deep breath into my lungs. How difficult did this have to be?

But there was no response.

'You spend a lot of time in here on that computer, don't you?'

She shrugged warily.

I walked towards her. 'What are you doing?'

'It's just my project, that's all.' She hung her body defensively over the closed laptop.

'Can I see?'

She shook her head and gripped onto the device as if I were about to rip it from her.

'Surely you don't mind me taking a quick look if it's just a school thing you're doing?' I rested my hand on the desk, and Charlotte recoiled visibly.

'You'll be able to see when it's finished.' Her words were rushed and mumbled, and I noticed a swift redness spreading across the bridge of her nose.

I moved my hand away from the desk and onto her shoulder for a couple of seconds. Her rigidity didn't let up. 'I just worry that you might accidentally end up on dodgy websites or something.'

Silence. She was such hard work. If she were my *actual* daughter, I would have forced her to let me examine her search history there and then.

'Anyway,' I said, 'you need to cut down on the screen time. For your own good.'

Unable to think of anything else to say that would illicit a meaningful response, I left the room and pulled the door closed behind me, knowing that as soon as I was downstairs she'd be back on that bloody machine, immersed in whatever it was that she was up to.

FORTY-NINE

BECKA

I hear the gentle pad of Freddie's footsteps as he goes downstairs to his office. The tapping of a keyboard and the click of a mouse. The opening of drawers.

Finally, I can open my eyes. Nothing has changed in the room, but it is dark outside now. The clock radio shows that it is half past nine. The door is open and, as quietly as I can, I get up and creep out to the landing. From there I can see Freddie sitting at his desk. I tiptoe back to retrieve the notes from my underwear drawer.

Charlotte. My daughter.

I stare at the phone number – the same one that is written on each piece of paper – and repeat it in my head over and over until it is imprinted on my memory, until I can hide the notes again.

Now I am ready.

In the en suite I wash my face with cold water. The noise of the running tap alerts Freddie, for he is here in the doorway within seconds, an anxious stance painted all over him. I turn and smile, reaching for the towel.

'Everything OK?' I ask. I will prove that I can act as well as he can.

He takes a step backwards. 'I thought you were...'

'I think I had a funny turn earlier. Just felt a bit faint, and don't know what came over me. Did you have to carry me up here?'

'Yes.' He gives me a careful look.

'Any chance of a cuppa? I feel so dehydrated. Maybe that's what happened earlier.'

'Yes. Of course.' Freddie moves into the bedroom cautiously. 'Shall I bring it up here for you?'

'No, I'll come down.' I force my voice to be light and cheery, giving no hint of all the things that are whirring in my mind.

I follow him downstairs, assessing everything I see on the way. My coat and shoes on the stand in the hall; the landline telephone on the desk in Freddie's office; the hook where the front door keys should be but aren't.

While I hear him getting mugs out of the cupboard I silently go and try the door. As I expected, it is locked.

'Becka?'

I jolt back. He's standing in the entrance to the kitchen, watching me.

'You should eat something. You must be starving.' He indicates that we go and sit at the kitchen island, where he has set out plates and cutlery and the bowl of salad that I started to prepare before Grace's visit.

Refusing wouldn't be helpful, I tell myself, so I settle onto a stool and watch as Freddie shares out the food.

'What did the woman want earlier?' he says casually.

'Woman?'

'Her from across the road.'

'I don't remember.' I scratch my head and dig a furrow between my brows. 'Did she bring a parcel? I thought it was strange that she came to the back of the house. And then, the next thing... I felt really faint.'

There is distrust in his eyes. Did he hear our conversation? Did he *see* the photograph?

'No. She didn't bring a parcel. It seemed like she said something that upset you.'

'I can't remember what she said.' I pick up my fork. 'Anyway, I *am* starving. Can we eat now?'

The conversation about Grace's visit is over. I look across to the bi-fold doors and see that the key is missing from the lock.

He watches me. He follows my eyes as I check out the exit and the place on the worktop where the knife block is missing. I flash a smile but he doesn't respond. His neck muscles are ribbed and tense, like mine.

My mind and body aches. I am trapped in this deceit, exhausted from pretending that I am Freddie's wife, pretending that nothing is wrong. He is with me for the rest of the evening, not leaving my side as we watch television. I am revulsed that my hand is nestled in his, that his body is pressed up against mine, but I cannot move away for fear of alerting him to my new knowledge. He tries to chat about the house move again, even suggesting that we could leave here before completion day: we could hire a cottage in the area so that we can feel the vibe of our new community before we move in permanently.

'No,' I say, horrified. 'I have so much more packing up to do.'

But he tells me not to worry about that: he can get the removal firm to finish off here. Get cleaners in to give it a once-over before the keys are passed over to the new owners. My nerves are stretched like elastic but I am too drained to argue.

* * *

That night, he holds on to me tightly in bed, his face at the back of my neck.

'I love you so much,' he whispers. 'You know that I'll never let you go, don't you?'

I cannot speak. I wait for him to lapse into semi-consciousness so that I can slip out of his arms and skulk downstairs to use the telephone, but every time I move, thinking his breathing and the weight of his body indicates a suitable depth of sleep, he clutches onto me again.

'I need the toilet,' I hiss, at one point during my restless night, and he reaches over to switch on the lamp, his eyes following me through into the en suite, where there is no escape.

He has me cornered.

While somewhere out in the world – maybe not too far away – my daughter, Charlotte, is waiting for me. She is thinking of me just like I am of her.

The anticipation is tortuous.

Soon, though.

He can't hold on to me forever.

Not now.

FIFTY

MAGDALENA

Charlotte must have taken some notice of our little talk. Perhaps she did respect me enough to listen and follow my advice, albeit to a limited extent. So instead of hiding away in her room she took to going off out for walks. I offered to accompany her, but she disappeared at odd times and without forewarning.

Initially, breaking her away from her laptop appeared to be a positive thing, until the arguments with Toby started, about the frequency and length of time that she spent out of the house. She missed meals. She ventured out in the most beastly thundery showers without an umbrella or waterproof garment. She returned home too many times after dusk, after Toby had bombarded her with frantic texts she couldn't be bothered to respond to. I wondered if she was meeting someone – a secret boyfriend or girlfriend – but no other evidence materialised to support that suspicion. When quizzed on her whereabouts, she claimed to be walking 'nowhere in particular, just around'. Said she liked the exercise and being out in the fresh air as it gave her space to think.

Toby concluded it was probably to do with working through her grief.

Me, on the other hand... Well, I thought she was up to something.

I discreetly followed her on one occasion and saw her standing at a bus stop that serviced a number of routes in and out of town. Later, she denied that she had been there. I checked her bedroom while she was at school but the task revealed nothing. No diaries, no notes, no bus tickets in the bin. Her laptop was locked with a password. Her phone was never left unattended.

Then, after a couple of weeks, things seemed more settled. The atmosphere in the house returned to a pleasant level of conviviality, and comfortable curt chitchat resumed at the dinner table. Back in the safety of her room, Charlotte became engrossed in her laptop, on her 'project' once more, telling Toby that it was connected with her business studies course, and the journeying away from home for hours on end diminished. We all went out as a family again, to the cinema, to an alpaca centre, for pub meals, where she was quiet and polite. It looked like she had turned a corner and the grieving process was coming to a natural conclusion.

I relaxed into the role of stepmother.

It was on a Sunday lunchtime, after I had made the effort to cook a proper roast lamb dinner with minted peas and dauphinoise potatoes, that things took an unsettling turn. A lighthearted conversation about the placement of the sofa in the living room – I had recently changed the furniture around in an effort to put my own stamp on the place – went off on a tangent, and Toby was led unwittingly into a discussion about the limited space in Charlotte's room. She needed a decent-sized desk for her studies; she needed a bigger chest of drawers; she needed a double bed as it was what all her friends had – only little kids had single beds and hers was just *embarrassing*. As she reached for another helping of balsamic-glazed carrots, I flashed a look at Toby and made the brave suggestion that we could look for another property. Move house. Get something that would better suit us all.

'Yes!' Charlotte's eyes lit up quite unexpectedly; and I bloomed with that little maternal pull inside my chest.

'You'd be happy to go somewhere else? Leave this old place behind?' Toby picked at a sliver of meat in his teeth.

'Well, for the right sort of house, obviously. Something in a nice area.'

'Little Miss Snobby,' Toby joked. 'And what area would be the right sort for you?'

Charlotte put down her cutlery and leaned into the table, absorbed in the topic. 'Well. The area out of town – you know if you carry on along from the sports centre? – and there's the road out towards the Peak District with some big posh houses?'

Toby was tilted on an elbow, nodding along to her directions. I felt a vague queasiness. Maybe too much lamb fat.

'Well, one of the avenues off that road – I think it might be Hardwick something, but I can't properly remember' – Charlotte glanced at me, at my discomfort – 'that's a nice area. I've walked down there a few times. There's a really distinctive house with a massive monkey puzzle tree in the front garden.'

I pushed my chair backwards and ran upstairs to the bathroom just in time to vomit the contents of my guts into the toilet. Sweating, panting, teary-eyed and holding back my hair, I pressed the flush as Toby appeared behind me.

'Are you all right?'

I forced a little laugh. 'Too much rich food, probably.'

He put a comforting hand in the space between my shoulder blades as I splashed my face with water. 'Well, me and Charlotte definitely enjoyed the lunch. It was a lovely meal.'

I returned downstairs, to Charlotte sitting at the table, her plate cleared.

'Thank you for a delicious dinner,' she said. A scanty voice, and the usual lack of eye contact.

I began to stack the plates. Toby reached over to take the slice of lamb I had left uneaten, and Charlotte slipped away to resume her project in her bedroom.

FIFTY-ONE

BECKA

I am trapped.

Despite trying my hardest to keep everything the same, it feels like everything has changed. Like playing a game of chess, I carefully have to consider every move, every vocalisation, every expression before making it, and it seems like he is doing the same. The tension is electric.

What does he know that *I* know? What does he know that I *don't* know? If I get away and go to the police what will they do? Help me, or charge me with Magdalena's murder?

He follows me around as we have artificial conversations about colour schemes for the new bedroom. We pack bags and boxes, discussing their contents and where the best place will be for them in our new house. I spend an inordinate amount of time near the windows, trying to catch sight of Grace, but, unusually, the net curtain is motionless and there is no sign of her.

In the afternoon there is a brief glimmer of hope when I hear Freddie in his office talking on the phone to the insurance company about our upcoming change of address. I grab a pair of shoes from upstairs and rush to make a sneaky getaway through the bi-fold doors: Freddie had been out only minutes earlier to empty the bin so I assume – hope – they are still open. With my heart thudding in my throat I tug the handle but the doors are stuck fast. Locked. The key is nowhere in sight.

My escape plan derailed, I return dejectedly to the pretence of clearing cupboards.

* * *

In the evening we open a bottle of wine and settle into the sofa. Freddie looks distracted, so I suggest a film we could watch, and caress his knee lovingly as I snuggle up to him. He smiles at me and puts his hand over mine.

'Hey,' I say casually, 'I think the garage might need locking before it gets dark. I'm sure I saw the doors open earlier.'

'Did you? I must have forgotten to shut them when I got the boxes out.'

'It's OK, I'll go and sort it.' I begin to stand, but Freddie is on his feet before me.

'You stay here. I'll do it.'

He's gone. But it's all right because I have a plan B.

I grab the landline handset from the living room and run upstairs to the bathroom. As I shut the door I notice – oh shit, what is going on now? – the little privacy bolt has been removed. Apart from Freddie's office, for which I never had a key, it was the only lockable room in the house. Why has he done this?

But I don't have time to speculate. I need to hurry. My fingers jab the number that is imprinted in my memory.

Quick, quick, please answer...

On the third ring I hear her voice. Youthful. Quizzical. 'Hello?'

And then I remember her. Pictures flood my brain and my heart and I see her as a baby, a chubby toddler, a smiling little girl with pigtails and missing teeth, a confident, pretty teenager in a school uniform.

'Charlotte,' I say, my eyes bulging with unshed tears. 'It's me. I'm your mum.'

There's an agonising wait of about two seconds before the squeals and breathless sobs of, 'Mum? Really? Is it really you after all this time?'

'Yes, it is.' My voice cracks and withheld emotions burn at my throat. 'I'm here, but...'

'Mum! Yes, yes! Oh gosh, it's your voice, it really is! Where are you?' she gasps. 'Oh Mum... you didn't drown. But... but what happened? Why have you left us?'

'I lost my memory. I couldn't remember you. I didn't know where I lived or anything. Someone tried to help me but then it all—'

'You have to come back. When are you coming home? Are you trapped somewhere?'

I hear the sound of Freddie slamming the garage door. I have to go; I can't let him hear this conversation.

'Quick, tell me the address,' I say. 'Where you are? Where I should be.'

'Birchwood Lane,' she tells me. 'Number fourteen. Please. Don't go yet...'

'Don't call me back, it's too dangerous. Trust me, I'll come to you. Soon.'

'I love you, Mum,' Charlotte says as she hangs up.

My tears fall then, and I hold myself over the sink, trying to hold back the sobs, hearing Freddie lock the door again as he returns from outside.

'Becka?' he shouts from the hall. 'Where are you? Are you OK?'

I take a deep breath and hide the telephone in my make-up bag. It will only hold charge for about a day, but it might be enough. I splash my face with water, gather a handful of tissues and make my way downstairs.

'Got something in my eye,' I explain to him. 'I needed the mirror to get an eyelash out.'

He watches as I dab my face. Watches as I go back to the living room to sink onto the sofa.

He sits again beside me and takes my hand, strokes his thumb over my new wedding ring.

'I love you, Becka,' he says. 'I always have and I always will. I feel like we're Romeo and Juliet. Remember the pact that we made all those years ago? We said that we would always be together, whatever happened. And we vowed that if anything ever threatened our relationship, we would *die* together. We actually recited words, remember? A love ritual. We were so insistent that we'd never be parted, ever.'

I look at him with alarm. 'A pact? You mean... you'd kill us both?'

'Yes, it's what we agreed,' he states. 'I'd do it. Absolutely. Obviously, it's all hypothetical at the moment, but I do have a plan for that eventuality.'

'A plan?' Horror drains the blood from my face.

He nods. 'I have a plan, and I have the means.'

My hand is limp as he lifts it to his lips to kiss my fingers.

FIFTY-TWO

MAGDALENA

Charlotte was too quiet again. Sneaking about listening to conversations, looking guilty every time I popped my head around her door, sending signals that she wanted me out of the way. Most people wouldn't notice what she was up to – and Toby certainly didn't – but I had got the measure of her. Little things, like putting the candles back on the mantelpiece after I had moved them to the windowsill during my room reorganisation. Tipping my favourite, expensive, foundation down the bathroom sink: I noticed a smear of it on the white porcelain and then found the tube almost empty. Swapping my bookmark to the wrong page. Eating chocolate that I had earmarked for a particular recipe. Throwing away my favourite black silk knickers: they had been missing for two weeks and despite me searching everywhere, I knew in my heart that it was *her* who had taken them.

I knew I had to stop trying so hard for Charlotte to like me. I had to stop obsessing over these small acts of defiance and make the most of my relationship with Toby, and eventually everything would settle.

A short period of medication might help, I decided, and I

rummaged through one of the boxes that I had brought along from my temporary lodgings, to find a batch of sleeping pills and antidepressants that I had been prescribed a couple of years ago. For a few days or so I self-medicated and chilled out, went for walks, tried out some new baking techniques. I tried to be myself rather than a sycophantic stepmother, not giving a toss if she'd had a good day at school. Toby sensed a change in my disposition, and, thinking that I was comfortable in my new family life and role, relaxed into a contentment of his own. But it was as if his guard was down, when one evening Charlotte asked him why there were no Cokes in the fridge, and Toby instinctively replied with, 'There should be some left. Your mother only went shopping on Thursday.'

I tensed and held my breath but Charlotte said nothing. She left the room graciously, and I mentioned the mistake to Toby, who apologised sincerely and abundantly before going to do the same with Charlotte.

'It's OK, she didn't get upset,' Toby told me afterwards. 'She's a good girl.'

But the next day I found my favourite china mug in the sink, its handle snapped off.

Three days later, Toby had popped out during the evening to fill the car with petrol and pick up a carton of milk. I was treating myself to a leisurely bubble bath, with my iPod softly playing chillout tunes in the background. Charlotte was in her room next door, avidly working on her 'project'.

Next thing, I heard her voice. Then squeals, excited shrieks of delight; the sounds of someone receiving good news.

I turned down my music and sat up in the steamy, fragrant froth, trying to tune my ears in to her conversation. Something about *fourteen*. Something like *don't go*. Then it sounded like *I love you*.

The conversation seemed to end there, being replaced by a bout of uncharacteristic yelling and *yes yes yes yes I knew it*. Feet stamping on the floor hysterically, like she was at some teenage concert.

Boom, boom, boom. The house rocked with the volume of the music she had just put on. I pulled out the plug and reached for the towel.

Charlotte was singing her heart out to the music, '*Rah rah, ah-ah-ah...*'

I dried my face and wrapped the towel around myself, stomped out of the bathroom and pushed open the door to her room.

'Turn. It. Down!' I shouted above the music.

Shocked, she scrambled across her bed to shut the lid of her laptop.

I pushed my way to her dressing table to pick up the speaker and find the *off* button.

Peace at last.

'There was no need for that,' I told her, tossing the speaker back onto the dressing table.

'Sorry,' whispered Charlotte meekly. She had both her hands on her laptop, as if I might go and wrench it out of her grasp.

'What was all that about?' I asked.

Charlotte shrugged and gazed at her fingers. 'Sorry.'

I fixed a glare onto her for a few seconds, even though she didn't see it, then turned and left the room.

FIFTY-THREE

BECKA

We are at the stage where life is a cat-and-mouse game. Freddie is watching me for my next move, and I am watching him for his. Neither of us is sure what the other knows. Neither of us trust each other.

Somehow I have to get away, get back to Charlotte. But how?

I cannot ring the police. Because I still don't know what happened with Magdalena or what my involvement was. But not only that: there is a gun in the filing cabinet, and Freddie has stated that he has a plan to kill us both if our relationship is put at risk. At which point would his crime of passion be executed? When police arrive at the door? If I try to run away?

And what might happen if Charlotte returns to the house?

Oh God, it doesn't bear thinking about.

But I have to escape. I can think of nothing else, yet I cannot think how to do it. All the doors and windows are locked, and Freddie follows me everywhere: the bedroom, the kitchen, the bathroom. Every small task is observed by him. I cannot clean my teeth or apply moisturiser without his presence overshadowing me.

He asks me why the landline phone is missing from the living room.

'I don't know,' I reply as casually as I can. 'I don't recall seeing it for a few days. Maybe it's in your office.'

He doesn't speak, but gives a tiny, terrifying shake of the head and I feel guilt colour my face.

The contents of the house are virtually packed. Cupboards are bare; the freezer is defrosted; the fridge is almost empty. Our lack of food surely means that we cannot remain confined here. Everything is in boxes: clothes, toiletries, crockery and cutlery, small appliances. All the pictures have been removed from the walls. My art from the hallway has been bubble-wrapped and packed along with the huge wedding canvas. I take cloths and glass cleaner upstairs to shine the bedroom window, and Freddie follows me up with the vacuum cleaner.

My attention is caught by odd activities across the road. There is a car in the drive and Grace's front door is wide open. I spray the window and begin to wipe as I watch the goings-on. Freddie's eyes are on me as he pushes the Dyson around.

Then, there's someone out on the front step. It's the woman I met before, Grace's niece, Jessica. She's speaking on her phone while the dog trots around on the front lawn. They go inside without closing the door, and then a few minutes later they come out again. She walks to the end of the drive looking up and down the street.

I swap to another cloth and continue polishing. Freddie unravels the vacuum attachments and cleans around the edge of the skirting boards.

Next thing, there's an ambulance pulling into the drive.

'What's so interesting out there?' he says, noticing that I have stopped my task to watch the events unfold.

'There's an ambulance over at Grace's house.'

He switches off the vacuum cleaner and comes to take a look.

'I hope she's all right,' I say. 'Maybe I should pop over.'

Freddie suddenly grips the top of my arm, harsh fingers digging into my flesh. 'You won't be popping anywhere. And this window is done now. You can go and clean the doors to the balcony instead.'

'What?'

'Now. Move away from the window *now*.' Freddie hisses the instruction between gritted teeth.

Dazed, I timidly pick up the cloths and the spray, and retreat to the other side of the room. Freddie remains silently watching the action for a while before pulling the front curtains shut.

Something feels very wrong.

Freddie unplugs the vacuum cleaner and winds up the cable.

'Come on,' he says.

'I just need to finish this door. It's still smeary.'

'Leave it.' His tone of voice leaves me no option but to gather my cloths and spray and follow him downstairs, where he goes into the living room and closes the curtains there, too.

I'm scared. Something – the sight of the ambulance? – seems to have triggered him into a new phase of hostile behaviour.

'Freddie, what's happening?'

He snatches the cleaning stuff out of my hands and tosses it onto the coffee table.

'We need to leave. Everything is done here now. Basically, we're just waiting to sign the last few papers and then we're sorted. But there's no point being here any more, so we might as well just get on the road now.'

'Why the urgency?' I ask.

'I didn't want this to happen to us.' He looks around, manically, wild-eyed, at the boxes stacked up in the room. 'Everything was going so well with the house move and the talk about babies – and we had a lovely time, didn't we? – and celebrating the wedding rings just like it was all real—'

'What do you mean, *like it was real*?'

'We should have left sooner. It's just... oh fuck, it's all going to go wrong.' He goes to the curtains and pries them a finger-width apart, just enough to peek through.

'Tell me what's going on, Freddie, please. Are you in trouble? Are *we* in trouble? Is this something to do with my accident?' I need to know everything, but I need to be careful. He is unpredictable, no longer behaving as if he is my devoted husband, and I have no idea what he is capable of.

Suddenly, he jumps back as his mobile phone starts to ring. He takes it from his pocket and looks at the number.

'Hi,' he says, answering it. 'Is everything OK?'

Maybe this is an opportunity for me to get away. I edge out of the room into the hall.

'That's great news,' says Freddie.

He's seen me. He's following again.

I put a foot onto the stairs and point up towards the bathroom.

Toilet, I mouth silently to him.

'Yes, that would be perfect. We could come in and sort it this afternoon.'

I scramble upstairs while his mind is engaged with his call. In the cupboard under the sink I rummage in my make-up bag for the landline phone. It's still there, and I pull it out with a spark of hope in my heart, even though I'm not entirely sure who to call.

Shit. Shit shit shit. The battery is dead. I jab at the unresponsive buttons as my spirit collapses.

My only solution now is to escape.

Footsteps on the stairs. I ram the phone into the cupboard and shut the door.

'What are you doing?' says Freddie at the door.

I wave my make-up bag at him. 'If we're leaving I need to take this with me.'

'Come on,' he says. 'We have to go now. That was the solicitor on the phone. I need to go in and sign a document before completion can take place.'

Suddenly, there's the sound of a siren outside. I go to the bedroom window and peek through the curtains to see a police car arrive, to park up behind the ambulance.

Then Freddie is behind me, dragging me away.

'What?' I say as we stumble back to fall onto the bed.

'Get away from the fucking window. Now!'

'What? What's happened?'

He holds on to me so that I can't get up. 'We can't let them see us.'

'Tell me what's happened. Please, Freddie.'

He groans and puts his hands over his face. 'Oh God, it's the woman across the road. Last night...'

'Grace? What happened last night?'

'I killed her.'

FIFTY-FOUR

BECKA

We sit there, stunned, listening to the last wails of the police siren outside. Then the mattress creaks beneath us, even though neither of us has moved for minutes.

'Why?' I ask, finally.

He tosses his shoulders sullenly, and his expression caves in for a moment.

'Why?'

He wraps his arms around my rigid body and buries his face in my neck. I feel tearless sobs ripple through his chest.

My heart is hammering, making me breathless. 'Tell me what happened.'

He sits up, not meeting my gaze. 'She was telling you stuff – putting stupid things into your mind – and I just had to stop her. She was spoiling everything: I could see our amazing life just crumbling away. It felt like we were so close to achieving what we should have done years ago. So I went over to her house after I put you to bed last night. She was wearing a scarf – like a silk thing around her neck – and I tried talking to her, but she wasn't having any of it. She got angry with me and I just... I just ended up getting hold of the scarf with both hands and pulling. Not intending... you know, I didn't mean to do anything bad. But then she was on the floor, and I'm sure that when I left her she was still breathing. I didn't *plan* to kill her; I just wanted to talk to her and tell her not to come spreading ideas and lies...' He looks at his hands that rest lifelessly on his knees.

I can't believe what I am hearing. Lovely old Grace, who had come to tell me about my daughter, is dead. Strangled by the hands that have caressed my body every night for the last four months.

'Don't hate me,' whimpers Freddie. 'I didn't mean to do it. I only did it for us, for you. So that you would always love me. Because I can't live without you now.'

My body is trembling. I can't think straight. Pictures fill my mind of Grace's throat being crushed as Freddie tightens her scarf. Outside, I can hear voices, urgent and instructional. The slam of vehicle doors. Boots on the drive. Jessica's dog, yapping playfully.

'That poor lady. I can't believe it,' I say.

And then I'm thinking, *will he kill me too, now that I know about it?* And I'm also thinking, *was it really Freddie who killed Magdalena and not me?*

'There's still a chance for us to get away,' says Freddie, as if he knows what I'm thinking. 'When the police leave we should get on the road. I'll withdraw a load of cash and we can just lie low for a while until everything blows over. They probably won't suspect me anyway, I mean, it could have been a burglary gone wrong, anything like that. We always said we would stay together in every eventuality, didn't we? We'd cover our backs and look after each other. And if things go wrong and we get discovered, then there's always our pact.' He mimes a gun to his head, letting his lips make a little *pop*.

I stare, open-mouthed, as he makes plans for us to go on the run, makes plans to kill us if we get caught.

'I'm thinking Scotland. There are loads of places where we

could get like a log cabin or a croft, and just escape from civilisation for a while.' He scratches his head. 'I'm not sure whether to go and sign the stuff at the solicitor's first though. It might look dodgy if I don't turn up.'

He's playing out some imaginary thriller in his mind. Romeo and Juliet. Bonnie and Clyde. Whatever happens, the outcome doesn't look good for me.

I make the decision that the safest thing for now is to go along with him. Pretend that I'm still in love with him, that I want to stay by his side. Give him something to live for, so that we don't have to die together.

'I need to tell you something,' I say to him as he's pacing around the room, constantly checking through the curtains.

'What?' He reels around, expecting bad news.

'I think I'm pregnant.'

He chokes in a lungful of breath and looks at me. His eyes wallow with tears. 'A baby? Just like we wanted? Ours?'

'Yes, obviously ours.'

He sits by my side again, his hand on my belly, his forehead touching my cheek. I can feel the vulnerability oozing from him and know that I should use it.

'Will you be honest with me?'

'I'm always honest with you,' he replies, his eyes shining in a way that now seems totally mad. I can't believe I was ever taken in by him. That I ever trusted him. But I need to know more.

'No, I mean... there are so many things about my accident and my loss of memory that I need to know. It's so confusing. I just think that if we're going to be parents together then we need a proper start. Get everything out in the open.'

His nostrils flare as he considers my request.

'We can't deal with all this chaos, and have a baby, and try to make a life miles away while I'm still in the dark about so many things. Our relationship needs to be solid. Doesn't it?'

Freddie nods reluctantly.

'So tell me then. Whatever has happened in the past, I can handle it, I just need to know. Tell me about *us*.'

'You were seventeen when I met you and I knew you were The One—'

'Stop it, Freddie. I've heard all this before. I want the *real* story about us.'

'It's true,' he protests. 'I have photographs of us together. We were inseparable. You painted that picture of *us*. We said at the time that we would always be together.'

'But something happened, didn't it? Something messed up our plans. We *were* together, but we didn't *stay* together, did we?'

Freddie hangs his head. 'My father died and left this house to me. But my stepmother and stepsister – Mags – were living here and refused to move out. I wanted this place for *us*. Me and you. I was so desperate. So I tried to scare them out with a fire, just a small one, just smoke really. I didn't intend to kill anyone. But it all got out of hand. And my stepmother... she died a few months later.'

Oh God, another death caused by Freddie.

And every excuse is that he did it for me.

Freddie continues. 'Your dad found out about us, about the fire, and he threatened me off. He was a pretty scary bloke. Then he made sure you took up the place you got at university and so you went to Glasgow to do Art. It's what you always wanted to do. But we never saw each other again.'

'So...' I am confused. How did I end up here after my accident? Was it Freddie who *caused* my accident? 'It doesn't make sense. How did we get back together?'

'Well,' says Freddie, 'that was all down to Magdalena.'

FIFTY-FIVE

BECKA

Magdalena.

The name that had instilled so much terror in me over recent times. The missing woman. I thought I had killed her, that she was buried in the back garden under the new turf.

Freddie told me that she was his stepsister. She had been my friend at school, the one who had introduced us. But things had gone wrong between us and she'd held a lifelong grudge against me, so that when she eventually bumped into me again after over twenty years, she felt no guilt in becoming my husband's mistress.

And then they began to plot my death.

'What?' It's like listening to the storyline for an ITV drama. 'What could I possibly have done as a teenager that would make her want me dead all these years later?'

'Well, for a start, you destroyed all her artwork so that she would fail her exam. She blamed you for not being able to get into university.'

'Well... I can see how someone might be angry about that. But to plot someone's death?'

Freddie's face has darkened. 'There was the fire, too. Her mother died because of it.'

'But *you* started the fire, didn't you? Surely the police were involved? Didn't you get charged with arson, with murder? Didn't you go to prison?'

'The police were involved, yes. And I could have been looking at a long prison sentence if I hadn't got away with it. But I think it was probably more to do with *how* I got away with it that pissed Magdalena off to the extent where she absolutely detested you and wanted revenge.'

There's a sinking sensation in the pit of my stomach. I don't understand what he's telling me. He's killed someone and escaped punishment for all this time, hasn't he? Yet Magdalena held a grudge against *me*...

'You rescued me, Becka. Just like how we had our pact, we looked after each other, did everything for each other' – Freddie takes my hand – 'You gave me an alibi. It's how I got away with it. You lied for me.'

I am physically and mentally trapped by him. Bound up with deceit and murder. I try to examine the depths of my missing memory to find something that will refute his claim, but there is only darkness, nothingness.

He peeks through the curtains again. I take in the strength of him, the broadness of his back, the solid muscle. His power against mine.

'So, tell me more about Magdalena,' I say. I am defeated. I need to discover how it has gone from then to now.

'Magdalena stayed here for a while. I took her in about a year and a half ago, when she turned up and needed somewhere to live and work from. I felt like I owed it to her really. Then it was sometime last October when she bumped into you and your... husband—'

'What's his name?'

'Toby.'

I remembered the dreams of me in the car with the water, with screams of *Tony* echoing in my head. Only it wasn't Tony, it was Toby. *My husband.* Was that the man with the coffee that I had recognised and followed in town?

'When Magdalena said that she'd found you... well, you can imagine how happy I was. Just to hear your name again and dream about what you looked like, how it would feel to have you in my arms' – he put a hand to his heart before continuing – 'then it was only a couple of weeks later that she was telling me about meeting up with your husband, how they were seeing each other behind your back and spending nights in cheap hotels. I didn't know what to make of it all or how to feel about it.'

'Did Toby' – it felt unnatural saying his name – 'ever come to this house? Did you meet him?'

'No, I never met him. I'd always had a policy that Magdalena couldn't bring men back here. I was uncomfortable about what was happening because she was still living here, still running her cake business, but on the other side of things my heart was telling me that if your marriage was on the rocks then there could be another chance for *us* to get together, if you and your husband split up. And then...'

'What?'

'Magdalena started joking about getting rid of you. So that she could go and move in with Toby. Marry him. She told me that you and Toby were going for a weekend away to a place by the side of the River Trent, and she had suggested that while you were there Toby could push you into the water and make it look like an accident.'

'She wanted him to kill me?'

'I know. I was horrified, but she just laughed about it and I thought that maybe she was joking and just trying to wind me up. But deep down I knew what she was like; I knew that she'd had a grudge against you for a long time. And although it had only seemed like a quick throwaway comment – most people would probably just say it was banter – I started to feel protective, like I could be your saviour, your angel in disguise.'

'So what did you do? Go to the police?'

'Well. It was difficult. You can see the position I was in,' he said. 'All I could do was monitor the situation because I had no real evidence to take to the police. I didn't know your surname or where you lived. And it wasn't like she left written plans around or anything. Hearsay, assumed threats, that's all it was. So I was basically tiptoeing around the house listening to her phone calls: it's all I could do.'

I waited for more information. Outside, there had been no more sirens. There had been no knocks on our door. Yet.

'So, what happened?'

'She'd been here with me that weekend of your trip away. She was so upset and jealous that you were together, but she was constantly on her phone, getting messages and calls about the awful weather and flood alerts. And then the call came through that your car had been washed away into the river, with you still in it.'

I shivered at Freddie's words.

'Mags was in the kitchen, sitting on a stool with a glass of wine and I stood in the doorway and heard her say something like "shit, so you've done it, she's actually dead?" and I just felt my blood run cold. I literally could have fainted. When she ended the call I asked her what was going on, and she told me that Toby told her you'd been washed away in the river, in your car. And then, at that point, I got so angry, I couldn't stand the sight of her or the thought of what had happened. But I felt helpless, and angry with myself too that I'd not prevented it happening. I told Mags to get out of my house, to pack up and go straight away. She laughed and said "don't be silly", thinking I was messing around, but I went and dragged her off the stool and threw her wine down the sink and told her to fuck right off. I gave her ten minutes to pack up and go. So she put some of her stuff into bags, and I forced her to hand over her house key. We had a blazing row on the doorstep, and I called her a despicable bitch and said she could never come back here again.'

'So, the bin bag full of clothes in the guest room cupboard,' I say then, realising what has happened. 'They weren't mine. They were hers that she left behind, weren't they?'

'I cleared out the room and took everything to the tip. All her belongings: television, bedding, clothes and personal things. She rang me, wanting to come and collect the rest of her stuff, but I told her I'd got rid of it all and that I would contact the police if she ever came back to the house. Thing is though, I'd cocked up, hadn't I? I'd forgotten to empty the utility cupboard with all the baking stuff, and I'd missed that bag in the linen cupboard, so I had to let you think it was yours.'

My skin starts to itch. I realise the cardigan that I am wearing is Magdalena's, not mine. And the underwear...

'Carry on,' I tell Freddie. 'I want to know how you found me.'

'I was desperate for news. I still had some contacts in the police from my time in journalism, so I rang around for information. The river had breached its banks in at least five villages. Roads were closed; properties had been evacuated. There were all sorts of rescue attempts going on through Lincolnshire and Nottinghamshire, and it was a logistical minefield because the lines of communication between the different emergency services were virtually non-existent.

'Then I got onto Google Maps to check out the path of the river and see where the issues were. I still clung onto the hope that you might be alive. I didn't know where you'd gone for your weekend away, so I drove south to one of the villages on my list, but there hadn't been any casualties or cars washed away there. Then I drove up to the next village, where the breach was worse, and someone told me that a woman had been pulled unconscious from the river and taken to hospital.

'I sat in my car and rang around all the hospitals, but obviously they will only give information out to family, so I had to tell them I was looking for my wife. That did the trick. I found out that a forty-year-old woman with hypothermia and head injuries had been pulled from a river and taken to Mansfield.

'I just knew it was you as soon as they told me. Like an instinct. And I had to go to you, even if your husband was there. Because if he had been there I'd have given him hell. I'd have let him know that he didn't deserve such an amazing person for a wife.'

'So, *did* you confront him?' I ask, imagining a fight between two grown men in a hospital café.

Freddie shakes his head. 'He wasn't there. He just never came. I waited there for days and days, sleeping overnight in that back-breaking chair in the waiting room. Spending hours by your bedside while you were in a coma. No one else came. No one else enquired about you. All the staff assumed *I* was your husband.'

It is sickening and bewildering to learn that someone can be abducted so easily. All it takes is a case of amnesia and family apathy, and anyone can walk out with a new partner.

And there was me, injured and vulnerable, believing everything he told me, leaving hospital to make a life with him, to have sex with him every night thinking that he was my husband...

'I basically struck lucky while the emergency services made the wrong assumptions,' says Freddie. 'There had been news reports which made me realise that the police had been looking for you in the wrong place, because your car was found miles away from where you were rescued. You must have been swept down river on the incoming tide, which then took your car further upstream when it went out again. You were so fortunate to survive. Other people whose vehicles got washed into the river at the same time had died. But because the river spanned a number of counties and police authorities, each village had been dealt with on a local level. So the other people that got rescued at the place where you got washed away were taken to Doncaster.

'Basically, the geography was what confused the issue,' says Freddie. 'People were still searching for you when you were actually in a hospital bed miles away, not knowing your own name.'

'Why didn't you tell them who I was? Instead of pretending that I was your wife?'

Freddie holds up his hands and smiles. 'It was as if it was all meant to happen. I'd been searching for you for years. You were the only one for me and I'd loved you for ever. And there you were: alive. Completely convinced that we were a couple after I showed you the pictures of us together when we were young. You even remembered our song, didn't you? So all I had to do was update your records at reception with your new address and my surname, and me as next of kin. It's easy enough to fake documents. And you were so happy with me, weren't you?'

'You tricked me! You took me away from my own family. You let them think I was dead.'

'No, no,' says Freddie. 'Your husband didn't want you enough to ring around the hospitals like I did. He wanted you dead, so that he could be with Magdalena.'

'So, Magdalena... when *did* I kill her? Because if she was still alive when I got swept away in the river...'

Freddie's face drops.

'*Did* she die? Or is she still alive? Did you tell me that I killed her just so that you could trap me here and pretend you were protecting me?'

Freddie takes a step towards me. I see the flare of his

nostrils, I see the anger coming off him like steam. He knows that I have found him out.

'Don't ask me any more questions,' he says through gritted teeth.

I bite my tongue and back my body up to the wall. I so want to mention Charlotte, my daughter. I want to ask him about her, about why he thought it was acceptable to take me away from her and let her believe that her mother had died, let *me* believe that I am childless.

But I can't. I have to be careful what I say because the wrong thing could trigger him, and I know that he is prepared to kill us both.

Every muscle in my body is rigid as I wait for him to say something else.

His jaw juts, and he stands and walks to the window, to peek through the curtains again.

'What's going to happen with our baby?' I ask. I need to remind him that we have good reasons to stay alive.

Freddie turns around. 'Our baby will be with us, whatever happens. We have to stay together. Nothing will separate any of us.'

'But surely, we can't just go on the run. I will need to have check-ups and things. Medical intervention.'

'You worry too much.' Freddie shakes his head. 'We'll cross that bridge later, if we have to.'

But it's good to keep up the baby talk, it focuses his mind on keeping me safe rather than killing me. He comes back over to the bed to sit and press his hand against my belly again.

'How long do we have to stay here?' I ask, because something needs to happen. We can't just remain trapped here for much longer.

The police are still across the road. There are people going into the house wearing white forensic suits; a constable standing guard outside; tape across the driveway.

'We'll go as soon as they do,' says Freddie.

'I'm starving,' I tell him, and he goes down to the kitchen to see what is left in the fridge.

He returns with a slice of Emmental cheese and three cherry tomatoes.

'That's all there is.' He passes the food to me and checks the window again.

* * *

By three o'clock it seems like things are winding down. The ambulance has gone and the forensic people have taken off their white suits on the front lawn and left the scene. I begin to get hopeful, thinking that we can get in the car and I will have more of an opportunity to escape once I am out of here.

I lie on the bed and stare at the ceiling. Freddie strokes my hair. He has already covered my belly with kisses, murmuring 'little bubby' over and over into the soft flesh. There is nothing I can do but allow it now that my life depends on being amenable to him.

Suddenly, there's a knocking at the door.

Freddie sits straight up, a finger across his lips. He reaches his other hand across to me and holds it against my mouth. There's no point trying to scream. For all we know, it could be the Amazon delivery man, and I wouldn't want to risk my life on him.

We wait.

Another knock, slightly louder.

Oh God, what if it's Charlotte? Please, don't let Freddie check through the curtains... But whoever it is has no further persistence and within seconds we hear the sound of footsteps retreating up the drive.

Two minutes later, Freddie is back at the window, his eye at the pleat in the curtains.

'It was the police. Probably just a normal door-to-door enquiry,' he says. 'But they've all gone now. Come on, it's time for us to make a dash for it.'

I follow him downstairs, and he goes into his office. At what point will I be able to run, to break free and finally escape him? When he unlocks the door and we go outside to get in the car?

But then I hear the slide of the filing cabinet drawer and know that he's getting the gun.

He comes into the hall and takes the keys out of his pocket.

'Remember our pact,' he warns me. 'We're in this together.'

I hold my hands up. 'Hey, I'm cool. You don't need to worry.'

I pull a smile. I am anything but cool. Tension knots inside me and I feel like throwing up. Something is about to happen but I don't know what and I have no plan. I know he has a gun and that he will use it if he thinks our relationship is threatened. All I can wish for is an opportunity, a few brief seconds where I can run and hide somewhere, knowing that I won't get a bullet in my back. Because my only focus is on getting away from this living lie and finding my daughter again.

He unlocks the door and takes my hand.

FIFTY-SIX

TOBY

The events of that weekend away still haunted him. He googled PTSD symptoms regularly, wondering how he could stop the flashbacks that would surprise him in the most unlikely of situations, bringing on intense bouts of sweating and nausea.

He found himself dashing out of work meetings and having to sit in his car while a fit of trembling subsided. He found himself thrashing around in nightmares in the dark early hours, gasping and struggling for air while Magdalena slept soundly beside him.

Would it always be like this? Were these memories embedded in him, never to dissipate?

'Toby!'

Becka's screams resonated around his head. He would never forget the sound of her voice, the anger and terror in it.

He would never forget what he did.

That night, though... He'd had to do it. Because who knows what *she* would have done to *him*?

He'd been in the car beside Becka as she tried over and over to start the engine. The river had been rising rapidly, the water lifting and pounding at the sills and underside of the vehicle.

She wouldn't listen to him as he advised her to stop pumping the accelerator. She was making everything worse, and all they could do was sit there, terrified, as the water came up through the floor.

He looked behind them at that point and saw the huge wave, the edge of it caught in the glow of the streetlights. They had seconds to spare before it would hit the car.

The fear must have shown in his face, because Becka turned and saw it too. She tried to open the driver's door to jump out, but the force of the water outside held it so that she could only push it a hand's-width.

Then the ice-cold water was rushing in through the gap, filling the car, making them both gasp and scream.

He'd grabbed her arm and pulled her back from the open door as she tried to wrestle him away.

Later, he'd told himself that he'd done it to stop the water coming in. That's all. He hadn't deliberately prevented her from getting out.

She'd screamed and punched him, scratching at his fingers to prise them off her arm. But by then the water was over the seats, up to their waists.

That's when Toby had opened his door, forcing it out with the strength of both his feet.

'Toby! Toby!'

He'd plunged halfway out of the door as Becka was climbing through the water, over the gearstick, behind him.

'No!' She'd seized his hair, his head, and it was as if she wanted to hold him there, to force him back in, under the water. To *kill* him. It really had felt like that.

So he'd lashed out. He'd elbowed her body and her arms to get her away from him. He'd slammed her head down onto the dashboard.

And then he'd stumbled out of the vehicle, dragging his legs through the dark rising water, tripping up the kerb to the far side of the road.

Through the open passenger door, he'd seen her slumped against the dashboard as the ridge of water hit the car, spinning it, filling it, lifting and turning it so that it floated up and off the road to where the edge of the river was.

Oh fuck, had he knocked her unconscious? Had he *killed* her?

He'd watched helplessly as the water surged so quickly that only a head and shoulder space of air was left in the car, as it listed and sailed towards the deeper water.

What could he do?

Frozen with shock, he'd pinned himself up against the wall of a house, knee-deep in the flood. He'd watched as the car was taken, a glint of light on the roof.

And then, with Becka still inside, it was gone.

Beneath the surface.

FIFTY-SEVEN

MAGDALENA

Thursday afternoon. Charlotte came in from school without bothering to say *hello* or *how was your day?* No smiles or pleasantries. I offered her a drink, and she turned it down with the usual shake of the head and 'I'm OK' before heading upstairs.

I followed her up with a pile of freshly washed laundry. There should have been some kind of award for me doing all that, but I was unlikely to receive any word of thanks.

She had just gone into the bathroom, so I put the stack of clean clothing on her bed. Then I noticed something.

On her desk she had left her laptop open. I crept over to it and nudged my finger over the touchpad. Remarkably it sprang to life, and because it had only been abandoned a couple of minutes ago, the password did not need to be entered. But there was nothing open apart from the Google search engine, and the box was blank.

I hesitated, almost feeling guilty. But the shower was gushing next door, so I knew that she wouldn't be back to catch me for a while yet.

I clicked on the search history.

Shit!

What was all this? A project about *me*?

I scrolled down all the searches that contained my name: restaurant websites, baking blogs, old social media accounts, Companies House information about my business and its previous registered address. The list went on and on before other searched pages started to crop up: a Facebook group for missing people; family liaison officer job description; villages along the River Trent; survival guides for flooding; local estate agents. I clicked on the Rightmove page, even though I had a deep suspicion that I would recognise the photograph.

Freddie's house.

An angle that took in the impressive front, the gleaming new windows, the block-paved drive with his car parked up. The monkey puzzle tree. And it was sold. He was moving on.

A black cloud of anxiety squeezed around me.

Although for the past couple of weeks I had suspected that Charlotte was up to something, this suggested a level of research more thorough than I could ever have imagined. What a dark horse she was. Quietly and meekly creeping around the house and around the town, all the while gathering some sort of evidence. What would she do with it? What did she know about me? Had she been to see Freddie; had she spoken to him? How much information would he have passed on to Charlotte? Enough to raise her suspicions so that she might go to the police?

My fingers shook on the laptop keyboard as I clicked out of her search history. The shower had stopped running; she would be back in here any time soon.

But then...

I spotted a piece of paper on the desk that had a phone number scrawled on it.

No, it couldn't be. Fuck, no.

I touched the word above the line of digits in horror and disbelief. No, it couldn't be. It wasn't possible.

Just the one single word.

MUM

FIFTY-EIGHT

BECKA

I am belted into the passenger seat. Freddie has taken my handbag and put it in the boot of the car with the rest of our luggage. He has the gun neatly tucked under his right thigh, within easy reach, as he takes the road around the edge of town. The satnav hasn't been programmed, and I have no idea where we are going. Scotland? Really?

'Do we need to stop at the solicitor's first?' I ask. 'I thought you said we had to sign something for the house.'

He shakes his head. 'We don't have time now. I'll ring them later and put things on hold, and we'll just have to wait it out until everything has blown over. Hopefully we won't lose the house, but we can't risk hanging around here or driving through the town centre.'

My thoughts of getting away during a visit to the solicitor's office are scuppered. And I can't risk doing anything stupid while we are in the car. He's too jumpy. As soon as my hand moves anywhere near the seat belt clip, Freddie's hand moves towards the gun. Freeing myself to open the door and scramble out at a point where the car is moving slowly enough seems impossible. I will just have to bide my time while I gain his confidence.

The traffic is flowing freely and I fix my eyes onto the road, looking for any points where the car might have to slow or stop for a moment, giving an opportunity for escape. But all the traffic lights are green and none of the roundabouts hold us up.

'Let's listen to some music,' I say, reaching to switch on the radio.

Freddie gives me a guarded look and touches the gun again. He is twitchy, wired. A different person from the kind, loving husband that he has been for the last few months.

He would now rather kill me than let me go.

I focus my efforts on keeping him calm, tuning into BBC 6 Music. Freddie pulls a face at the indie track that is playing. The beat doesn't synch with him; he only ever listens to dance music from twenty years ago.

'Let's not bother,' he says, switching off the radio.

We sit in silence for a while, and before long we're on the dual carriageway heading towards Sheffield, the car racing along in the outside lane. I see a flashing patrol vehicle on the opposite side of the road and my spirit becomes hopeful for a second, until I realise that if we are forced to stop by the police then Freddie will probably kill us both.

* * *

We have been on the road for about twenty minutes when suddenly there is the sound of a ping from the dashboard. Freddie hits the steering wheel with the heel of his hand and says, 'Shit! We need petrol.'

This means we need to find a filling station. A place where the car will stop and Freddie will get out. I think of the excuses I could make for going into the shop. A pregnancy test? It's unlikely that they would be sold there. Food? We have hardly eaten all day and the journey could be a long one. I will suggest that I go and buy sandwiches for us.

Two miles further along the road and a petrol station sign is shining, like a beacon. We pull onto the forecourt and Freddie looks around, surveying the pumps, the shop, the other customers. He puts his hand on the gun and transfers it furtively into his pocket.

'Stay in the car,' he orders me as he takes his bank card out of his wallet.

It has a pay-at-the-pump facility which limits my opportunity for escape. Freddie stays with the car. I check out the other stationary vehicles: a white van at pump six, a small Fiat at the first pump near the shop, and a tatty Ford Focus with the rear windows blacked out facing the opposite way beside us. The woman filling up the Focus has smudgy charcoal eyeliner on, and her hair is purple. She's wearing a short black dress that is covered with buckles and zips. She has a tattoo on her neck and three silver rings in her nose. She has attitude. I start to feel tearful – she looks like a person who could save me.

Freddie throws me a final warning look as he gets out of the car. 'Don't do anything stupid.' He taps his pocket.

His back is turned as he attends to the keypad on the pump. Carefully, I unclip my seat belt and quietly slide it back into its housing. I sit forward and pull the catch for the door. Immediately, Freddie turns, and I pop my head out of the car, one foot on the floor.

'Shall I go and get us some sandwiches for the journey?' I say, trying to make my tone genuine and relaxed instead of displaying the fear and panic that storm within me.

'No!' He looks towards the shop, then back at me.

'I could do with using the toilet as well,' I try.

'Get back in the car,' he hisses. 'We'll have another stop further on for food and toilets.'

I retreat back into the passenger seat and pull the door so

that it's almost closed but not clicked shut. Freddie begins to fill up the car with petrol. On the other side of us, the purple-haired woman has finished at the pump and is now in the shop. I scan the vehicles again: the Fiat has driven away and a motor-bike has taken its place, and a silver estate car has just pulled up on the other side of Freddie.

There must be something I can do. I gaze towards the shop windows, searching for the purple-haired woman. She is standing in the queue, holding a pack of biscuits.

Look at me, look at me, I silently urge her, hoping that I can convey my precarious situation with an expression of dread that she will understand and find some way of acting on. But she doesn't turn, doesn't meet my eyes. Her attention is focused on the packet of biscuits as she examines the nutritional values.

Freddie has finished. I hear the pump click off. He shakes the nozzle and puts the cap back on.

Please, please... I look around wildly for some way to escape because my time and opportunity is running out...

'Hey, mate, is this yours?' There's a shout from the guy who has got out of the silver car.

'What?' Freddie turns his back to the driver's door.

Is this my chance?

I push the passenger door open a little and step a foot out again, keeping my sight fixed on Freddie's back.

'There's a credit card on the floor.' The man walks towards Freddie.

Freddie moves to where the man is pointing.

I slide my body out of the door and squat beside the car. The purple-haired woman is leaving the shop. She beeps her key fob and her car indicators flash.

'Have you dropped it? I didn't know if it was yours.'

On the edge of my vision and with the car between us, I see Freddie bend and pick up the credit card. 'No. It's not mine.' He hands it to the man.

I am running out of time.

Move.

Do something.

Quick!

The man reads out the name on the card and still has Freddie's attention as I grab the rear door handle of the Ford Focus beside me. Scrambling inside, I pull the door shut at the same time as the purple-haired woman gets into the driver's seat.

She clips on her seat belt and starts the engine.

'What the fuck?' She jumps as our eyes meet in the rearview mirror.

'Please drive,' I beg her. 'I'm getting away from the man out there. He was going to kill me.'

She looks out at Freddie, wary of my story.

'Please. Don't let him catch me.' I realise there are tears suddenly spilling down my face.

Outside, I see Freddie moving away from the man, turning back towards his car...

'Yeah. He does look like a wanker.' She puts her foot down, and the vehicle screeches out of the petrol station and into the flow of traffic on the dual carriageway.

'Oh my God.' My hands are shaking. My body is shaking. I turn to look out of the rear window and see that Freddie's car is still on the forecourt with a pickup truck trying to manoeuvre around him, blocking his exit.

'Thank you, thank you! Oh my God. You've saved my life.' I sob, and as I touch the purple-haired woman on her shoulder she smiles at me through the mirror.

I've done it!

I'm free.

FIFTY-NINE

MAGDALENA

'Are you two sickening for something?' Toby said as he tucked into the steak pie I had made. He'd got home from work just after seven to find Charlotte in bed with a headache and me so nauseous with anxiety that I couldn't eat anything.

For the past two hours I had been debating whether to tell him about my discovery in Charlotte's bedroom. Her search history.

And the piece of paper with the phone number on it.

Because that was the thing. I realised afterwards that I recognised the number. It was Freddie's landline.

What did it mean?

Was it just Charlotte, deviously playing mind games with me?

Was it that the number gave her access to information from Freddie about her mum?

Or was Becka not dead after all? Oh God, what would happen to me and Toby if it were true? What the fuck would happen?

I couldn't bear to think about it, let alone discuss it with Toby. Surely it couldn't be true, it just wasn't possible. I told myself this over and over as I made pastry for the pie. I didn't believe it and there was no need to start a conversation about it. What would be the point of us panicking over something that Charlotte had probably made up to distress me? It must be some kind of set-up and she wanted me to find the piece of paper; she was taunting me. No, I wouldn't get stressed. I would call her bluff and leave things for now. Carry on as normal.

'It's not like her to get headaches,' Toby said with his mouth full of pie. 'Shame to miss out on this gorgeous food.'

I shrugged my tight shoulders. It was probably just attention-seeking behaviour rather than a genuine migraine.

After he had eaten, I followed Toby as he went upstairs and poked his head round Charlotte's door. 'All right, sweetheart?'

There was no reply. Her eyes were closed. She was probably feigning sleep. I flashed a look towards her desk. The laptop was closed and there was no sign of the paper with the phone number on.

Toby approached her bed and pulled the duvet back a little, placing his hand on her forehead.

'She said she was tired and had a headache,' I explained. 'Although she was fine when she first came home from school. Washed her hair, did some homework.'

Toby bent over and listened to her breathing. He gently shook her shoulder. 'Sweetheart?'

She gave a murmur that was barely audible.

'It's not like her,' Toby told me. 'D'you know if she's been sick?'

'No. No, she's been fine. Teenagers,' I said with a dramatic roll of my eyes. 'You know what they're like.'

We went downstairs and Toby opened a bottle of wine. I lit a candle and put on some soft music. If only it could have just been the two of us. If only. I wasn't sure any more about the benefits of the extended family.

'You just worry about them, don't you?' Toby said. 'You know, viruses, meningitis and all that.'

'Yeah,' I agreed, still feeling the nausea of the afternoon tainting my insides.

But it set me thinking.

Would a life-threatening illness be such a bad thing in the circumstances? If she really was ill and we didn't get her to the hospital in time...

The next day was bright and warm. I let Toby get out of bed first, because I hadn't slept well, and he went downstairs to make coffee. I lingered under the duvet, listening to him clattering around the kitchen, then his footsteps on the stairs. His elbow on the handle of Charlotte's door as he carefully carried three mugs of coffee.

'OK, sweetheart,' I heard him say. Mumble, mumble, something about school that I couldn't catch. 'Yeah, I'm sure that will be fine.'

'How is she this morning?' I asked as Toby set down my coffee on the bedside table.

'Mmm.' He waggled a flattened hand. 'Not tip-top. Says she's feeling groggy. There's a virus going round at the moment and she's probably picked it up at school. I suggested she stay at home today, and she didn't argue. You don't mind her being around, do you?'

'No, of course I don't.' I faked a smile. My stomach churned.

Toby decided to cycle to work as the forecast was good. I got dressed and popped a couple of slices of bread into the toaster to take up for Charlotte and check in on her.

She was asleep when I took the plate up to her room. I shook her shoulder gently.

'Hey, how are you feeling? I brought you some breakfast.'

She opened her eyes and slipped an arm out of the duvet. 'Sorry. I'm not really hungry.'

She'd left half the coffee that Toby had taken up earlier. Her phone was beside the mug, and I noticed the corner of a piece of paper sticking out from underneath it. I knew immediately it was the one I had seen on her desk the previous day. Busily, I made a show of removing the cup and rearranging her phone in order to put the plate of toast down, and the whole fluster of a scene – where she watched me fervently – resulted in me accidentally knocking the offensive note onto the floor.

Suddenly, and despite her supposed illness, she came to life, throwing her upper body over the side of the bed to snatch up the paper.

'What's wrong?' I said as her shoulder bumped my leg on the way up.

'Nothing.'

'Is it a love letter?' I laughed and playfully tried to reach for the note.

There was a brief little tussle then, during which Charlotte actually shrieked and shouted 'No!' before I stood over her, looking down at the number in my hand. At that revolting word:

MUM

'What is this?' My eyes drilled into the brimming ones that couldn't meet mine.

'Nothing.'

'It's a phone number. And it says *Mum*.'

She shrugged as a helpless, fat tear spilled onto her cheek.

'Where did you get this number from? How did you get it? Tell me what all this is about.' I had to get to the truth.

'She rang me.' She sobbed the words out softly.

Fear lodged in my throat; a shiver trickled down my spine. I put my hands out to the wall as my knees started to buckle. Bile rose up into my mouth. 'Don't be silly. We've been through all this before and it's just not possible. Someone is playing tricks on you and it's a scam. It's what happens in cases like this. There are some really horrible people around.'

Charlotte's chin quivered. 'It sounded like her. She said she was going to come back.'

I shook my head and clenched my teeth together as hard as I could. I scrunched up the paper in my fist. Then turned and stumbled from the room.

* * *

Downstairs, anxiety fermented inside me like a knob of yeast. I noticed the racing of my heart, the hollowness of my breaths, the way my skin felt tight and tingly as if it could be popped with a pin. I made the decision to dial the number and find out what was going on. Despite Freddie blocking me on his mobile, it appeared that he had forgotten to do the same with his land-line. The connection was made; it started to ring out; I waited for someone to answer. Would it be him? Would it be her?

After ten rings it went to answerphone. I tried dialling again. And again. There was obviously no one there. I remembered that he had sold his house.

I really didn't know what to make of my conversation with Charlotte about the claim that she had spoken to her mother. It couldn't be true, could it?

Could it?

These mind games of hers were intended to damage my relationship with her father. I told myself that over and over. Mind games. That's all they were. There couldn't possibly be any truth in what she was saying. Unless she was trying to get me to confess to something so that she could go to the police...

Oh God, my head was spinning. I couldn't focus. I couldn't think what to do. I knew what Charlotte wanted me to do: ultimately, she wanted me out of here, away from her father. She was trying to force me out.

But I couldn't bear the thought of leaving Toby.

All these years of flitting around, and I had finally found my soulmate. I couldn't leave him. And in reality, I had nowhere else go; it would mean starting all over again finding a home, a job, a partner. I really didn't want to end up living the same sort of life that my mother had.

I needed to stop Charlotte, so she couldn't carry on with this bizarre research, or go to the police, or damage my relationship with her father. Permanently.

The idea held so much potential. All I required was a recipe.

* * *

I had all the ingredients in front of me. Strawberries, ice cream, vanilla extract, sugar, whipped cream. The house was silent as I took the pills from my pocket and crushed them with a pestle and mortar.

I tipped everything into the blender and whizzed it up. Took the lid off and sniffed. Yes, it smelled delicious. I poured out a glass and took it upstairs.

'Sorry about earlier.' I put on my most apologetic voice and set the milkshake down on her bedside table. The plate of toast was untouched.

Her eyelids opened for a moment, and I reached out and stroked her hair. 'I was just angry that someone would try and trick you into thinking that your mother is still alive. As awful as it is, you have to face the reality that she's not coming back.'

A tear ran over the bridge of her nose and dripped onto her pillow.

'Come on, sit up. I've brought something nice for you.' I jostled her shoulders until she was in a half-sitting position with the pillows behind her, and proffered the glass of milkshake towards her mouth. 'Give this a little try. It's lovely.'

She took a sip and swallowed, and I waited a couple of seconds before pressing the glass to her lips again. Another tiny mouthful and a dribble onto her chin before she pulled a face.

'It tastes a bit funny.'

I put my face in the glass and then touched the liquid to my own lips to demonstrate that everything was fine, but she shook her head and wiped a hand across her mouth.

'I'll drink it later,' she said, adjusting her pillows and sliding down into the bed once more.

'OK.' I smiled and pressed my hand against her cheek. 'You do need to remember to keep your fluids up if you're feeling poorly.'

I went back downstairs, where I scrubbed the cooker clean and vacuumed the living room. Reorganised the kitchen cupboards and disinfected the sink.

Later, I quietly tiptoed upstairs and looked in on Charlotte. She was asleep and an inch of the strawberry milkshake had gone. A positive sign.

* * *

At lunchtime I went again to check the progress of my plan. Charlotte's eyes opened a little as I put my head round the door to tell her that I was going out and would be back later.

'How are you feeling now?' I asked.

'OK. But a bit dizzy.' Her speech was slurred.

'You need to keep drinking,' I told her, nodding at the glass beside her. 'Ring me if you need anything.'

Leaving her to sleep, I took my coat and bag downstairs and stepped outside. Putting the key in the front door, I locked it behind me.

SIXTY

BECKA

'So, where were you heading to?' The woman who saved me is called Jo and she has already told me that she shares her time around rescuing cats and working on her friend's market stall selling CBD oil.

I shake my head. 'I don't know where he was planning on taking me. I need to get to my daughter... and I don't know the way or how I would even do that. I don't have money or a phone—'

'Can you tell me the postcode or the address?'

'It's Birchwood Lane. Number fourteen. Oh, I would be so grateful if you could take me there. And also... Could I use your phone? Please? Do you have a phone?'

Jo fumbles in the handbag on the passenger seat. Pulling it out, she swipes the screen of her phone so that I can make a call, and hands it over before programming the address in the dashboard satnav.

Despite all the manic events of the day, Charlotte's number is still in my head. It rings out, over and over, before going to voicemail. I try one more time, and thank God, she picks up.

'Mum?' she says with a weak voice. 'Help me. Please! I

think Magdalena has spiked my drink. I feel really ill. Come soon. She's gone out but I'm scared what of what she might do when she gets back.'

'What?' I don't know what is happening any more. My life is spinning chaotically, ricocheting around murder and abduction and deception. How have we ended up in this cycle of lawlessness? 'I'm coming as quickly as I can. Charlotte, please just hang on until I get there... No, wait, I'm going to ring the police or ambulance, or...' We're going under a bridge and the signal is lost. I try to call back but there's just a beeping noise and it won't connect.

Jo puts her foot down, recognising the urgency.

I am trying to dial 999 but every time I think I've got through the signal cuts out. I put my hands over my face and muffle a moan of panic with my palms. Not Charlotte, too. How can it be that on the same day both of our lives are in such danger?

'Just try the police again,' says Jo as she breaks the speed limit.

I redial, and finally this time it's ringing properly.

'I need the police and an ambulance because my daughter's in trouble.' My words are garbled, and the call handler asks me to slow down and repeat them. I give out the address and attempt to explain what is happening with Charlotte.

'Can you tell me where you're calling from? Is this the same address where you require assistance?'

The phone drops out of my hand as Jo brakes suddenly to avoid a truck that's swerved into our lane, and I scrabble to retrieve it from the floor. A blank screen confronts me when I pick it up, and I yell the address into it, not knowing if anyone has heard. I jab at the nines but lose the signal again, and I'm tearing at my hair and whimpering in desperation...

'Calm down.' Jo reaches behind to lay a gentle hand on my

knee. 'We'll be there in six minutes. The police will probably be on it anyway – you told them the address, didn't you?'

Yes, I did. I take a long, full breath and lean back into the seat.

Soon, Charlotte. Hang on for me.

SIXTY-ONE

BECKA

We race around some tree-lined avenues as Jo follows the satnav's instructions.

Then, *'You have reached your destination.'*

Where? I'm looking at the house numbers and we're outside number four, but there's a dustbin lorry blocking our way and I can't see where number fourteen is.

'Get out,' shouts Jo. 'Go!'

So, I'm out, slamming the car door and dashing down the road and then it's all coming back to me: I recognise the gardens and the porches and the driveways like I have never been away. The memories are flooding into my head and I know this place: I don't even need to look at the numbers because it's the one with the box hedge and the black gate that I'm fumbling with. The catch seems to be stuck and I'm yanking and lifting and I know deep in my mind that there's a special technique to getting it open, but I'm desperate to get through, so desperate to get to her...

'Charlotte!' I scream up to the bedroom window that I know is hers. I kick the gate again and twist my wrist trying to force the catch. 'Charlotte, I'm here!'

A face appears. Then she's hammering her fists against the glass, yelling to me, but I still can't get through the gate, and then there's a woman behind her and my eyes click with the woman – Magdalena – and I'm filled with the realisation that she is the one, the one with the grudge against me, who is behind all that has happened.

From across the street there is another shout. I turn to see a man on a bicycle – oh my word, it's him, the man that was in my dream: the man that I followed around town that time – Toby – and he looks at me with such an expression of terror that drains all the colour out of his face.

Suddenly, he's on the floor, smacking down onto the concrete with his bike toppling and tangling between his legs, and I can't see what's happening because the dustbin lorry has moved between us, and I am trapped in a surreal rotation of looking up at Charlotte but being unable to get to her and turning to find out what is happening with Toby. My husband.

Five seconds. I'm still shunting my body against the gate. Ten seconds. Magdalena tries to pull Charlotte away from the window. I must get to her before she is harmed. Then, it's like another part of my memory returns and I remember that I have to simultaneously lift and pull the gate back on itself to get it open.

The dustbin lorry rattles away down the road. Jo's car pulls up outside the house, and we both look across to where a pedestrian is on his knees attending to Toby. A woman stands beside them both, on her phone. The bike has been moved. A patch of blood is pooling around Toby's head.

What do I do? Who do I go to first?

There's only one answer. Charlotte. My daughter.

'Toby!' It's an unwitting squeal as the front door opens, and Magdalena pushes past me to run towards his unconscious body.

I lurch into the hallway and then she's there: Charlotte, at the bottom of the stairs, childlike and so huggable in her pyjamas, reaching for me as she collapses into my arms.

We are locked in our embrace as we hear the screech of tyres and then the thud.

More screams.

The slam of car doors.

'What the fuck?' It sounds like Jo's voice shrieking out at the front of the house.

Charlotte's body tenses in my arms. I press my cheek to hers and stroke her hair, inhaling the familiar citrusy smell of her shampoo.

'Stay here, darling,' I tell her. She has to be shielded from whatever carnage is out there, and it's me that is going to protect her because I'm her mother, and I'm back.

I shove the front door shut so that we don't have to see or hear what chaos is happening out there. The shouting, the running, the blaring of horns. All the noise.

All I want to do is be here, holding my girl.

Suddenly, there's a metallic sound, a yank of the gate, the thud of urgent footsteps outside, the shouldering at the door as the handle is forced up and down, up and down.

'Becka! Becka, let me in! I need to talk to you.'

NO!

Please don't let it be him!

Freddie's face is pressed up to the glass panel as he kicks and hammers his fists on the door. 'Becka, please!'

'Leave me alone!' I scream as I pull Charlotte away from the door and into the living room.

'Who is it, Mum?' she whimpers, but utter fear prevents me from answering. This nightmare can't be happening – not again after everything else – and I wrap my arms around Charlotte's head and wedge her into my shoulder, and we cling onto each other, praying that the door is strong enough to keep Freddie away from us.

There's a frantic blare of sirens. A screech of brakes.

Suddenly, a gunshot.

Screams, out on the street.

Screams in here, and me and Charlotte pressing together in terror as the front door is bashed open.

That's it. We're done for.

SIXTY-TWO

BECKA

I dare not open my eyes; I cannot look at him.

He's going to kill us because we made a pact all those years ago. Those stupid words we said to each other in the naivety of young love.

I feel his presence in the room as he closes in.

I wait for the cold gun to touch my head.

Suddenly, there's a firm hand on my shoulder and I wrap my arms rigidly around Charlotte, because even though he will shoot me, I can't let anything happen to her. I have to take the bullet.

'Mum,' she's saying as she tries to pull away from me. 'Mum, Mum.'

I cling on and there's an animal sound in my throat and my eyes are still squeezed shut to block out everything that's happening, and the noise out on the street is excruciating...

'Mum, Mum it's OK. Look, we're safe.'

I turn and slowly, boldly, open my eyes.

'It's all over, love. We've got him out there,' says the policeman. 'He can't hurt you now.'

* * *

There are two ambulances and three police cars on the street. Jo's vehicle is blocked in, so she waits inside the house with us, to pace the floor and express incredulity about the events of the day.

'I'm not saying I didn't believe you about the guy when you climbed into my car at the petrol station, but to think that he chased us all the way here and then tried to shoot the lock off your door so that he could get you... Wow, my head hurts with all the stress, the what-ifs. It's a good job that you rang the police before we arrived, so that they were quick enough to come and catch him. I mean, if he *had* got into the house...'

'I don't want to think what might have happened,' I say.

'And that woman who was here. She just ran out without looking and then, next thing, that guy's car had hit her.' Jo looks through the front window. 'Maybe I shouldn't have parked there? Maybe I blocked her view or something?'

'It wasn't your fault,' I tell her, then whisper, in disbelief, 'she nearly killed my child.'

I look down at my daughter, curled into the foetal position with her head in my lap. She has stopped shaking now and a numbness has set in. I hold her as best I can, stroking her arm, her face, her hair.

'Do you think Dad is OK?' she asks in a small voice.

'I don't know. But he's got the paramedics there and they'll do all they can.'

She sighs and I feel her breath on my leg. 'I just want us all to go back to normal again. That's all I want.'

Being normal again seems a completely unachievable outcome. But my daughter is here, with me, in the place that seems vaguely familiar. Although surely that armchair never used to be in the bay window.

There is a rap on the door and Jo goes to answer it. She's the closest thing I have to a best friend, even though we've only known each other for not much longer than an hour. A female police officer comes through, to check what's happening indoors, because she's had an unclear report about a child being poisoned.

'I think I've been here before,' she says, gazing around the place. 'Months ago. In relation to a missing person suspected drowning case.'

'Well, you've got some catching up to do,' I comment sarcastically.

There's another knock on the door. Another police officer. There are going to be questions, lots of them. It feels like this could be a very long day. I gently ease Charlotte away from my lap and go to put the kettle on because I have just remembered where it is.

* * *

The street is now clear of emergency vehicles. Jo has gone home, promising to keep in touch. Darkness has pressed up to the windows and the curtains have been drawn. Charlotte and I have the house to ourselves; we're on the sofa, holding on to each other as life spins around us. Everything feels like a surreal, scary dream, a story that happens to someone else, and it seems as if all we want to do is be silent even though we've spent the past few hours in constant conversation.

But at least we are safe and we are together.

Freddie has been arrested and is behind bars. He cannot reach me any more. Our pact is broken.

Charlotte has been checked over by a paramedic and everything is fine now: fortunately, she vomited up the small amount of milkshake she drank, so plenty of fluids were recommended to flush the remaining toxins out.

'It's so wrong,' says Charlotte. Her mood has been a rollercoaster, veering between melancholy weepiness and exhilarating relief. 'It should have been the other way round.'

Maybe it should.

But karma is a strange thing and doesn't always take the logical route.

Because today, her father, Toby, died. Although a head injury was initially suspected, it turns out that the most likely cause was a heart attack. The shock of seeing me, back home again after he had left me for dead.

'I have *you* back, though.' She smiles through her tears.

I start to cry, too. 'It's because of you that I'm back. You never gave up trying to find me.'

'I never would have stopped looking. I think she guessed I was up to something. *Her.*' Charlotte pauses and lets out a breath. 'I'm not sad about *her*. Not at all. She deserved it.'

I pull her close. 'She held a grudge against me for a long time. It can't be good, keeping that much bitterness inside you. Whatever you thought about her... just let it go. Don't let it stay with you and spoil *your* future. She's out of our lives now.'

Magdalena was indeed out of our lives, hit by Freddie's car as she ran to Toby's aid. She had been taken to hospital and was in an induced coma in intensive care. Just like me, all those months ago. The difference, though, was that she had broken her neck. She would recover but be paralysed for ever, unable to move from her bed, unable to live a normal life. On the plus side, there was no brain damage and no memory loss.

She would remember *everything* that had happened.

SIXTY-THREE

BECKA

We're doing fine now.

It's nearly a year and a half since I was pulled out of the river, and mine and Charlotte's lives have changed beyond all recognition.

If anyone ever thought that our experiences might cause us to retreat into ourselves, to become mistrustful and timid, they would be wrong.

We've blossomed.

Charlotte's method of combatting her grief saw a frenzied bout of revision and coursework, resulting in a fantastic set of exam results. She's in sixth form college now, doing A Levels in Maths, History and Sociology, because ultimately, she wants to go to university and study Criminology. Her amateur sleuthing has given her the bug to pursue it professionally, and she gets hooked on all the true crime documentaries on Netflix. The local gym has become her second home and, determined to be able to look after herself, she's got into boxing in a big way. Already, there are two shiny trophies on the mantelpiece from competitions she has won. The pride I feel for her is indescribable. She won't ever drink strawberry milkshakes again, though.

And I have returned to art. It's a love that has surprised and captured me, waking me in the night to whisper ideas and colours and themes so intensely that I have to switch on my lamp and reach for the sketchpad beside me to gather the mental images that may elude me by morning. Watercolours, acrylics, charcoal: the conservatory has been taken over by my mess of materials, and I am absorbed daily in creating canvases of all sizes and subjects, most of which are snapped up in the local galleries. I am making a credible income from something that I only ever thought could be a hobby.

'You're so talented,' my mother says, every time she sees a new sketch or painting on the easel. 'I always said you should have made a career of it after doing your degree.'

My life is enriched by having my mother back. She's a strong, independent woman who is always there when I need her. Not an interferer or a busybody and she doesn't really do fussing, but she is just someone that Charlotte and I are grateful to have in our lives. And to think that I believed for all those months that both my parents were dead... But I can't dwell on the mental cruelty that Freddie inflicted on me: I have to be positive and move on.

It's strange though, how sometimes I feel as if I miss him. Maybe, in different circumstances he might have been the perfect husband for me. If we could have loved each other without the backdrop of deceit, if the fire had never happened... Who knows?

Stop it, I tell myself. Yo-yoing between these love-hate thoughts aren't good. And I'm especially thankful that I never got pregnant because that would have added a whole new layer of turmoil.

No, it's just me and Charlotte now. And, like I said, we're doing fine.

. . .

'Do you think we should move from this house?' Charlotte asks me one evening. We're having our usual Mum and Daughter Thursday Night, which means that we order in a takeaway and light the posh candles and make time to chat about any subject. We do a lot of speculating on life: sometimes the past, but mostly the present and the future. Which is good.

'Well... I always thought you were settled here. With school and friends and everything.'

'I think after everything that happened I've sort of fallen out with this place. I've got good memories but there are bad ones too. Maybe it's time for us to have a fresh start. We could stay in the area. Although it wouldn't bother me if I had to change schools. We could just go somewhere random. Like Wales.'

My senses are triggered. There's a stab of something strange – Horror? Nostalgia? – at her words.

'Why did you say Wales?'

'No reason. As I said, just somewhere random. Chill out, Mum.' She laughs and throws a cushion at me.

Relief. It's not often that I get sparked; I've done well considering everything. 'Hmm. Yeah, maybe we could consider looking. Your room would take some sorting out though if we moved house.'

'My room's not that bad!'

'You'd easily win the award for Hoarder of the Century if there was one.'

She snorts and laughs until tears run down her face. 'I thought at first that you said Whore of the Century.'

We like to joke. Hearty laughter is good for us. Sometimes we're like a pair of kids.

It makes me think, what she said about moving. Maybe Charlotte is right. We should go elsewhere. I've had a large payout from Toby's life insurance: a gasp-out-loud surprise amount. The solicitor had looked at me with one raised eyebrow as he talked me through it, mentioning how fortunate it was that I had taken out the policy only two months before my own accident. 'Really?' I'd said, but he remained professional and made no further comment on it.

So, yes. It will be easy to afford a much nicer place.

She's a good girl. Bin bags, old boxes, cleaning stuff: Charlotte takes them all upstairs and makes a start on her walk-in bedroom wardrobe. She packs everything up for either the bin or the charity shop, leaving only the essentials behind. Four and a half hours later, it is done. She loads the bagged bric-a-brac into the hallway and comes through to the kitchen.

'Guess what I found?' There is a genuine grin of disbelief as she holds something behind her back.

'What?'

She places a laptop on the table. 'Voila!'

'What?'

'It's yours!'

'Mine?' I stroke my hand over the black plastic before opening it up.

'Needs charging, obviously. But after you went missing, I took this and hid it in the bottom of my wardrobe. It was just... I don't know... some kind of instinct. I didn't want *her* looking through it or taking it away. She'd conned her way in saying that she was working with the police, but I didn't trust her even then.'

'Have you used it?' There's a foamy, glittery feeling inside me: intrigue, anxiety, or maybe the start of an old memory breaking through.

'No, I couldn't get on. I didn't know your password.'

Neither do I. But I plug it in to charge regardless.

* * *

Four days later, numerous failed attempts, and the elusive password still keeps me out.

'You need to do the muscle memory thing again,' Charlotte tells me, because I was able to do the code number for the safe behind the microwave without thinking, finding over five thousand pounds in cash encased within it. So I place my fingers over the computer keys, trying to relax my brain, but they are unable to type the right combinations of letters and numbers.

'Maybe I will have to take it somewhere to be unlocked,' I finally surmise.

But it's only a matter of hours later – during the first waves of an early night's deep sleep – that I wake with the magic word imprinted in my mind. I'm sceptical, massively so, that this could be the right one to get me into it. It's still worth a try, though.

I sit up in bed and fire up the laptop. The screen asks for my password. *Here we go,* I think.

Bec&Fred

I type in the box.

There's a flicker and a whirr, and the little circular thing spins for a worryingly long time, as if it's seriously questioning my authenticity.

Then, bingo! I'm in.

A wedge of doubt lodges under my ribcage. I arch my back and take a sip from the glass of water beside me to quell the queasiness. Nervously, I click through the Documents file, then the Pictures file. Plenty of holiday photographs. Silly snaps of me and Charlotte that look like cartoon animals. There's nothing untoward.

I sigh and stretch my neck to one side. There is obviously nothing on here that I need to be concerned or excited about. Charlotte says that I never bothered with social media. But...

What about emails?

I click on the icon. Bizarrely, my muscle memory works on the email password, and I wade through pages of spam, deleting everything. Finally, I am back to the dates before my accident. There are emails between me and the host of a riverside cottage, letting me know about a key safe. Another thread from a canoe hire firm about a session that I booked for Toby to take place the day after my accident. I click on the link to their website and see that the company has an incredible number of one-star reviews, slating the firm for their poor safety standards. Scrolling further back I find documents relating to the life insurance policy that had been taken out only eight weeks earlier. And then...

It's been buried in a bundle of unread spam. An unopened message from '*Postmaster*' telling me that my email hasn't been delivered. I click back on the thread to see the original that I had tried to send.

My blood runs cold as I read the first line of the email. It begins,

Dear Freddie,

My chest constricts. I look at the date on the screen. Two months before my accident. What was going on? I take another gulp of water before reading the whole message.

Dear Freddie,

I don't know if you will remember me. We had a thing together years ago when I was seventeen. I hope you don't mind my getting in touch after all this time, but not so long ago I bumped into Magdalena and it triggered some memories. Do you still have anything to do with her? Anyway, I googled your name and found out that you're a famous

photographer now, so I got your contact details from your
website. I see you are living in Derbyshire, the same as me.

So... I just wondered if you fancied meeting up? A drink
together, maybe some catching up, reminiscing. Let me
know.

Becka x

My hands are trembling as I click out of the email. I notice
that I had spelled his name wrong in the email address – Fredie
instead of Freddie. I had tried to contact *him*. But he never got
my message.

I shiver and pull the duvet up around my shoulders, and
read the email one more time before deleting it. Had my relationship with Toby been in jeopardy? Did I know that he was
having an affair with Magdalena at that point? And was there
any relevance in the date that the insurance policy was taken
out? Had *I* planned some kind of accident for *Toby* during our
stay by the river?

My heart is beating so loud that I can feel it pumping in my
ears. Who even was I, before the accident?

Stop it, I tell myself. There is no point in speculating. Just
stop it.

I sign out of the email account.

Along the corridor, I hear Charlotte's sleepy footsteps and
the creak of the bathroom door. Minutes later, there's a tap
before she sticks her head into the room.

'It's the middle of the night,' she whispers. 'Why is your
light still on?'

I point to the laptop. 'Cracked the code.'

'Ahh, go, Mum! What are you looking at?'

I shrug. 'Just thought I'd browse some properties. You know,
your idea about moving?'

'Yeah. You up for it, too?'

'You bet.' I wink and hold my arms out to her. 'I've found a fabulous place with a hot tub.'

A LETTER FROM HAYLEY

Dear Reader,

Thank you so much for choosing to read my second psychological thriller, *Such A Loving Couple*. After the excitement of my debut, *The Perfect Girlfriend*, which was published only four months ago, this year has certainly been a rollercoaster!

If you enjoyed either of these stories and have a spare moment to leave a review, I would appreciate it hugely. It makes such a difference helping new readers discover my writing.

To keep up to date with all my latest book news, just sign up at the following link. Your email address will never be shared and you can unsubscribe at any time.

www.bookouture.com/hayley-smith

You can also connect with my Facebook profile, through Twitter or Instagram. I chat about all sorts of things – particularly books, music, and my allotment – and would love to hear from you.

Thank you again for reading.

Love,

Hayley

KEEP IN TOUCH WITH HAYLEY

facebook.com/Hayley.Smith.Writer
twitter.com/WriterHayley77
instagram.com/HayleySmithWriter

ACKNOWLEDGEMENTS

I am so grateful to everyone that has been involved in the writing and publication of my second psychological thriller.

Firstly, the remarkable team at Bookouture. What an amazing publishing imprint to bring this story to life – the absolute best that I could wish for. THANK YOU so much to my fabulous editor, Susannah Hamilton, whose creative ideas and insights just shimmer with brilliance, sharpening everything that I do (yes, even the hefty deletions!).

To my publicist, Sarah Hardy, who keeps me informed on all the marketing stuff with emails that make me smile ☺.

I owe huge gratitude to Lizzie Morris who is such an amazing motivator. Faced with lots of blank pages and a looming deadline, our writing days really helped to get my word count up. The wine and lunches were the best bit.

Thanks to my fellow writers in the Bookouture Author's Lounge for fun and constructive conversation. I initially joined thinking there would be velvet chairs and gin, but alas, not. However, the discussions on how to hide a body have been so useful.

To my fantastic children and their partners – Nicola, James, Joel, Loz, Abbie and Josie – who always encourage and support me. I really appreciate it. Extra thanks again to Nicola for all her patience and help with social media. I will try to improve!

And as always, the biggest thanks go to Michael who has put up with me locking myself away for months to write another book.

Made in United States
Troutdale, OR
03/11/2024

18396932R00202